BROKEN GROUND

A Novel

Karen Halvorsen Schreck

HOWARD BOOKS
An Imprint of Simon & Schuster, Inc.
New York   Nashville   London   Toronto   Sydney   New Delhi

Howard Books
An Imprint of Simon & Schuster, Inc.
1230 Avenue of the Americas
New York, NY 10020

This book is a work of fiction. Any references to historical events, real people, or real places are used fictitiously. Other names, characters, places, and events are products of the author's imagination, and any resemblance to actual events or places or persons, living or dead, is entirely coincidental.

First Howard Books trade paperback edition May 2016

HOWARD and colophon are trademarks of Simon & Schuster, Inc.

For information about special discounts for bulk purchases, please contact Simon & Schuster Special Sales at 1-866-506-1949 or business@simonandschuster.com.

The Simon & Schuster Speakers Bureau can bring authors to your live event. For more information or to book an event, contact the Simon & Schuster Speakers Bureau at 1-866-248-3049 or visit our website at www.simonspeakers.com.

Interior design by Davina Mock-Maniscalco

Manufactured in the United States of America

10   9   8   7   6   5   4   3   2   1

Library of Congress Cataloging-in-Publication Data
  Schreck, Karen Halvorsen.
Broken ground / Karen Halvorsen Schreck.—First Howard Books trade paperback edition.
  pages ; cm
  I. Title.
PS3619.C4619B76 2016
813'.6—dc23   2015028887

ISBN 978-1-4767-9483-9
ISBN 978-1-4767-9485-3 (ebook)

For Randi Ravitts Woodworth and Mark Woodworth

Now farming became industry, and the owners followed Rome, although they did not know it. They imported slaves, although they did not call them slaves: Chinese, Japanese, Mexicans, Filipinos. They live on rice and beans, the business men said. They don't need much. They couldn't know what to do with good wages. Why, look how they live. Why, look what they eat. And if they get funny—deport them.

—John Steinbeck, *The Grapes of Wrath*

You won't have your names when you ride the big airplane, All they will call you will be "deportees."

—Woody Guthrie, "Plane Wreck at Los Gatos"

PART I

March 1934–August 1934

ONE

Charlie wakes me as he rises, mattress springs creaking beneath his long limbs. This early in the morning, with the sun yet to come up, shadows cloak our small bedroom. But I can make out the sleepy shape of him sitting on the edge of the bed. I can smell his warm skin. Ivory soap and, beneath that, the gritty hint of Lava. Charlie starts with a cake of Lava when he returns from the rig each night— all but sandpapers himself clean—then finishes with Ivory because he knows I like that scent better. Only when he's shed oil, grease, and dirt like a second skin does he draw me into his arms. "Mrs. Warren," he says then, because he still can't believe our good fortune. "Mr. Warren," I say back, because I can't believe it, either. Here we are, just three months married, with an oil camp tent house to call our own, complete with kitchen, bedroom, front room, and a privy out back. There's hardship all around us, out there in the big beyond, and close at hand, too. Our own pantry with its slim pickings, our well-worn clothes and hand-me-down furniture—this very creaky mattress, which was Charlie's aunt's before it became ours—are testaments to the times taking their toll. But two months before our wedding, Charlie found a job as a driller on this East Texas oil field. He came on down here without me and got to work. The few hours he wasn't on the rig or sleeping, he readied this place—slapped up wood walls and a tin roof, laid planks for a floor, cut out the window over there. And now here we are, as happy as any pair of newlyweds can be. John D. Rockefeller, richest oil baron of them all, couldn't be happier. He's less happy, I'd lay odds. John D. Rockefeller doesn't have Charlie in his life.

A mourning dove calls outside our open window, from the scrawny honey locust tree that grows beside our home. The shadows are swiftly paling to just that mourning dove's gray. Sun's coming up. The curtains on the window hang stiff as planks of white board; not a breeze stirs. It's going to be another stifling day. A deadly heat wave in March. Who'd have thought. Then again, who'd have thought this winter, and early spring, too, would prove dry as a bone—the drought so bad that some days the black blizzards roll east from the Texas Panhandle and right over us, then on to places as far-flung as New York City and Washington, D.C. Just last week, according to accounts, a fog of prairie dirt shrouded the Statue of Liberty. The White House, too, turned less than white. On the worst days, Charlie says he and the other fellows on the rig measure visibility in inches, not feet. Static electricity crackles in the air. Blue flames leap from metal equipment and barbwire fences, making dangerous work all the more so. One man bumps against another, they generate a spark so powerful it can knock them both to the ground.

Charlie doesn't complain, but round about noon every day, even when the sky is a stark blue ceiling marked only by the searing sun—no dust to be seen, not even on the far horizon—I'll turn sick with worry. Sometimes the dust gets so thick in the nose and throat, a body can barely breathe. Sometimes, unattended, that thickness turns to dust pneumonia, and then a body simply can't. And then there's heatstroke, the most common ailment.

Maybe today I'll hitch a ride out to Charlie with a jug of cold water and a towel. It won't be easy. "Woman on the rig!" the warning will sound, and the roughnecks and roustabouts—men of a different ilk than Charlie—will whistle and worse. But the sight of my husband cooling off, his head thrown back as he drinks from the jug, the muscles in his throat rising and falling as he swallows—well, I'd walk through hot hell for that. Let them whistle and worse. I'll pour water on the towel and rub it down the length of Charlie's arms. Down to the tip of his callused fingers, I'll work my way, wiping away grime, tending his sun-scorched skin.

I press my hands to my chest, where my heart suddenly punches. "Charlie?"

He has tipped his head toward our window in an attitude of listening. The mourning dove—that's what he's trying to hear. Charlie loves the sound of that bird, but his ears ring more often than not these days due to the noise on the rig. He says you haven't heard a ruckus until you've heard a gusher let loose. Twenty-two years old and he's losing his ability to make out discreet sounds. The mourning dove's muted, throaty coo. Me softly saying his name. The yearning in my voice. He's missed all that.

I take hold of Charlie's arm and say his name louder. He turns. "Well, hello there." His hand settles warmly on my waist. "Didn't mean to wake you, Ruth."

There's enough light now to see the freckles emblazoned across his sharp nose and high cheekbones. The coppery strands burnished into his curly, auburn hair. The fine lines at the outer corners of his blue eyes, which are just the color of the bellflowers that grow in the field behind my parents' house back in Alba, Oklahoma. Flowers I used to sink down into when things inside the house got hard. Now Charlie's gaze is all I need for solace, along with the wondrous rest of him.

I hear myself sigh. Wistfulness, that sigh could be interpreted as. Or desire, which would be the truth.

Charlie smiles. "Stay in bed. I'll get the coffee going."

He moves to stand, but I keep hold of him. "Our Bed Is an Island," I say.

It's a game we play. We want to see the ocean together one day. For now, we pretend instead.

"Ruthie." Charlie regards me. "You know what day it is." A smile tugs at the corner of his mouth. "Not Sunday or Christmas. A plain old Monday in March—that's what day it is. If I had one magic wish, I'd make it otherwise, believe you me."

"It's barely five." I peer at the round-faced clock on the bedside table, sitting squat on its three little legs. "Why, it's not even a quarter till!" I beam at Charlie, triumphant. "We have time. We don't have to—you know." I snuggle down under the hand-stitched wedding quilt that was a gift from Miss Berger—the librarian in Alba, my previous employer— who unpacked it from her hope chest and gave it to me for mine. Miss Berger, who's decided she'll never marry, wanted the quilt put to good use. Well, then. I lift the quilt's edge, so Charlie can join me under its interlocked rings of bright fabric. "We could be here a little longer. All tangled up in each other. You know."

Charlie knows. He knows that if he returns to me under the quilt, our bed will become an island surrounded by an ocean we most often call the floor. Hawaii, our bed will become, or Barbados, Bermuda, or Bali. Or maybe one of the Galápagos would be nice, or the Cyclades, or the Canaries. Places we once mapped in geography lessons, the names of which I savor like candy on my tongue. Castaways, that's what Charlie and I will be, and we'll dreamily drift, lost in each other, far from civilization, free from dust, drought, and demands.

Charlie leans toward me, the low sound in his throat somewhere between a purr and a growl. The round identification tag he always wears—it belonged to his father, who died in the Great War—slips free of the confines of his pajama shirt to dangle from its leather cord in the air between us. Gently the silvery tag swings, steady as a hypnotist's watch. Charlie draws nearer. I stretch my arms above my head, relish the waiting. Any moment, we'll be all tangled up.

But then, when he's nearly close enough to kiss, his expression twists, and he draws away. "Nope." He tucks the quilt around me. "We're drilling on a new tract of land today. I've got to get an even earlier start."

Still, I don't let Charlie go. Moments pass, my hands doing this and that, all the while holding on, until finally he tickles me nearly to death and I have to release him. Then he's up like a shot, and our island is just a bed that he's not in, and our ocean is just a floor he's crossing, and the other side of our far horizon is just the kitchen in which he's making coffee.

And so it's begun, Monday. The camp town awaits me, for better and worse, and the oil field that never quits awaits Charlie. There he'll give orders, and take them, and work himself to the bone, breaking up and drilling down, drawing up the black crude that helps men like John D. Rockefeller get rich, and helps people like us get by.

WHILE CHARLIE DRESSES, I pad barefoot in my nightgown to the kitchen. No time to waste now; breakfast needs making. I heat the stove, whip up some biscuits, fry the last three of our eggs. We like them fried hard, make a big show of calling the crackly edges bacon. I cook a can of beans, too. What with the long day Charlie faces, beans and a biscuit will satisfy me.

He sits at the table as I'm setting down our two plates. I join him, and we clasp hands. Skin against skin like this, I can't help but notice the obvious differences between Charlie and me. My skin doesn't freckle in the sun like his. Instead, never mind how much I try to cover up, I turn as brown as the biscuits on our plates. My hair is brown, too, except in the summer, when it's streaked with the sun's yellow. But nothing, not even the sun, will change the color of my eyes, which are as black as my mood used to get before Charlie and I married and moved away from Alba. There's nothing bellflower blue about my eyes; they more reflect a stormy night. I'd like to change that about myself—my black moods most of all—but Charlie says this difference in our natures is a fine thing. "Put a glass half empty and a glass half full together, and you've got the whole glass," he teases. Once I shot back, "Half empty, my dainty foot. I'd be empty without you." But the look he gave me was worried, not playful, so I never said that again.

Sometimes, holding hands with Charlie, I feel like a child, cared for and protected, which is a warm feeling indeed after the cold comfort of my growing up. Sometimes I have to remind myself that I am grown up. This provides the single (so far) source of tension between Charlie and me. "Make yourself heard," he said once, his voice heated. "Don't kowtow to me."

"Let's pray," I say now, my voice clear and firm, loud enough to be heard, no matter the state of Charlie's hearing. Together, we thank God for food and work and each other. As always, I add a silent prayer of thanks for this, the *we* of our prayer, which, since Charlie and I have been married, has made me feel closer to God than ever before. The *we* of our prayer is entirely different from what I heard growing up, at home and at the Holy Church of the Redeemed, which was established by my father, along with a few others who felt the rest of the churches in town weren't good enough. They rented a small building, called themselves Elders, found their preacher, and established their covenant. At the Holy Church of the Redeemed, *we* means the Elders, who speak for everyone else.

"Amen," Charlie and I say.

Charlie digs in first. Or starts to. Biscuit nearly to his lips, he hesitates, eyeing my portion. Then he sets down the biscuit, scoops a heap of egg onto his fork, and reaches for my plate. I snatch my plate away. "I'm not hungry."

"You're as hungry as me."

"Keep this up, mister, and I'll take my breakfast on the front porch." I look at him in a manner most queenly. "Alone."

Charlie shakes his head and laughs, egg cooling on his fork. But I see the resignation in his eyes. He knows I mean it.

For further emphasis, I snap my fingers. *"Tempus fugit!"*

Dutifully, Charlie slides the egg back onto his plate. "I had to go and marry the one gal who actually remembers her Latin."

I shrug. "I liked Latin. The little we learned of it. Which is to say, if you'd paid attention, you'd remember your Latin, too."

"You liked *geometry*, Ruth. Proofs and all that. Heck, you liked everything, from kindergarten to twelfth grade."

What Charlie knows and doesn't say is that from the get-go, I've been hungrier for learning than I've ever been for food. In spite of Daddy. Because of him, maybe. Maybe that's the gift Daddy's given me. Take something away, or make it hard to get, or put limits around it—barriers of judgment that say *This is evil and so is that* and *The only good book is the Bible*—the desire only grows greater. Long before Charlie and I got married, I wanted to go to college and become a teacher, share knowledge and information even as I kept on learning myself. But then there was Charlie, who'd always been there, my best friend, only this time he had a ring and a promise: *We'll leave Alba. We'll move far away. We'll see this big old world.* I still want to go to college. But now I won't go alone. Charlie will come, too.

He cocks his head at me, grins. "You know very well why I didn't pay attention in school, Ruthie."

The upturned corners of his mouth draw me closer. Our bed could still be an island.

"Because our teacher was stern and stuffy?" I know this is not the answer (though it is one aspect of the truth). But I want to hear him say it. And he does.

"I was too busy looking at you."

With my fork, I pretend to wave his words away, though I cherish every last one of them. "We both know you paid more than enough attention in school during science. We were always different like that."

Different from most of the other students, I mean, as Charlie well knows. Most of the other students were there because they had to be. Charlie and I were there because we wanted to be.

He shrugs and keeps eating. He wants to be a doctor someday, he's always said. Now that we're married, he's more likely to qualify: "If I can." *If.* Depends on how long these hard times linger, and on how the money comes in, that's what he means. And there might be a baby first, if God wills and the money comes in. No, simply if God wills: a baby.

It's only sometimes, when the chores are all done and I'm alone, drifting a bit, that I let myself daydream about college first and teaching right after, before a baby or anything else. I'd be an *interesting* schoolteacher, unlike our teacher, Mrs. Himmel. Sometimes, I think we learned despite Mrs. Himmel, not because of her. Miss Berger, the librarian, was my real teacher. In fact, last August, right after Charlie and I got engaged, when he was working as a farmhand and I was working at the Alba public library, Miss Berger got Charlie and me to apply to college. "You *must*," she said. "As an intellectual exercise. An experiment, if you'd rather put it that way." I grabbed Charlie's hands like we were about to set off on a great lark. But then he said, "No money, no point in exercising or experimenting either one," and I felt my shoulders sag. "Maybe someday," he added quickly. "But we'll let you go first, Ruth. I don't need to go right away. There's only one thing I need right away. One person." He put an arm around me, drew me close, and for some days, distracted by the question of money and the answer of each other, we forgot about any old college application.

But Miss Berger didn't give up. One September night, she sat Charlie and me down and slapped two manila envelopes on the library table between us. The envelopes each held an application to Union University in Pasadena, California. Miss Berger, way back when, considered attending this college. It's a good school, she told us, with strong programs for future teachers and doctors both. "Fill out the applications as a favor to *me*," she pleaded.

So we filled them out, goaded by Miss Berger, and sent them off in the mail. And I usually only dwell on this—that our applications are out there somewhere, on someone's desk or file cabinet in faraway California, when I'm alone in the afternoon, chores all done, drifting and daydreaming.

I take hold of Charlie's shirt, pull him close, kiss him full on the mouth. We taste like biscuits and us. Who needs jam? Who needs college? Who needs anything but this? When I release him, yellow dirt dusts my fingertips. East Texas soil. So different from Oklahoma's red clay. He kept his promise. We did move—not far, far away from Alba, exactly, but far enough.

I wipe the dirt on my napkin. "I'll do laundry today. Promise."

Charlie shrugs. "You don't have to if you don't want to. This pair of dungarees will make it to Wednesday before they stand up of their own accord."

He's not kidding. After a few days' work in the field, his clothes are as stiff as can be, caked with oil, gasoline, dirt, and sweat. Thus, the necessary cake of Lava and the bar of Ivory soap for me.

"Monday is wash day," I say firmly. I've almost finished cross-stitching a set of tea towels that testify to this fact and others: *Monday, Wash. Tuesday, Iron. Wednesday, Clean*, etc. Beneath reminders like this, I've cross-stitched little animals for decoration. Monday's animal is a lamb. Tuesday's, a goose. Wednesday's, a cat. I have yet to stitch the others. But since Thursday is *Mend and Sew,* I'll be done soon enough.

Charlie takes his empty plate and cup to the kitchen sink. I stand, too, though I'm nowhere near done. "I wish you wouldn't eat so fast." I can't keep the missing-him-already out of my voice.

Charlie picks up his lunch pail. "I'd just be putting off what's inevitable."

"That's not what I mean. I'm talking about your digestion."

He leans over and, playful as my cross-stitched lamb, nips at my ear. He pretends to chew and swallow, then pats his stomach, satisfied. "My digestion is fine."

Together, we go to the front porch. The sun shines brightly. Other birds are singing—black crows, brown thrashers, blue jays—but the mourning dove has fallen silent. It'll be dusk before she sings again, and soon after that, Charlie will return home.

We tell each other I love you. We hold each other for a long moment. Then what else can we do? We say good-bye.

I'M KNEELING IN a skittering strip of the honey locust tree's shade, scrubbing a pair of Charlie's dungarees on the rub board while his shirts soak in a pot, when I hear the high, thin voice of one of my neighbors. "Two plus two equals five."

I smile down at Charlie's dungarees, the knees worn paper-thin. My neighbor knows better. I've taught her better. She's teasing me.

"Very good, Edna Faye," I tease her back.

Surprised silence from behind me. I press my lips together to keep from laughing, then start scrubbing again. Almost, these dungarees hold the shape of Charlie. Almost, I can feel the curve of his bones when he kneels or bends.

"Three plus three equals seven."

"Excellent." Working at the frayed hems, briskly rubbing left hem against right, I tell Edna Faye that she is the brightest girl for miles around.

At that, her bare feet patter against the dirt, and the late-morning glare softens. She's standing behind me now, lending her skinny shadow to that of the honey locust. "You're not listening, Mrs. Ruth."

From what I've seen, Edna Faye has spent most of her six years not being listened to by anyone—especially anyone in her family of nine. The one constant in the life of a roustabout's child is change, and in the case of Edna Faye's family, constant change has yielded constant chaos. As the middle child of the brood, she's particularly lost in the shuffle. Maybe a month ago on a Monday, Edna Faye drifted over as I stepped outside. She hungrily eyed the pot I was carrying, seeming to think it might hold soup. It held only hot water and laundry. Still, when I smiled at her, she began prowling the yard in ever diminishing circles, evaluating the situation. Finally she sidled up and sat right down on the ground next to me. I asked what her name was and told her mine, and that was all it took. Edna Faye has barely stopped talking since.

"Four plus four equals nine," she says. Her voice breaks

with temper or tears, I can't tell which. I can't bear the thought of her unhappy under my watch, so I turn around and take her small grubby hands in my wet ones.

"Do we need to review your addition tables?" In spite of my best intentions, I sound stuffy and stern, a younger version of Mrs. Himmel. But if Mrs. Himmel's methods worked for me, I guess they work for Edna Faye, too; at least they do today. She nods solemnly, blinking her round gray eyes. If she weren't so thin—dangerously thin, her belly a taut ball bulging beneath her flour-sack shift—her pale face, framed by a milk-colored corona of hair, would resemble nothing so much as a full moon. As it is, the hollows at her cheeks and temples betray a very hungry child.

"Well, then." My voice gentles. "Let me hang up Mr. Charlie's clean things, and we'll get to work on your math."

Edna Faye smiles, exposing the crooked, gray nubbins of her teeth.

I hang Charlie's dungarees from the clothesline, along with several pairs of socks that have soaked long enough in a bucket of bleach and, on *Thursday, Mend and Sew,* must be mended and sewn. Then I take Edna Faye's hand and lead her into the house. I set a piece of paper and a pencil on the kitchen table. "Addition. The ones. Do odds first and then evens, *opposite* of usual." I stress this because Edna Faye likes variety. Or variety is all that is familiar to her, all she's known over the course of her brief but everchanging life.

Edna Faye bows her head over her work. 1+1, she writes carefully on the paper's top line, her tongue working inside her mouth, pushing her cheek to nearly full-moon full. I take a pitcher of milk from the icebox and peer down into it. I can spare a cup, at least. I pour milk into an empty canning jar, then cut a slice of bread and spread molasses on thick. I set all this before Edna Faye, and she breathes in deep. Smelling is the next best thing to eating, and she's clearly learned to live on the scent of food alone. The smell of bread, molasses, and milk sustains her through the odds and well into the evens, too. It's a good while before she takes her first bite, her first gulp. And then, like that, the plate is empty; the jar, drained. Edna Faye eats faster, even, than Charlie. Soon as I can afford to buy the ingredients to bake a pie, I'll bake two and let this child and my husband battle it out in their own personal pie-eating contest.

Edna Faye covers her mouth with her hand like I taught her before she burps. "Excuse me," she says. I taught her that, too. She's still hungry as a bear cub, so I pour more milk. "Take it slowly, now," I say, and she does her best to obey while I review her sums.

"Well done." I smile. This time she deserves the compliment. "Perfect, in fact."

Edna Faye licks the milk mustache from her upper lip. "Subtraction now."

This is what I like most about Edna Faye. She wants to learn. She *needs* to.

Time passes, the only sounds the ticktock of the clock and her pencil's scratching, and I eat my own little lunch, the twin of Edna Faye's.

"Here," she finally says, handing over her paper. And now I'm the one bowed over the smudged numbers, calculating differences.

Edna Faye has made a few errors on her eights and nines, but really, she does a fine job for a child who's only in the last handful of weeks learned methods for making things increase and decrease predictably. As a reward, I invite her into the front room to sit on the sagging sofa that Charlie and I found by the roadside. It must have fallen from some traveler's overburdened truck; it threatened to fall from ours. But we got it here, and it's become the lesser island in our lives.

Here on the sofa—as the sun peaks in the sky, then begins to sink lower, and shirts soak too long in the pot, dungarees and socks dry on the line, and little shadows begin to gather in corners again, which means the minutes truly are ticking toward the time when the mourning dove coos and Charlie returns—I read a tale to Edna Faye from my copy of *The Fairy Tales of the Brothers Grimm.* We choose "Rapunzel," her favorite and one of mine, too. "Why do you like this story so much?" I asked her once. "The tower," Edna Faye answered. As if the greatest joy in any life would be to be locked away alone, all by oneself in a quiet place, with only hair to grow and a guard to deliver regular meals. I like the story for an entirely different reason: the escape. Edna Faye probably would be content if we never got to that part, but I always read on to the happily-ever-after end.

I read on. The sun sinks. The shirts soak. The minutes tick-tock. The shadows gather, deepening, clinging to one another. I turn page after page.

It hits me near the happily-ever-after end. My teaching got the best of me. I neglected to hitch a ride out to Charlie, bearing a jug of cold water and wet towels. It's too late now. I will visit him on the rig tomorrow.

I turn another page, listening for the mourning dove.

Instead, there's a sound like I've never heard before—a sound like trains colliding. Our little house shifts, the sofa lurches, the window rattles. The jar from which Edna Faye drank falls from the kitchen table and shatters on the floor.

SILENCE FOLLOWS THE sound. The tornado that hit Alba in 1930 left in its wake such a silence. But this silence stretches even longer. This silence becomes its own kind of terrible noise.

Something moves beside me, breaking whatever spell has kept me frozen in place. I look down. Edna Faye. Her gray eyes seem to swallow her hollow moon face. "What was that?" she asks.

I shake my head, and once I start, I can't stop. Shaking my head, I walk to the front door. I open it. Even now there's not a sound to be heard. No one stands in the silent road. Any birds in the trees—black crows, brown thrashers, blue jays—are stunned dumb. Our mourning dove . . . I hope she flew far away from here this morning. I tell myself she flew far away. She will return at nighttime, when Charlie returns, because Charlie was working in a new field today, a faraway field, a safe field, far away.

I stand on the porch and watch for him, though it is not yet time for him to come home. In fact, time seems to have stopped, which no doubt will delay him all the longer.

I look toward where the sun should be, fixed to a

standstill on the horizon, and where the sun should be looms a black cloud of smoke rising, rising, enormous already and ballooning bigger. I smell it then. Burning oil. And something else—something like scorched meat and singed hair.

I clap my hands over my nose and mouth to block the smell, to suppress the cry thickening in my throat, and time starts again. Neighbors spill from tents and homes like ours, women and children and men—men too old to be working or injured men unable to work—who are shouting. "Blowout!" Over and over I hear the word, but no matter how many times I hear it, I can't think what it means.

Someone tugs at my dress. "I have to find my ma."

Edna Faye's high, thin voice is solemn with understanding. I drop to my knees. We are eye to eye, and she is the teacher. "What happened?"

"Blowout," she says.

Something in my expression—impatience? anger?—makes Edna Faye wince. She is afraid. I don't want to be another adult who makes her fearful. I should smile reassuringly and tell her to go find her ma. Instead, I grab her shoulders and yank her close so I can hear her every word through the noise of lamentation rising all around us.

"What's a blowout?"

"A fire. A big fire. A bad fire." She's crying now. "Killed my uncle and my grandpa, too, up in Whizbang a while back."

Whizbang, Oklahoma, she means. The boomtown that sprang up almost overnight around one of the biggest gushers ever discovered—nearly as big as the gushers here. I heard

about Whizbang. I heard about that fire. It destroyed everything in its path. It almost destroyed Whizbang.

I look to the horizon again. The fire is in the west.
Which way did Charlie drive this morning after he folded
himself into our truck's front seat? I watched him walk to
the truck, his lunch pail swinging at his thigh. I watched
him climb inside. I raised my hand and blew him a kiss. He
blew a kiss back. Waving, he backed the truck toward the
dirt road that took him in whichever direction he went. But
I didn't watch him drive away. Already, I'd turned back to
the house. Because today is Monday. *Monday, Wash.* I had
to get busy. And there are his shirts, soaking in the pot.
There are his dungarees, hanging from the line, and his
socks, clothespinned into place. The East Texas wind has
dried them already. But I will wash them again—*Monday,
Wash*—because look: faint tendrils of oily, black smoke,
black as any dust storm's blizzard, black as any mood, snak-
ing around the dungarees and socks, and the shirts still
soaking in the pot—clothes that Charlie will wear against
his skin. My husband's skin smells like Ivory soap, and beneath that, a hint of Lava. I can't have him heading off to
work smelling like something—*oh, God*—like someone
burned.

This is what I'm doing when a man comes and tells me
that Charlie is dead, killed in the blowout. I'm scrubbing
Charlie's shirts, dungarees, and socks. The man talks to me.
He talks to me. Talks to me. To the back of my bowed head
he talks, to my rounded shoulders, my body heaving with effort. I hear "husband," and I hear "dead," and that is all I
hear. That is all I need to hear. Now I must get busy. Never

have I worked so hard at one simple task. Monday's task. I work at it.

But I cannot get Charlie's clothes clean enough. I cannot wash them white as the snow that I have seen only a few times in my life. One time I was with Charlie. This was eight years ago. He was fourteen. I was thirteen. We were walking home from school late one January afternoon, when the moon already hung in the sky, as the moon must hang in the sky now, only that January moon was hidden by clouds and this March moon is hidden by smoke. Charlie and I were walking and talking, discussing a comment Mrs. Himmel had made about the sixth day and Adam and Eve. In a low voice, Charlie told me about something he'd read on the sly, tucked away in the corner of the Alba public library where one day I would work. Charlie had read bits and pieces from a book by a man named Darwin. This man Darwin thought seven days wasn't all it took to make the world, and Charlie wondered what I thought about that. I was thinking on what I thought, and Charlie was waiting for my answer, when snow began to fall like manna from the sky. "Look!" Charlie said. And we raised our mittened hands like hallelujah, and the white flakes dusted the wool. Charlie's hands were big. Mine were small. Charlie's mittens were blue. Mine were red. I remember this. We gazed at our mittened hands, at the crystals sparkling against the wool, each as unique as a human soul, shining fiercely, swiftly extinguished. "It's a miracle," I said, and Charlie said yes. A miracle. Our first snow together, a miracle we shared, and we promised each other we'd share many more.

Our first snow together was when Charlie and I fell in love, I realize as I wash his clothes all through the dark, smoky night. I wash holes into the knees of his dungarees and bigger holes into the heels of his socks. I wash the cuffs and collars of his shirts to shreds. I wash my hands raw. I wash my hands bloody.

The day Charlie and I fell in love. The day of the one and only miracle in my life.

TWO

Mother's scuffed brown lace-ups appear in my field of vision. "It's time, Ruth."

I sit on the floor in the spot where our bed used to be an island, but now I am lost at sea. The bed is gone, given to someone who needs a bed big enough for two. The room is empty. Our house is empty, and what's left of my life.

My parents and Charlie's mother, Margaret, made the decisions about what to sell or give away. I saw them do so as if from a great distance while the black fog encroached from where it lurked at the corners of my eyes, the back of my mind, the outer limits of my heart that beats dully on and on. I heard the three of them talking, also as if from a great distance. Their voices rose and fell, pitched high and low with varying emotion, but their words remained indecipherable, distorted, like a gramophone played at the wrong speed.

Days have passed since the blowout, possibly weeks—

don't know, don't care—and all this endless, senseless time, I've been waiting for the black fog to cover me completely. I've been waiting to vanish, as Charlie did. Charlie was incinerated, Margaret told me, weeping as I have yet to weep. Tears fail me. Dry-eyed, I watched Margaret's mouth move. "The flames consumed him."

Let the black fog consume me.

Mother's thin hand settles on my shoulder. She gives me a shake. "Your daddy has a meeting."

I slide down the length of her words into the back room off the sanctuary where Daddy and the other leaders of the Holy Church of the Redeemed hold their meetings. There is the cone of yellow light cast by the lamp that hangs over the table, and there are the men who keep the Covenant—Daddy and the others—heads thrust forward, shirtsleeves rolled up, fingers pointing.

"Oh, for heaven's sake!" Mother's voice shrills to anxious. "Margaret left some time ago. She wanted to reach Alba before dusk. At this rate, we'll arrive tomorrow. He'll miss his meeting, Ruth, and you know we don't want that."

With a strength that surprises me (Mother's strength always surprises me), she grabs my arm and pulls me to my feet. Out the empty bedroom, down the empty hallway, past the empty kitchen and the empty front room, and across the threshold over which Charlie carried me, Mother drags me. Back to before, she drags me. Back to Alba.

Shock of sunlight. Then someone says my name. "Mrs. Ruth."

For the first time since the blowout, a voice I want to

hear. I wrench my arm from Mother's grasp and turn to Edna Faye.

She stands beneath the sagging laundry line, staring at me. *O,* her mouth makes, and her gray eyes, big as they've ever been, brim with dismay. And there's Edna Faye's family—all but her father, who is now a name in the alphabetical list of names that precede *Warren, Charles,* a name etched on the black slab of granite laid down by the oil company beneath a tall sweet gum tree outside of camp. Edna Faye's siblings have piled onto the mattress that lines the bed of the dilapidated wagon hooked up to their jalopy, tent poles strapped to its running board. Edna Faye's mother, who seems to have aged twenty years in however long it's been since the blowout, sits hunched behind the steering wheel. What unbelievable quiet for such noisy kids. They lean into their belongings—blankets, buckets, boxes, two battered bicycles, and an old cookstove—and keep the silence of the dead. Where are they going? West? I've heard about West on the radio, read about it in the papers and on the fliers distributed by the farm owners, which promise work and better weather. I've seen evidence of west-bound refugees on the road, too. So many fleeing their homes and farms, driven out by dust storms, drought, and dissolution, rattling on toward where the sun inevitably sets. Mother's closest friend from her childhood back in Guthrie had to go west; Mother has told me so time and again, until the telling has distilled into a kind of refrain: "Alice Everly and her family were far better off than us. If they turned homeless, what are the odds we'll do the same?"

Take me with you, Edna Faye. Anywhere but Alba. Take

me there. I wrench my arm from Mother's grip and go to her. We clasp hands.

"One plus one equals two," she says.

I nod. *Take me.*

"Two minus one equals one," she says.

I close my eyes against this difference.

"Don't give up." I hear my voice for the first time since the blowout. Really hear it—rough and thin as a piece of paper torn in half. "You hear me, bright girl? Keep learning."

Mother's hand settles again on my shoulder. Edna Faye releases me, and Mother steers me toward Daddy's car. Next thing I know, I'm in the backseat. I watch through the window as Edna Faye climbs onto the mattress in the truck's bed and burrows down beside her brothers and sisters.

Edna Faye is crying. Out the window as we pull away, I watch that little girl, my bright girl, do a woman's work of tears.

SPRING CREEPS IN, as it will. Blossoms open on the redbud by the road; I see them from my bedroom window. A flash of blue streaks by one day—an indigo bunting whistling its sharp, clear song. The bellflowers out back will bloom soon, no doubt. All things blue recall Charlie's eyes. Mother says I am blue. "Pray. You're not praying hard enough. You must end this blue mood, Ruth." Darker than blue, I think. Darker than Charlie's eyes. Black, the color of my eyes. Black fog punctured by occasional birdsong, the flickering movement of pink buds on a brown branch tossed by the wind—the wind that used to remind me of God's spirit encompassing me. Mother is right about one thing: I'm not praying hard enough. I'm not praying at all. I've tried. I can't. And if God speaks in a still, small voice, well, I can't hear God for the wind.

I lie in bed days and nights. I don't sleep much.

"ENOUGH IS ENOUGH!"

Out of nowhere, Daddy's voice. It's the first time he's spoken to me since our return to Alba. I open my eyes, look toward the bedroom doorway. There he stands, wearing a denim shirt and a pair of hickory-stripe bib overalls, as he does every day of the week but Sunday. Dim light fills the bedroom; outside, the rooster, Captain, crows. It must be early morning. How long have I been lying here, awake?

Daddy strides to my bed, stands over me. He rubs his hand roughly over the gray stubble of his beard. "Free ride ends now, Ruth. Understand." A statement, not a question.

He's gone then, leaving Mother in his wake. She pushes her thin hands through her thinning red hair. "You heard your daddy." She's mustered sternness, but a thread of pity laces her tone. "Let's get on with it. Get on with life." She glances at the wedding band I still wear. "Time to take that off, put it somewhere safe. Don't you think?"

I tuck my ringed hand under the bedcovers—a reflexive gesture, the kind a child would make. My expression must say, *Never,* because Mother sighs. "All right, then. Just get out of bed, Ruth, if you know what's good for you. Your daddy made his demands clear. You don't want to go messing with that. You know what I mean."

At her rising urgency, the black fog lifts a little, and I do know what she means. Mess with Daddy and live to regret it.

So with Captain still crowing, I get out of bed. For the first time, I take stock of the bedroom. Somehow, the little bit left of what I had with Charlie has been unpacked and put away. Mother did this, more than likely. Here I am, right back exactly where I was, as I was, before. It's as if I never left Alba. It's as if my life with Charlie was a beautiful dream.

My nightgown is rank; I've been living in it. I give Mother a look, and she complies by leaving the room and me to myself. I strip off my nightgown and drop it in the empty basket that will soon hold other dirty laundry now that enough is enough. I put on the black dress I wore to the memorial service for Charlie and the other lost men. Then, without much more than a sip of coffee from the cup that Mother sets on the kitchen table before me, and a bite of milk toast from the bowl she puts down beside that, I say, "I'm going out."

"Already?" Mother draws back in surprise. "Well, good." Sounds like she's saying the opposite.

"I'll be back soon." If only I were saying the opposite.

Out I go.

On the front porch, I stop. Beyond out suddenly seems impossible. Then the door bangs shut behind me, shaking the brittle Christmas bough that still hangs there, scattering a shower of dead needles at my feet, propelling me toward the porch steps and down them. Across the patchy lawn I go. One foot in front of the other, headed toward what's most familiar I go, leaving footprints in the red dust that coats everything all around. By the time I've walked the four blocks to Central Street, the dust coats me, too. A block down Central, the one-room brick building that is Kickingbird School has, from the dust, turned the color of dried blood. Across from the school, the Alba Public Library, a small fortress constructed of rough-hewn stones, has turned from yellow to orange.

The wind rises. I lean into it. I lean toward the library, toward Miss Berger. I keep going. With each step, my footprints disperse, swept from this earth as Charlie was, his life no more substantial than a grain of dust. But here is the library, a small fortress. Here, its door—red, like those of certain churches. Pull, pull hard, and the door opens against the wind. I am inside. The wind may buffet the windows and hiss at the door closing behind me, but inside, all is still and calm. Miss Berger sits at the front desk, a red bandana covering her short, gray hair. She leaps up at the sight of me—her lean, rangy body taut with barely contained energy— knocking her chair to the floor. Disregarding this, she's upon me in a moment, pulling me close. My head rests on her bony chest, and I hear her heartbeat, vigorous and vital.

"I'm sorry, Ruth. I'm so sorry." Her words are close to comfort—the closest any have come. She pats my back. "You're shivering, and it's hot as blazes out there. Are you ill?"

"Just cold." As I say this, I realize it's true. "Always cold." That's true, too.

Miss Berger guides me to her desk, rights the chair, sits me down, then retrieves her green wool shawl from the bottom drawer and starts to drape it over my shoulders. I lean away. "The wind and dust. I'm filthy."

She gives an impatient huff and wraps the shawl around me, firmly securing the ends in a thick knot that hangs, a warm weight, against my ribs. Now she darts off to her little office, just behind the desk. I hear her lift the kettle from the two-burner unit, then pour out what's inside. Next moment, she presses a full steaming mug into my hands. "Just brewed this. I was going to pour it over ice when it cooled, but it's put to better use this way." She resolutely tugs her bandana down on her forehead. As usual when the weather warms, she wears a white cotton T-shirt neatly tucked into a long khaki skirt. When Charlie was a boy, he once told Miss Berger that she looked like she should be going on safari in this attire. To which she said that the library was adventure enough. Her work here—she loves it. It was all she's ever needed out of life and all she'll ever need.

I thank her for the tea. As I take a scalding sip, she nervously clasps and unclasps her hands. "I was one day away from coming to your parents' house, Ruth, never mind your daddy."

Daddy doesn't like Miss Berger, in spite of the fact that, as my previous employer, she paid me twice a month without fail for my work, and my wages helped us get by.

Miss Berger's fingers are trembling. With a hiss of exasperation, she gives them a shake. "Now's as good a time as any, I guess."

She opens the top drawer of her desk and takes out two envelopes, then holds them right before my eyes. The tea's steam momentarily clouds the formal handwriting, but after a moment the words come clear. One envelope is addressed to Mr. Charles Warren, c/o The Alba Public Library. The other is addressed to Mrs. Charles Warren, c/o The Alba Public Library. The return addresses on both envelopes read:

Admissions Office
Union University
Pasadena, California

Wet heat sears my thighs. Miss Berger drops the envelopes on the desk and swiftly extracts the dripping mug from my hands and sets it on the floor.

"Look what I've done!" My voice breaks with emotion far greater than what's called for. "I've gone and spilled all over everything!"

"Not *everything*." Miss Berger yanks off her bandana and hands it to me. Her short hair stands on end; she clearly couldn't care less. "Go ahead, use it." She gestures at the bandana. "No, don't worry about the chair. Take care of yourself first."

Dutifully, I try to dry my dress. Then Miss Berger uses the bandana to wipe down the mug. She whisks off to the back room, returns to freshen my tea, and picks up the envelopes again. They might as well be glass, the way she holds them.

"Came about a month ago, before I got the news about Charlie," she says. "I've been keeping them safe, as I promised I would. But now I can't wait any longer. Please, Ruth. Open them."

Any moment, it seems, the envelopes might *do* something. Leap from her hands. Levitate. Speak. Bite. But of course, they simply wait to be acted upon. Outside, seeping in, the wind hisses and buffets. It stirs the encroaching black fog. "I only did this for Charlie and me. That's why we both did it. For *us*. College doesn't matter anymore."

"It most definitely matters! Despair is a coward's choice, Ruth, and you're no coward." Miss Berger gives me a glare as scalding as the tea. I look away; the cooling stain on my dress becomes something to study. Last time my clothes got wet like this, I was doing wash. The time I want to remember—not the smoky night, but the clear day—there was Edna Faye, bravely working away at her math, tackling problems others might dodge. Not so long ago, I prided myself on being as brave as Edna Faye. Not so long ago at all.

I set the mug of tea on the desk. I take the envelopes from Miss Berger. While she watches, I carefully open one envelope, then the next. Side by side, I scan them. The words are nearly the same.

Dear Mr. Warren, one letter opens. *Dear Mrs. Warren,* opens the other. Then they both read: *After much deliberation, we are pleased to offer you a full scholarship to Union University.*

The letters continue from there. *Intelligence, potential,* and *congratulations.* Those are the words I can take in.

"We're accepted." My voice sounds flat.

"Indeed, and not only that, your way is paid!" Miss Berger gives me a fierce hug, then releases me. "Do you know how rare this is? What a gift—a gift for which you longed, Ruth. Now it's yours, and you must receive it. You have to say yes."

For a long moment, we are quiet, so quiet that, along with the wind, I hear something scurry across the floor. The library is often overridden with mice. When it is, they wreck havoc on the books, nibbling covers and pages. We got good at catching mice, Miss Berger and I, wielding brooms and boxes. I was the one who usually carried our captives outside. It was satisfying to see them shake off their trembling and bolt, their sleek brown and gray bodies darting into bushes, disappearing among twigs and leaves. By some kind of grace they could not possibly understand, they were free.

"A gift." I try on the word for size, wondering whether it will ever fit.

HOME AGAIN, I walk past the front door and around the side of the house, past the cackling chickens, past strutting, glittering-eyed Captain. I go to where the bellflowers bloom. At least Mother said they were blooming some vague, immeasurable time ago—the time that constitutes the days before today. I expect flowers glowing on long stalks in the noonday light, such as the light is, for the sky is opaquely gray behind a scrim of dirty air. Still, I *expect* flowers. I expect them to remind me of Charlie's eyes. But there are no blooms, not anymore. The wind and dust have stripped them away and beaten the stalks to the ground. Nothing remains of the bellflowers but a messy pulp.

I sink to the ground. Lost as I've been in black fog, I missed the chance to see that blue again.

Go.

Not a still, small voice but one that reverberates to my

marrow. Beneath the opaque sky and low-hanging haze, upon a bed of broken bellflowers I listen and hear it again: *Go*.

   Go, Charlie said once upon a time. *Go*, Miss Berger said only today. *Go*, God seems to be saying now. *Go*, says a woman I don't know, the woman I am becoming, the woman I must become. *"Go."*

THREE

I write the letter I must to Union University, declining Charlie's scholarship. I am able to do this only with Miss Berger's help. She stays by my side, encourages me when I falter. Words are insufficient to describe all that has happened, but even in their insufficiency, they work a terrible magic on me. Writing things down makes them true. Charlie's death becomes a fact fixed on a page.

Almost as an afterthought or a postscript, I accept my scholarship. "Could you qualify your acceptance a bit?" Miss Berger asks. "Could you *gladly* accept it, or *gratefully*?" At this, I draw the line. I seal the envelope, affix the stamp, and send the letter off in the mail. The next day, I return to my old job at the library. I tell Mother and Daddy about this last—it's what they wanted, after all, for me to get on with it. But I don't tell them about my college plans. Tell them about college now and I'll get such grief that, come mid-August, I'll be too weighed down to leave the house, let alone take the train to California. Tell them come mid-August, when I'm due to depart, and I might actually do just that. Depart, mouse from captivity, Rapunzel from tower. Not glad or grateful, but going.

My hours at the library are every day but Sunday, as long as I care to work. I arrive before the library opens and stay after the library closes. There's no place I'd rather be, cataloging and shelving books, leading patrons through the stacks to find what they're looking for, sending them on their way. Over my lunch break, I read voraciously. I read far more than I eat. I stay busy at all costs, for when I am not busy, I am consumed by distraction, worry, and sadness—not necessarily in this order. The black fog hovers, waiting for an unguarded, opportune moment to descend. Hope tastes tainted, at best bittersweet, without Charlie sharing the cup.

The library isn't the busy place it used to be. The people of Alba, including the children, are increasingly busy scrabbling for necessities. When that's the case, a leisurely trip to the library becomes yet another unaffordable luxury. So Miss Berger and I spend our days poring over publishers' catalogs, trying to make the best book selections for the few remaining patrons, parsing out the meager dollars left in the budget. We do other things too, of course. We fix the building's plumbing when we're able and hunt down volunteers when we aren't. We clean the toilet and sink, wipe away the red dust that seeps through crevices and cracks in the walls, and settles on every surface—on book covers, bindings, the edges of every page. We wash the windows. We mow the grass and tend the few flowers that have managed to survive. We maintain the library inside and out, and in doing so, we become better friends. Widowed, I'm able to be a better friend. The girl I was—consumed by the *we* of *us*—died with Charlie. I have to make room for others at the table or I'll eat alone for the rest of my life. It's right that I should first try doing so with Miss Berger, and she's kind enough to help me know how.

Working side by side from day to day with her, I confirm what I already assumed: Miss Berger is quite the freethinker. Years back, when Charlie wanted to talk more deeply about Darwin, she was the person to whom he turned. I knew about their exchange; Charlie relayed their conversation to me. But now I witness other examples of the confidence Miss Berger inspires. When women are in trouble—say their husbands are drinkers, or gamblers, or violent; or maybe their husbands are fine upstanding men, but the women are having health problems that lead to medical tests, and their husbands and doctors won't let them see the results, or let the women give their opinions on the results—for *whatever* the reason (and there are so many), women come to Miss Berger for advice they can't get elsewhere. At least a few times each week, Miss Berger pulls *Grey's Anatomy* or an *Encyclopaedia Britannica* from the shelf, or one of the few scholarly journals the library owns, and reads and interprets information that might prove helpful to the person in need. "It's the least I can do," she says when anyone tries to thank her. "You'd do the same for me if our situations were reversed."

One night in early August, my thoughts on my imminent departure—the packing I have yet to do, the conversation with Mother and Daddy I have yet to endure—I'm about to flip the library's sign from *Open* to *Closed* when a faint knock sounds. I open the door, but no one is there. Only when I hear the knock again do I realize it's coming from the other entrance—a narrow side door. People never enter there. I doubt most know the door *is* there, hidden as it is by dusty shelves inside and by tall, dense holly bushes outside. The library shelves that conceal the side entrance hold our oldest bound newspapers, dating from the early 1880s until just after the first Oklahoma Land Run in 1889. The few people who peruse these volumes are typically engaged in land disputes, heatedly challenging who staked what claim, settled where, and when. They're much too worked up to notice a door off to the side, more an afterthought than a door, no doubt a last-minute addition to the architect's plan. Miss Berger and I use the side entrance when we take out the garbage. Otherwise, it stays shut.

The knocking grows more insistent. I start toward the sound, but from behind her desk, Miss Berger shows the flat of her hand: *Stop.* She hurries to answer. So stealthily does she slip behind the shelves that she appears to be going into hiding.

Moments pass, during which I hear bits and pieces of a whispered exchange. Then Miss Berger emerges. Two women and an old man follow her.

No wonder they knocked at the side door. *Whites Only*: That's the library's unwritten rule, implemented by Alba's Powers That Be, to Miss Berger's fury, and these folks—the women wearing carefully pressed if well-worn dresses, along with hats and gloves; the man wearing a faded gray suit and carrying a battered gray fedora—are Negro. I would have distinguished them as *colored* until a few weeks ago, when I used that word in conversation with Miss Berger and she set me straight. We were deciding which books we might donate to the traveling library, a truck that passes through the Negro side of town about once a month. Miss Berger chose a volume, *The Souls of Black Folk*, by Mr. W. E. B. DuBois— a thinker and spokesman for his people, she explained, adding that I'd learn a great deal if I read his work. "Mr. DuBois would say that *Negro* is the current, correct term, preferred by himself and other members of his race," Miss Berger said, and laid *The Souls of Black Folk*, our library's only copy, atop the stack of other donations. As the book was up for donation, I wasn't sure how I'd be able to read it. I mentioned this to Miss Berger, and she said that we'd get another copy as soon as soon as the budget allowed. "But given the choice of here and there, I choose there," she said quietly. "It's a crime to keep the work of Mr. DuBois locked up inside this place, languishing on a shelf. This book needs to be shared with those who might not otherwise have access to it."

Could it be that one of our three visitors selected *The Souls of Black Folk* from the limited offerings of the traveling library? I wonder about this as Miss Berger hustles them into her small, windowless office and then beckons for me to follow. I have to edge my way into the room, which holds a cabinet of library supplies, the two-burner unit, the often contrary loose-leaf copy machine (manufactured in 1902), rolls of dated maps, three towers of moldering books in need of repair, and a crate that serves as both umbrella stand and Lost and Found. The room barely contains Miss Berger and the two other women, who are nearly as tall as she and big-boned to boot. In comparison to them, the elderly man seems a bird, perched on the edge of the table that holds the copy machine. When I tuck myself in beside him, he leans away from me. He's uncomfortable standing shoulder to shoulder with a white woman. He grips the rim of his hat so tightly that his fingernails pale. I wish I could reassure him, but I don't know where to begin. His female friends regard me, their expressions flat and unrevealing, as Miss Berger closes the door, and the small space becomes still more claustrophobic.

"Well." Miss Berger expels a long, shaky breath. "Here we are. But what happened to ten o'clock tomorrow night, as we'd planned?"

"This couldn't wait." The taller woman's voice is grim. She shoots a smoldering glare down her long, hawkish nose—a glare which rakes over me, then Miss Berger, then fixes on me again.

"Now, Minah." Miss Berger's voice is firm and calm. "This is Ruth, my reliable colleague. You can say what you need to say in her presence. No need to beat around the bush."

"There's real trouble this time. Can't afford any unnecessary risks." The woman—Minah—doesn't take her gaze from me.

Miss Berger says, "Ruth's not a risk, and, Minah, you know there's always trouble."

"This is different." Minah sucks in a breath. "Wolf's at the door."

For one long moment Miss Berger holds perfectly still, and I swear I can hear the beating of hearts other than my own. Then, "Say it," Miss Berger says.

Minah turns to her friend. "It's yours to tell, Susan."

"No, it's Papa's." Susan, round as a barrel, has a lushly plump face that shines with perspiration. She reaches across our tight circle to touch the elderly man's sleeve, and he gives a nod of permission. "But since he can't . . ." Susan clears her throat. "Papa was walking home from the Thorne place last night around about eleven. They kept him late, chopping wood and such."

The man's scarred, arthritic hands don't look like they could wield an ax. But I must underestimate his strength. You don't get calluses like he has from doing nothing.

"The Thorne place is way out, west on Central, where it's just dirt road. You probably know that." Susan's hands are the opposite of her father's, fleshy and dexterous, working the air. "So Papa has some miles to walk at the end of each day. He passes the Homestead." Susan hesitates, and her hands go still. "Well, you do know about the Homestead."

"Indeed," Miss Berger says.

Everyone knows about the Homestead—the first claim staked in this area during the Land Run. Rumor has it that Timothy Bradford, the man who took possession of the place, was actually a Sooner; he jumped the gun and snatched up prime property before others had crossed Territory lines. Timothy Bradford's descendants still live on the Homestead, though they've long since leased portions of their fields to tenant farmers. After three generations of wealth, they're as strapped as any other local landowners, I've heard, with harvests being what they've been in these last years.

"Papa smelled the smoke." Susan's hands, working again. "Then he saw it rising above that windbreak of cottonwoods off the side of the house." She lowers her voice. "Papa's no fool. He didn't go close. But he heard them singing. He heard their horses neigh and stomp the ground."

Miss Berger looks at me. "Do you understand, Ruth?"

Minah interrupts the answer I do not have. "No time for explanations, Sarah. Not now. White people get hungry enough, desperate enough, they get blameful. Next thing we know, it'll be Tulsa 1921 all over again."

"Papa and me, we did our time in Tulsa," Susan blurts. "We came here because of it. We don't want another Tulsa."

Thanks to Miss Berger, I know about Tulsa 1921, too. But before Miss Berger informed me, I'd heard nothing about the race riot that occurred over the last day of May and the first day of June that year. That's when a mob of white people attacked the Greenwood District, the wealthiest Negro community at that time in the United States—"it was also known as 'the Black Wall Street,'" Miss Berger said—and burned it to the ground. "The violence went on for sixteen hours," she continued, her eyes glittering with some emotion I didn't fully understand. "In the end, eight hundred Negros were admitted to white hospitals, because their own hospitals were in ashes. No one ever figured out how many people died—somewhere between fifty-five and three hundred. That's what I've heard, though the authorities put it at thirty-nine. Ten thousand folks lost their homes. Thirty-five city blocks were destroyed. All because Dick Rowland, a nineteen-year-old Negro shoe-shiner, startled Sarah Page, a seventeen-year-old white elevator operator, in the elevator of Tulsa's Drexel Building. That's the so-called justification for the riot. That and the history of these United States."

I was eight years old in 1921. It seems like a long time ago to me, and the Tulsa of that time like a backward place indeed. A race riot like that wouldn't happen now—not one that big, for the world to see. At least, that's what I've thought until today, until right this moment, when tension such as I've never known charges this cramped, airless room. All I want to do is get out of here, run far. But there's no way out. Not without pushing and shoving, making a general fool of myself and disappointing Miss Berger. Not without ignoring Susan's papa, who has balanced his gray fedora atop the loose-leaf copy machine and, like his daughter, now shapes the air with his hands. As he gestures, he opens and closes his mouth, trying to speak, emitting grunts instead. I catch a glimpse of where his tongue should be, but isn't; it's a pink nub of muscle instead. And now Susan responds to her father with similar gestures—sign language, I realize. They're *talking* to each other.

"'Case you were wondering," Minah says to me, biting out the words, "that man could talk good as you before the riot. But during it, he said something someone with a knife thought he shouldn't have, and that was the end of that."

Nausea rolls through my gut.

"Papa wonders about this new mayor." Susan is focused

intently on her father, ignoring Minah and me both. "He's heard some good words."

Miss Berger nods. "Your daddy's heard right. He's a decent man, Mayor Botts. Or he wants to be. That's my perception. We'll talk to him." Susan and Minah cut eyes at each other, and Miss Berger corrects herself. "Sorry. *I'll* talk to him. Botts seems to be more . . . well, as mayor, he has to keep up certain appearances, but he's got enough Choctaw running through his blood to understand situations like this better than any city official before him. And he's thick as thieves with the new sheriff, who swears up and down he's not like the old one." Miss Berger turns to Susan's father. "Any other suggestions or questions, Jubilant? Please share them if you have them."

Jubilant flashes his hands. "Don't wait," Susan translates. "Talk to Botts soon as possible."

Jubilant picks up his hat, then runs a brittle finger along the bottom of the rim, wiping away the red dust that must have settled on the copy machine without either Miss Berger or me noticing. The fedora has left an imprint on the machine, as perfect a circle as any crown.

"I'll go straight to the mayor's house." Finally, Miss Berger opens the door and, as air drifts in, gestures broadly, ushering us from the office. "I promise I'll talk to him tonight."

Minah, Susan, and Jubilant leave the way they came, out the side door. Miss Berger doesn't waste a moment after their departure. She snatches her pocketbook from beneath her desk. She's nearly to the front door when I manage to catch up to her. "Wait! What was happening at the Homestead? Who—"

"KKK." Next moment, Miss Berger is out the door.

I stay nearly two more hours at the library, searching out and reading everything I can find about the Ku Klux Klan and the Tulsa race riot. Turns out, even Miss Berger hasn't been able to acquire much on these topics.

THE LITTLE TIME left passes, leaving only a handful of hours before I board the train for California—the hours of tonight, tomorrow, and tomorrow night, to be exact. The day after tomorrow, soon after dawn, Miss Berger will drive me to the station. Perhaps then we'll have a chance to talk more about her visit to Mayor Botts. So far: "He listened." That's all she's said. I try to bear in mind that we haven't had time for conversation, with so much for me to finish up at the library before I go. Not that Miss Berger is demanding extra work from me, but as a thank you to her, I want to do it. I want to give the place one last, thorough cleaning and spruce up the grounds. I want to set every shelf in order, type up the story-time schedule for the fall, make necessary adjustments to the card catalog. I do these things. And I catch and release two last mice.

Now it's the end of today, closing time, the last time for me. I flip over the sign. My fingers are stained with ink from all the typing. My cuticles are torn from the scrubbing, dusting, weeding, and pruning. My hands are shaking. *Closed* has never felt more *Open*, on the precipice of a great unknown.

I turn, startled to find Miss Berger not at her desk but standing right before me, as she did on the dust-ridden, windy morning of my return last spring. She takes my hands in her own, contains their shaking. "You'll tell them tonight?"

It takes me a moment, but then I nod. I'd prefer to relay the news of my departure only after I'm entirely packed. But I know I shouldn't. In fact, I can't. It's not only that it wouldn't be fair to Mother and Daddy. There's a practical component: I've tried packing in the dark dead of night. Mother or Daddy always awake at the sound of me stumbling over or bumping into or dropping something. Bleary-eyed, they'll charge to my room (Daddy) or waver in the doorway (Mother) and ask what's what and why. I always make up some sorry excuse about end-of-season cleaning, to which the reply is always *Do it in the light of day, why don't you?* Tomorrow I will pack in the light of day. Tonight I'll tell them what's what and why.

Miss Berger catches her breath at some shift in my expression. "Oh, Ruth. Don't worry so. It will be all right. If they don't want this for you, know that I want it for you enough for both of them."

Throat tight, I manage another nod. Satisfied that my hands are steady again, Miss Berger releases them.

I FIND MOTHER and Daddy at their typical posts in the front room after dinner—Mother in her rocking chair, thumbing through her dilapidated book of handwritten recipes; Daddy in his easy chair, working on the Sunday crossword puzzle. They are listening to Gene Autry and Smiley Burnette, singing on the *National Barn Dance* show out of Chicago. Chicago sounds a stone's throw away; the radio signal always comes in loud and clear on nights like tonight, when, perfectly centered and framed by the open window, the bright moon hangs in the star-studded sky. A clean-cut hangnail moon tonight, and Chicago just down the road. But California—I don't believe we've heard a peep or a rasp of static from California. It might as well be on the other side of that moon.

I sit down on the overstuffed sofa—the fabric coarse and stiff, nothing like the lesser island of Charlie's and my once-upon-a-time life. I take a deep breath. "I'm going to college." There. I've said it.

A june bug drones against the window screen, trying to get outside where it belongs. Daddy pencils another word into little squares. He doesn't look up, nor does Mother. Smiley Burnette's accordion swells, so I raise my voice a bit. "I'm leaving in two days. For college."

Now Mother looks up, her finger set on a recipe to mark her spot, her expression muddled. She blinks in my direction. Daddy checks the worn-down nub of his pencil's lead. "Come again?" he says.

"'Whoopi-ty-aye-yay,'" Autry yodels. "'I go my way . . .'"

I leap from the sofa, turn off the radio, face them again. "I received a full scholarship to attend a four-year college, Union University in Pasadena, California. I accepted the scholarship. I leave for California day after tomorrow."

The recipe book slips from Mother's lap to the floor; stained, wrinkled index cards unglue themselves and scatter. Daddy is on his feet, towering over me, newspaper rattling in his hands. "You'll do no such thing."

I lift my chin to meet his eyes, just the shade of mine. "Try to stop me." I want to shout, but this squeaks its way out.

For a long moment, I think Daddy might do just that—try to stop me. He casts the newspaper to the floor and lifts a hand, stiff and flat, to slap.

"It'll kill me staying here." I manage to say what I've practiced these last weeks. "If I stay, I may still be breathing, but I'll be dead inside. I have to go."

He lifts his hand higher, level with my cheek.

Mother steps between us. She thrusts me back, away from him. When he dodges to the right, she shadows him. To the left, she does the same. Mother has never been more agile than at this moment, keeping her husband and her daughter apart. In the face of her resistance, Daddy seems to deflate. His expression shifts from enraged to incredulous to disoriented. His hand lowers to hover awkwardly at his hip. He resorts to words. "Rebellious," I hear him say. "Ungrateful." And something about the Fifth Commandment. Something more about sin.

Still, Mother will not step aside. "Go to your room, Ruth." She's the one who shouts this, in a tone that seems to reflect Daddy's summation of me: *Bad girl.* But I know differently. Mother is trying to protect me, not shame me. I tell myself this as I go to my room, as I lock myself inside.

I SPEND WHAT'S left of daylight packing and, after a restless night in bed, I'm up with Captain the next morning. Accompanied by his crowing, I start to pack. It doesn't take long. By the time his relentless revelry has dwindled to the occasional boastful squawk, my big, old suitcase is full. It holds everything I now call my own. My few clothes and toiletries. My Bible and my *Brothers Grimm.* The three photographs of Charlie and me: seven and six years old, dragging a wagon; just graduated from high school, brandishing diplomas; on our wedding day, clasping hands. And our wedding gift from Miss Berger—the quilt with its bright rings of fabric. Breathing a prayer—an unformed sentiment somewhere between *thank you* and *help*—I close the suitcase and lock it with a key. I tuck the key into my pocketbook, hide my pocketbook under the bed. Only then do I unlock my door and open it a crack. I hover there, listening, until the sounds of the house establish themselves. Daddy's not here or I'd have heard something from him—brusque word, rough movement, heavy footfall. Mustering courage, I slip down the hallway to the kitchen.

Mother sits at the table, weeping into her hands.

"Please." I sit beside her. "Forgive me."

"Why?" *Why should I?* I think that's the implication, but then Mother adds, "For what?"

"For leaving you."

Mother lowers her hands, revealing her ravaged expression. When she is upset, she tugs at her thinning hair; her interlaced fingers are tangled with dull strands of gray and red, a scant cat's cradle.

"You're not ever coming back, not really." She plucks at the strands, trying to free her hands of them. "With Charlie, I always thought you might. When your babies came, I let myself think, you'd need my help. Finally, I would be a real help to you. And maybe those babies would see me as something other than who I've let myself become. Maybe they would see me as brave and strong, the grandma who never scolds, who only does right by them. Maybe I would have been a good grandma to your babies, Ruth, as I've never managed to be a good mother to you."

"You *are* a good mother." I long to weep with her, but as ever, my eyes are dry. "You were so very good yesterday with Daddy—brave and strong."

"Once maybe. Once maybe I was."

"No! Not just once. More times than I can count."

She ignores this. "Mine has been half a whole lifetime of weakness. But for your babies, the other half, maybe I would have been different."

I close my eyes, but still I see them, the babies, tottering—*first steps!*—through the bellflowers with Charlie and me close behind and Mother watching from the back door, a radiant smile on her face. She looks younger than I've ever seen her, and Charlie and I are as we were before the blowout, almost kids ourselves, and our children, a boy and a girl and, yes, a baby in my arms, are the perfect combination of us two. They have Charlie's blue eyes, and my hair when it turns honey-colored in the summer sun, and his long limbs, and my smooth, clear skin. Maybe the little boy has freckles, because I love Charlie's freckles, tracing them with a fingertip until there's the reward of a smile. Little feet pound unsteadily against the earth; the flower stalks stir; the baby is a solid weight in my arms; the baby smells of milk and Ivory soap; the baby looks up at me with blue eyes so big I could fall right down into them. I could drown in those eyes.

I gasp like I'm coming up for air, and Mother's face swims before me. Abruptly, she stands and goes to the kitchen clock that long ago stopped keeping time. She takes the clock from the wall and fiddles with it until off pops the back. From the belly of the clock, she removes a slip of paper. She sets the slip of paper down on the table before me.

"What is it?"

"Look."

I look. "A check?" I look again. "A check."

Mother gives a sharp nod. Her expression has hardened to grim.

"Two thousand dollars," I say slowly. "A check from the oil company, payable to me." I look up at her again. "Mama?"

"Charlie must have been thinking *what if*. A good man watches out for the what-if."

"Life insurance?"

Mother nods, sinking back down in her chair. "Your daddy considered it his, as we've been putting a roof over your head, and it appeared we would be doing so for some time. But that's not the case after all. Your daddy still wants the check, I imagine—he had some kind of plan for it, you can bet on that—but I don't want it. It's not right to want it. Not anymore. Never was, really. Take it, Ruth."

"But—"

"Take it with you to California. And take this, too." She pulls a scrap of paper from the pocket of her apron. She's written a name there, Alice Everly, and beneath that a California address and a phone number. "That friend I told you about who went west with her family? It took a little doing, but I tracked her down. I spoke to her on the phone, Ruth. I told her you were coming, and she said to call as soon as you arrive. You won't be alone out there, not if she can help it." Mother presses the paper into my hands. "Do that for me, Ruth, promise? Call Alice Everly. Go see her when you're able. I want you to have some folks out there, our kind of people, who can help when need be."

"I'll call her for you if for no other reason. I promise."

Mother's expression softens with relief. Her eyes go misty again; she looks quickly down at the clock and gets busy fiddling with the back. When the back clicks into place, she seems like she doesn't know what to do next. She's exhausted, I realize. She probably hasn't slept a wink. So I take the clock from her, hang it on its nail on the wall, tilt it this way and that.

"Even now?"

She nods.

I wrap my arms around her. "You sure?"

"Sure as I've ever been," she says.

EARLY THE NEXT morning, the sun a cusp of orange on the horizon, Miss Berger's elegant if aged gray Zephyr ferries me down drowsy, dirt roads, and then onto busier, paved streets. Instead of her typical T-shirt, khaki skirt, and bandana, Miss Berger wears a neat bottle-green suit jacket and skirt and a matching hat. She's taking herself out to lunch, she informs me during our drive. She doesn't get into Oklahoma City nearly often enough; she's going to see a bit of what there is to see. In particular, she'll visit the library. They have entire shelves devoted to new books, and she wants to browse them.

Miss Berger parks the car near the city's brand-new

depot, and we make our way inside. Upon hearing my destination and departure time, a porter whisks my suitcase away, leaving me to carry only a picnic basket of food packed by Mother and my pocketbook, which holds the oil company's check, the scrap of paper with Alice Everly's information, and all the money I managed to save from my summer at the library—just enough for a train ticket to Los Angeles.

I start toward the ticket booth, but Miss Berger steps in front of me. With a flourish, she produces from her jacket's pocket the very ticket I intend to buy. "For you," she says.

I shake my head, stunned.

Miss Berger shrugs. "No refunds allowed."

"But I can't accept it! After all you've already done—"

"Well, I've got no use for it. You know how I feel about clutter, Ruth. Guess I'll just have to dispose of it." She manages to make a little tear in the ticket before I snatch it from her hands.

"Thank you." That's all I can come up with. When I try to express my gratitude more eloquently, Miss Berger fairly shudders with impatience and, without further ado, draws me into the waiting area. It's a grand place. She launches into a description of the architectural elements—which she read up on last night, apparently—the art deco details and terrazzo floors, the metal and glass chandeliers with their chevron designs, the bright and colorful ceilings painted with American Indian motifs.

Only a few minutes until my departure now. There's so much I want to ask Miss Berger, so much I want to know—

about American Indian motifs, sure, but also about her life, her work, how she came to help the people she helps and why. Never mind escaping Alba. At this very moment, I don't want to say goodbye.

"Do you see that long narrow rectangle spanning the far wall?" Miss Berger points; I see it. "For the Choctaw people, that rectangle symbolizes the road of life that one travels in his span on earth." She flicks me a glance. "Or her span on earth, as the case may—"

"Please," I blurt, clutching her arm.

Her eyebrows arch in surprise. "Yes?"

What to say with so much vying for my attention. *Choctaw*. The word lodges in my mind like a pebble in a shoe. "How did you know Mayor Botts is part Choctaw?"

This is not what I wanted to ask at all. But Miss Berger, patient with most any question, cocks her head, considering. "I could see it in him, and he confirmed it," she finally says. "I know quite a bit about the tribe, actually. My mother was Choctaw through and through. She grew up on a reservation and met my father, who was French Canadian, and then they came and settled in Alba, where there was land to be had . . . but not a lot of acceptance."

Here is something I want to hear. "I didn't know." I'm still holding on to her arm. I don't want to release it. Not yet. And she doesn't draw away from me. She looks at the far wall, the rectangle there. But her unfocused gaze suggests she sees something entirely different.

"My parents died in a car accident when I was sixteen. Since then, I've spent a lot of time trying to learn things they might have told me. It's been a bit of a compulsion, in fact. I probably know more about my heritage now than I would have if they'd lived."

I swallow hard. "What did you do when they died? Besides *learn* things, I mean. What did you *do*?"

Miss Berger sighs, her gaze still distant. "I tried to raise myself as I believe they would have if they'd lived. I never forgot them, but I got on with my life. I didn't go to college, as I'd hoped to do, but I worked my way into the position I hold now." She winces as if something pains her, and I loosen my grip on her arm. For a long moment, she is quiet; she feels she's said enough, I'm afraid. But then she takes a deep breath.

"I think about my mother every time I enter the library." She turns to me, present and attentive again. "The building was constructed before the Land Run as a mission school for Choctaw children, back before people became concerned about the 'Indian Problem.' Soon after the Run, the number of white children in the area surpassed the number of Choctaw—or so it was said—and the school's mission changed accordingly. The Choctaw children were removed from the school, some of the older ones forcibly, and sent to the reservation, all but uninhabitable territory, not so far from the Thorne place. I take it as no coincidence that the Klan holds their meetings at the reservation's doorstep. I also take it more than a little personally."

"I didn't know." I feel like a fool, repeating myself.

Miss Berger smiles at me, and her smile is kind. "But that's why you're going to college, yes? To learn things. To know more. To understand." Only now does she withdraw her arm. She tugs at the cuff of her jacket, trying to smooth the wrinkles I've made in the sleeve. "Let's find your platform, shall we?" Her voice is bright and energetic. "Don't want to waste that ticket."

I hurry after Miss Berger. In a matter of moments, we stand by the train. It hisses and gusts fumy steam, readying for the journey.

"Well," I say for something to say, "I guess this is it, then."

Miss Berger turns abruptly and clenches my arms. With quiet urgency, she says she trusts me, but there are my parents and the rest of Alba to worry about. One misspoken word from me, and other people could suffer more than they already have. But now I'm leaving, so now she'll tell me, as she's wanted to since the other night. "Wolf's at the door," she said in so many words to the mayor. And then he, along with the new sheriff and the two remaining officers who weren't already draped in white sheets, drove out to the Homestead, where they had a little talk with the Klan.

Miss Berger leans closer to me, and her voice becomes quieter still. "Let me be clear. The *mayor* and the *sheriff* talked, and everyone else listened, as people are apt to do when guns are pointed their way. I'm not saying it's the right way to do things—threatening violence with violence—and I don't think that's ultimately what doused the fire under the kettle. I think what did it, at least temporarily, was Botts's real threat. He promised that if there were any more such gatherings or related actions, he would go straight to the governor. He'd go higher than that, if need be. He'd contact the press out east and name names. I wouldn't put it past Botts to do something like that. He's a decent man. He knows how it is to be on the other side of the majority. So for now, at least, certain folks can sleep a little easier. I wanted you to know this before you left, Ruth. I realize it's been troubling you. I hope you can rest easier now, too."

"Did the mayor tell you all this?"

Miss Berger gives a small shrug. "Oh, I went along for the ride. I didn't get out, mind you, didn't let those lunatics see me, the only woman there. But I rolled down the car window and got an earful, believe you me. Now." She heaves a sigh, a mixture of relief and sadness. "It really is time for goodbye."

I set down the picnic basket, and we hug each other close.

"Write me," Miss Berger says, her arms still around me. "And not just postcards, either. 'The weather is beautiful! Wish you were here!' Not that. I expect full-blown letters."

"You'll write to me, too?"

"Of course."

"You'll tell me if things change? For better or worse?"

"I will." She draws away from me, her expression soft with understanding. "It's good you want to know. Keep on wanting to know as much as you can about everything you can, you hear me?"

I nod, my throat too tight to speak.

"And don't you worry, Ruth. I'll check in on your mother."

I manage once again to thank her.

A whistle blows. "All aboard!" a conductor shouts. "Last call! All aboard the Antelope, express to Kansas City!"

Miss Berger gives me a gentle shove. Next thing I know, I'm on the train. Dazedly, I find my place by a window. The aisle seat is empty, so it is easy enough for me to sit down—collapse, really—drop the basket of food at my feet, and peer through the smudged glass. There is Miss Berger, a tall figure in bottle green, walking back to the waiting room. She pauses at the entrance, looks up and all around. She is taking in the architecture again. She isn't missing a thing.

My vision blurs.

Go, she said, Charlie said, God said, I said. And now here I am, going.

The train lurches forward, and crying, finally crying for the first time since Charlie's death, I am gone.

IN KANSAS CITY I have to switch trains—and quickly. Flustered, I hustle to a platform. Turns out to be the wrong one. I barely make it to the right one, where, accompanied by the screech of metal wheels, gearing up to go, and a conductor's reprimands, I jump onto the Atlantic Express. I take my seat—again by a window—as the train jolts forward. My companion for this leg of the journey, an elderly man, is already hunkered down by the aisle. He's sound asleep, grizzled chin to sunken chest, gnarled hands twitching in his lap. With some effort I manage to settle into place without awakening him.

All the way across Colorado, New Mexico, and Arizona, all the way to Braxton, California, the Atlantic Express has no scheduled stops. The hours stretch before me, and as they pass, the elderly man sleeps so deeply he might as well be under a spell. I, on the other hand, am wide awake, jittery with excitement and nerves. Can't focus to read or write a letter. So I watch the country roll by. After Kansas City, the towns dwindle from sparse to next to nothing—a crossing gate here, a depot there. A solitary platform flashes by. There's the occasional gas station or trading post, a few ramshackle houses. Deeper into the plains, an uneven brown line appears in the distance. Mountains, maybe? There will be canyons and deserts to come, I know, and occasional bodies of water, and always the changing sky, like nothing so much as an enormous bowl turned upside down. And there will be my memories.

Late afternoon, we pass the first Hooverville, constructed beneath a bridge. Then another under a viaduct. A few hours later, one right out in the open, no shade or shelter to be found. In these places, men, women, and children squat in lean-tos, big boxes, broken-down trucks, abandoned freight cars, fashioning some semblance of safety and security. Come sunset, they huddle around ash can fires. Sometimes, when Route 66 runs parallel to the tracks, I catch sight of jalopies and pickups straining beneath the weight of more people than they should carry, plus their worldly goods. They're heading west. Okies, like me. Arkies, like the man beside me, I learn when he finally snorts himself awake around ten at night. Motivated by a handbill, or a newspaper account, or a rumor, they're escaping someplace that just might kill them if they stay. It's foolish, I know, but every time we pass one of those vehicles, burdened with tattered families, I look for Edna Faye.

I nibble at the food Mother provided—ham sandwiches, boiled eggs, a peach, two slices of watermelon, a handful of oatmeal cookies, a jug of water, and a thermos of coffee that goes from hot to cold over the course of the trip. A wealth of food, the kind of food my parents can't afford. Mother took a risk, buying such things. If Daddy finds out—well, I don't want to think about it. I offer to share the wealth with the elderly man. He politely resists until around midnight, when he accepts half a cup of cold coffee and a ham sandwich. In a heartbeat, he downs both, and then again he sleeps.

I doze off and on, too. I dream of Charlie. When the dreams are sweet, we are all tangled up together, we are reading together, riding this train together, going off to college together. But when the dreams turn bitter, more like the truth, we are falling, drowning, burning, dissolving, vanishing, gone. Charlie is so present that each time I open my eyes, I turn to the elderly man beside me, expecting my husband instead. The shock of this doesn't diminish, nor does the dismay that follows.

I am fully awake at dawn. Outside it's desert, pure and simple. How the earth has changed color over this long ride—red to brown to all the many shifting shades before me now—but always cracked and parched. The vegetation has evolved, too. Patchy, struggling farm fields have yielded to tenacious scrub, tumbleweed, and cacti. There's the occasional blooming thing as well—blurred splotches of pink, yellow, or red that must be cactus flowers.

At Braxton, the Atlantic Express finally slows to a stop. I'm considering standing, climbing over my still-sleeping seatmate, stretching my legs, when suddenly, the conductor appears, grabs the old man, and drags him down the aisle and out the door. As fast as that it happens. Then there's a scornful shout from the conductor—something about a ticket. I twist in my seat and see the old man sprawled on the cement platform, arms and legs akimbo, a look of resignation on his face. The wind lifts his battered hat and pushes it, haphazard as a tumbleweed, onto the tracks. "All aboard," the conductor shouts, and the train lurches forward again.

There's a billboard above the platform where the man still sprawls:

JOBLESS MEN KEEP GOING!

WE CAN'T TAKE CARE OF OUR OWN.

BETWEEN BRAXTON AND Los Angeles, the towns increase in size and activity. Palm trees thicken, as do other tropical plants that I cannot name, and flowers. In between the towns, lush farms spread. People of all ages work the fields—people who resemble me as much as anyone, or my previous seatmate, or Edna Faye and her family. Okies and Arkies, they look to be—probably still bone white where their skin is covered; otherwise, sunburned tender pink to harsh red—tending crops low to the ground or fruit trees in rows, too, bending and rising, reaching and plucking, gathering harvest that would be considered heaven-sent back home. In spite of that billboard, it seems to me this land is very much taking care of folks, whether they're originally its own or not. I hope that all the others I've witnessed trying to get here will find such reward. There's work if a body wants it, surely, and food to be eaten, and a place to rest.

Just outside Los Angeles, I try to pray. I pray for myself. I start there. But then I pray for the old man who accompanied me from Kansas City to Braxton. For Mother and Daddy, Miss Berger, Minah, Susan, Jubilant, and Mayor Botts, I pray. For Edna Faye. For safety and mercy. For hope in the future.

It's evening when we arrive. The Los Angeles train station proves immense—or it feels that way to me. It's something of a mess too, damaged by a recent earthquake. And it's crowded; harried people running every which way, jostling and pushing as they pass. With the help of an impatient porter, I locate the electric trestle train that will take me across something called the Arroyo Seco, then on to Pasadena's Santa Fe depot. What at other times might be a short jaunt seems nearly as long as my previous cross-country trip—I'm that anxious. I learn one thing along the way, which I will try to remember to write to Miss Berger: The Arroyo Seco is a vast canyon unlike anything I've ever seen before. Canyon crossed, the trestle train makes its way into Pasadena and the depot. And like that, I am where I will be, I imagine, for four years to come. Wobbly-legged, I step off the train and into my new life.

But I don't know which way to go. So I follow the lead of other passengers, who hurry on, familiar with these surroundings. We wind up at the baggage claim. Swiftly, the others collect their belongings, and then they're gone—out the depot's exit and off into the evening. I'd like to follow them, ask the kindest-looking of the bunch directions to Union University. But my suitcase is nowhere to be seen.

I find a young, snub-nosed attendant, who does some scrounging in the Lost and Found, then checks my ticket again and nods knowingly. This happens all the time, he says, with passengers who've switched trains over the course of a trip as long as mine. Another train from Los Angeles will pull in about an hour from now. Most likely my suitcase will be on it. "Most likely," he repeats. "Not a promise. You'll have to wait and see."

Suddenly, I am exhausted. The Lost and Found has gone a bit foggy. I pass my hand over my eyes, but the fog, which holds my own particular gloom, doesn't seem inclined to fade away.

The attendant points at a nearby bench, suggests I take a seat. When I don't muster myself, he takes me by the arm and escorts me there. He regards me for a moment, his brow furrowed with worry. "Where are you heading?"

"Union University. I think."

"You think?"

"I know."

"New student?"

I nod.

"Know how to get there?"

I shake my head.

He pulls a tablet from his pocket, rips off a piece of paper, and draws a little map. "Turn right here and then head straight down here." He traces the way with his finger. "Can't miss it."

"Thank you." At least there's this: a map to follow.

"If I'm still here when you leave, I'll give you a ride."

My skin prickles. This is the kind of situation Mother always warned me about. "No, thank you."

The attendant shrugs. "Skittish, huh? Probably wise, country girl like you." And then he strolls away.

I'd close my eyes, but yes, I'm skittish—so skittish that I tuck my pocketbook beneath my rump and clutch Mother's empty basket like a shield to my chest. I grow increasingly weary, and, at the same time, increasingly edgy. It's an unpleasant combination—my bones like lead, gravity pulling me down. Even as my nerves ping, I strain to glimpse any questionable stranger.

Perhaps a quarter of an hour into the waiting, a burst of activity causes me to leap to my feet. Here it is—whatever bad thing is going to happen. Several official-looking men in suits and hats stride into the depot and take up posts outside the entrance to the train platforms. They are followed by two policemen, blackjacks drawn, leading perhaps thirty people. Two other policemen bring up the rear of this group. When an elderly couple falls behind, they prod them forward. There are men and women of all ages, boys and girls, babes in arms. They fall into an uneven line, all the while remaining strangely silent. Only a few murmur exchanges, and these are shared so sporadically that it takes me awhile to realize many are speaking Spanish. The people are well dressed, well groomed, and brown-skinned, not sunburned. Mexicans, I suppose they are, given the fact that this is California. Watching them, I can't help but think of the circle of people I saw with Mother and Daddy late last spring, soon after my return to Alba. The people were gathered together in a field near the Thorne place. We heard the sound of their drums before we saw them dancing. It was Good Friday. We were driving to a nearby town where a church was presenting a reenactment of the Crucifixion. "Some kind of powwow," Daddy said scornfully as we passed the gathering in the field. He blared the horn in an effort to disrupt their meeting. As we drove on, I watched out the rear window, unsettled by the dancing, the drums. The whole affair seemed of another time, another world altogether. When the gathering was finally out of sight, I sank back into my seat, vaguely comforted that I was me, not one of them.

What would Miss Berger have thought of such comfort? What would she think about the comfort I'm feeling now? *Whatever bad thing is going to happen is not going to happen to me after all.* What would Miss Berger think of the line of people before me? I shiver, though the air is anything but cold, and sit down again on the bench.

The people begin to shuffle toward the platform entrance. As they pass beneath the archway, the adults in the group hand slips of paper to the official-looking men, who make notations on thick documents clamped to clipboards. "Step on it!" a police officer occasionally snaps, or "*Vámonos!*" At this, some of the people start, casting anxious glances to either side or over their shoulders. "No dallying!" "Don't waste time!" a police officer says. "Eyes forward." Lot's wife, turned to salt all because she looked back—the story from Genesis flashes through my mind. But this is no hurried flight from fire and brimstone. This—whatever it is—is conducted with practiced efficiency by the officiators and docile resignation by those officiated.

The last people pass through the platform entrance, and porters soon follow, pushing trollies stacked with luggage, trunks, and crates. The group's belongings, I gather. There are surprisingly few items for so many people.

There's a sharp whistle and the now-familiar screech of brakes against metal wheels. A train is approaching; there are its last gasps of steam. I glance at the clock on the wall and leap to my feet. The porter's promised hour has come to pass. This must be the train that may—*will*—hold my suitcase. Maybe it's the same train that will take these people away. But I don't want to think about them now. All I want is my suitcase—retrieving it, and what's inside: my clothes and toiletries, the photographs of Charlie and me, my wedding dress and veil, the bright quilt beneath which we slept. Find my suitcase and I'll be so relieved that a late-night walk through this unfamiliar city will be a breeze. I have a map, after all. Finding a place to sleep—my dorm room, I hope— most likely waking a sleeping roommate I've never met . . . all this will seem no real challenge at all once my suitcase is in hand.

I head toward the platform, intent on locating what's left of my life. I'm almost there when one of the officials spots me. He rushes over, blocks my way. "What do you think you're doing, Miss?"

Mrs., I almost say. *Or ma'am, if you prefer.* But then I remember what I want and consider my best plan: Make him a certain ally. I smile at the man. Beneath the brim of his snappy hat, his features reveal themselves as those I've come to think of as particularly Californian, handsome yet generic, like the Hollywood stars I've seen on cinema posters throughout the years. His face has the broad appeal of buttered bread or vanilla ice cream—deliciously palatable, easily digested. Still smiling, but suddenly aware of my disheveled state, I pass my hands over my hair, gone lank from the long trip. "My suitcase might be on that train. I need to find it."

"Well." The man flashes what I suppose is his winning smile. "There's government work going on here. Can't let you interrupt that." To my amazement, he chucks me under the chin. "FDR wouldn't like it, see. I'd have to tell him about you, and he'd take real offense." As proof of his connection to the president, he flashes a document bearing a government seal. "So take your basket, Little Red Riding Hood, and hurry on back to your seat. I'll rustle up your suitcase if it's there. But we got to get these people boarded. They're going back to where they belong, courtesy of the United States government. Back to Mexico."

"Why?" It's risky to ask—I might irritate him. But I'm curious.

"Repatriation, that's why. It's what these people have wanted and needed for a long time—a free ride back to their Mother Country. We're giving it to them. And we're making more jobs for Americans to boot."

I think of all those people in the Hoovervilles, U.S. citizens with nowhere else to go. The old man sprawled on the train platform. Edna Faye. "Oh. Well, that's good, then, but . . . you won't forget my suitcase?" I try not to sound pushy. Needy, maybe. But not pushy.

The man glances at something behind me. "Looks like

you're missing something other than a suitcase. You might want to scoot on back there before you lose that, too."

I whirl around. My pocketbook. I sat on it to keep it safe—the insurance check inside, along with my earnings and Alice Everly's address—and then I left it right out in the open for anyone to steal. You can't tell from looking. Anyone might need extra loot. Anyone might be desperate enough. Any of the Mexicans. I bolt back to the bench.

That's where I'm waiting some twenty minutes later when the Mexicans begin to board the train, and the man, handsome as a movie star, friend by proxy of FDR, swaggers toward me, my suitcase in his hand.

PART II

September 1934–April 1935

FOUR

My dorm room door bangs open and my roommate bursts in, her soft blond curls a tangle of leaves and twigs, her suntanned arms filled with flowers. Helen St. Pierre inclines toward theatrical entrances, and exits, too; makes sense, as she's a member of the drama club. Like me, she has declared herself an education major, and she hails from Oklahoma (albeit Heritage Hills, a posh Oklahoma City neighborhood). Our home state is where the similarities between us end. Just look at us now. I'm in my nightgown, working at my desk, which faces Helen's by our turret window, hot tea gone cold in my cup. The room and I smell of nothing so much as dusty books and stuffy air. Dazed and bleary, I've been studying all morning. I've forgotten to eat lunch again; I may have forgotten to wash my face and brush my teeth. My hair, raked by my fingers as I work, is most certainly a frizzy brown mess. Helen, decked out from head to toe in blue and gold (school colors, down to her saddle shoes), smells of citrusy perfume and fresh air. Her green eyes glisten; her red lipstick smacks of *freshly applied*. Except for the fact that Helen's hair has turned nest, she could be a poster girl: *Union University Freshman Coed*.

"Up and at 'em, Ruth."

I twist my wedding band around my ring finger. Sometimes, faced with Helen's enthusiasm, I briefly forget who I am. I forget, for instance, how much older I am than Helen and the rest of the freshman class. The three years' difference typically feels like three decades, except for those rare times when Helen's energy turns contagious. Take right now. Her enthusiasm, like strong coffee, makes my knees jiggle nervously beneath the desk. In a flash of blue and gold, she's distracted me; I'm discontent, sitting here like I have every Saturday since school started, my nose in a book, a pencil in my hand, notepaper at the ready.

"I'm up." I press my knees together to stop their jiggling. "And at 'em, for that matter." As a testament to this, I tip my textbook, *Introduction to Educational Practices,* toward my roommate.

"Oh, for heaven's sake." Helen strides to my desk. She slams my textbook closed, plucks a pink carnation from her bouquet, tucks it behind my ear. "We've got things to do and places to go. And I won't take no for an answer."

It's happened before; it could happen again, right here and now. She's spirited me away several times. And then in the middle of doing who knows what, who knows where—going for sugary coffee or a lazy stroll, playing badminton or Chinese checkers, baking angel food cake in

the dormitory kitchen, listening to a conservatory student's oboe, viola, or tuba recital, riding in cars with boys
whose names I can never remember; in short, playing the
typical freshman coed—memories will descend with a
vengeance. *Empty,* I'll think. And encroaching in an instant, the black fog. There goes my desire for the present
and my hope for the future, both of which are bound up in
the work I'm supposed to be doing. Reading, studying,
learning—that's what I can count on to keep the black fog
at bay. Not play.

I pointedly reopen my textbook.

Again Helen shuts it. She pulls such a clownish grimace
that I can't help but smile. Heaven help me. Smile and next
thing I know, she'll have me laughing, and next thing after
that, we'll be off. I force my expression into a disapproving
glare. "You raided the chapel's flower beds again?"

"Absolutely not." Helen tosses her head as if insulted. "I
raided other gardens this time. I am nothing if not equitable
in my thieving."

Hel Fire is Helen's nickname. She and I have lived together for nearly a month now, and I can attest that she
takes on life with red-hot zeal, her will expressed more
often in impulsive rampages than intentional choices. Already, Helen is notorious for her ability to wreak havoc on
campus with her clandestine pranks and shenanigans. (Can
freshmen steal the senior bench, layered with decades of
painted signatures? At Helen's prompting, she and her
friends can. Should anyone even think of making off with
laboratory mice and releasing them onto the stage during an
all-school meeting? Sure, why not.) Helen's nights, extend-

ing far past curfew, and multiple flirtations are becoming the stuff of legend. College, for Helen, is nothing more than a wild ride. And she makes no bones about the fact that, in addition to a BA, she is intent on earning an MRS degree by the time she graduates. I don't imagine she will have a problem achieving either. Helen is smart enough to earn her BA—possibly with honors, if she would only choose to study and attend classes. And she is winsome and lovely enough to find a husband, if that's what she desires. She quickly captures everyone's affection. The first time I saw her, standing at the entrance to the Student Union, flanked by two clearly smitten fellows, she captured *my* affection. "Ruth Warren! Comrade in arms!" she cried, abandoning the boys and running down the steps to where I stood. "I've been waiting and waiting for you, and finally, here you are! Why, you're wearing exactly the same cute blouse as in the photo on our dorm room door! How smart of you, to make it so easy for me to pick you out in a crowd!" I didn't mention that I don't have many blouses to choose from; Helen figured that out soon enough.

Now she drops her messy bouquet of flowers on top of my desk, scattering leaves and petals across my book and papers, then sashays over to her closet and takes a crystal vase from a shelf. She goes to the little sink in the corner of our room and fills the vase with water, then returns to my desk and carelessly arranges the flowers, tossing broken-stemmed and wilted castoffs to the floor.

"It's homecoming." She says this almost as an aside as she dusts my cup of tea with a lily's pollen.

"I've heard." I take the carnation from behind my ear,

breathe in its spicy scent, plunk its stem into my tea, and then bury my nose in my textbook again. I *will* be prepared for Monday morning's exam. It's my most important class, Introduction to Educational Practices. I don't want to disappoint myself or the teacher, a man by the name of Professor John Tobias, who is nearly as charismatic as Helen—at least to me—but for entirely different reasons. Professor Tobias radiates intelligence. He's taught me more about teaching in this past handful of weeks than I dreamed I'd ever know. Helen, who's in his class with me, says I hang on his every word. She, on the other hand, hangs on his every physical feature. His good looks, she's told me, are the reason why Introduction to Educational Practices is the one class she never skips.

She gives the flowers a final fluff. "It's the biggest game of the year."

"And that holds some appeal?"

Helen ignores me. "Last night's spaghetti supper, fine. You were allowed to miss that. But not this." She sets the flowers on top of her dresser, then returns to her closet and takes down one of my favorites of her many, many articles of clothing—a belted blue dress that is both too short and too fully cut for Helen but fits me just right. She lays the dress across my unmade bed. "There is only one freshman year, and it has only one homecoming football game. You will attend. There's an open dorm afterward, and I've told everyone the best party is happening right here in our room." She dusts her hands together as if every problem has just been solved. "It's a kind of mountain-and-Mohammed setup, don't you know. Go to the game and join the party, Ruth. You might as well. Or soon enough, the party will come to you. I don't care if you're still in your nightgown. I don't care if this room is still a pigsty. I'll make you join in, one way or another."

Heaven help me, I'm eyeing that dress. Its beautiful color makes everything else look dreary, dull, and drab. Everything but Helen and her bouquet of flowers. I force my gaze back to the book; the words swim before my eyes. "I need to study."

"*If* you come to the game, Ruth," Helen blithely continues, "I will spiff this place up while you get dressed. That way you won't be embarrassed. Because, unlike me, who couldn't care less about the state of things, you will suffer acute shame when our slovenliness is made public. I know you will, and you know you will. Might as well give in."

In the face of hard times, keep a neat house, Mother always said. *Monday, Wash; Tuesday, Iron*—I've let things go. Shucks, if Helen isn't right. I don't want anyone but my roommate to see me in this state.

"Cruel girl," I say.

"Terrific!" Her face brightens as if I've paid her the finest compliment. "I'll get the room ready. Once you're dressed, I'll get *you* ready."

"I'LL SAY THIS." Helen gives me the once-over outside the football stadium, adjusts the blue dress's belt buckle so that it's centered on my waist. "You clean up real nice."

"I should." I duck my head, dodging the compliment. "You only spent an hour on me."

"Not so. I spent twenty minutes on the room and thirty

minutes on you." Helen tosses back her shining hair, free of twigs and leaves. "I spent the other ten minutes on me. Really, though, you should let me dress you up more often."

"I'm not a child."

"Every morning, for instance." Helen is as good at ignoring things as she is at taking things by storm. She gives a nod to the group of upperclassmen eyeing her, and me, too. "Just look at the attention you're getting."

Not even on my wedding day did I wear lipstick, as I am now (Helen's, waxy-tasting). On my wedding day, I simply swept my hair up into a loose bun. Whereas today Helen, having combed through the rattails, has crimped it into loose waves that "frame my face and graze my shoulders," as she put it.

Charlie never cared about such things. Charlie loved the way I looked, plain and simple. I wipe the back of my hand across my lipsticked lips, suddenly ashamed.

Helen glances at me. "Oh, sweetheart." She's heard me calling out in the night; she's been startled awake by my bad dreams; she's held me while I cried. Her expression softens. "Come on." She pulls a silk handkerchief from her dainty pocketbook and wipes the smeared lipstick from my mouth and chin, then links her arm through mine. "Let's find us a seat where there's less scrutiny."

We show our student identification cards to the barrel-chested, blue-uniformed campus guard at the gate, whose jolly "Welcome, ladies," uttered through the bristles of his gray mustache, belies his threatening appearance. Helen navigates us through the crowd gathered at the concession stand and onto the sidelines. From there, she leads me halfway up the wooden bleachers, where we sit down. Soon she's engrossed in a conversation with a fellow bearing a blue-and-gold Fighting Spartans pennant. To my relief, they allow me to keep to myself. This first football game will be my last; I might as well take in the scene. It does feel good to be outside on this balmy, clear day. The warm breeze carries the minty hint of eucalyptus. Flatlander that I am, I'm struck, as always, by the mountains that ring Pasadena. And there, in the distance, rises the Rose Bowl, a horseshoe-shaped structure that dwarfs this little stadium. The Rose Bowl glints in the sun, winking whitely at me. I've heard that in a few months the mountains will be white, too—capped with snow—but for now they're as brown and dry as the turf of the football field before us. Turns out Pasadena—all of California—is also weathering a drought. The dust isn't nearly as pervasive as it is back in Texas or Oklahoma; there are no black blizzards here. But the amount of water it would take to make this field green is beyond the university's means. The surrounding parks and lawns have gone brown, too; they will stay that way or get worse until streams flow in the arroyos again. Only flowers flourish under the care of watchful gardeners—and there are fewer flowers than usual, I've heard (though to my eyes, vivid blooms accent every open space on campus). *Flores*. That's what the gardeners say, tending the beds.

Flores. Arroyos. Seven weeks ago, I would have known these things only as flowers and canyons. But now, without even trying, I have Spanish words on the tip of my tongue. The language is everywhere, on street signs, churches, and missions, in shops and cafés. And everywhere, people speak it, not English. I should have expected this, given my experience at the depot on the night of my arrival, but the fact continues to take me by surprise. "What country are we in again?" I sometimes ask Helen and she sometimes asks me. But we've learned that California was Mexican Territory about as recently as Oklahoma was Indian Territory. So I guess that explains why.

Helen clutches my arm. "It's starting!"

The game, I realize, blinking at the football field. That's what she means. That's why we're here, after all.

The bleachers grow crowded as the game goes on and on and on. Though Helen tries to explain the rules, talking of downs and yards, offense and defense, I grow antsy. My books, the exam, the letter I owe Miss Berger—these things seem to exert a magnetic pull. Finally, as the crowd's shouting crescendos, Helen leans over and tells me that we're nearly at the end of the second quarter. "Halftime's coming right up!" From her tone, this is a good thing. "Does it take another half to make a whole?" I ask in all seriousness. Helen gapes at me and then laughs. Her laughter is my answer.

I try to watch the cheerleaders. Young men wearing blue and gold sweaters and neatly pressed slacks flip young women wearing blue and gold sweaters and shin-length skirts into the air. There's additional gymnastics and a whole lot of shrieking. *U-N-I-O-N S-P-A-R-T-A-N-S!* Repeatedly, they spell the words, until I can't think what they mean. I lean my elbows on my knees, clap my hands over my ears, stare blindly at their antics. Let my posture connote relaxation for Helen. Actually, I'm trying to muffle the din and let my mind wander anywhere but here.

My mind wanders to wondering, to *if*. If Charlie had boarded the Antelope with me, if we'd changed trains in Kansas City together, if we'd traveled across the rest of the country to Los Angeles, if we'd made our way through the train station there (marveling that the earth could heave and quake as it did less than a year ago, leaving such disrepair), if we'd settled into one of the college apartments set aside for married students, if we'd plunged into freshman year together, if we'd been older than most everyone else together, if we'd *been* together . . . would we have spent this Saturday afternoon taking a break from our studies? Would we have gone to a football game? Would we have felt more at home at homecoming together than I feel on my own? Or would we have stayed in our apartment, shared popcorn for an afternoon snack, quizzed each other for tests, napped when we got tired? Would we have said "Our bed is an island"? Would we have drifted together on an ocean of our own making?

"For heaven's sake!" Helen whispers urgently into my ear. "You're shivering. Are you okay, Ruth?"

I hug myself tight.

"You're cold like you get." A statement not a question. Helen knows. She puts her arm around my shoulders. "Look, it's halftime. You stay put, and I'll go get us some hot cider and donuts. They make the donuts fresh here. They're always nice and warm."

With the pennant-waving fellow at her side, Helen descends the bleachers at a brisk clip. Much of the crowd has proceeded her, leaving me and a few other stray souls to mind belongings and seats.

The university marching band is milling about the field, playing a jazzed-up version of a popular ballad I've heard on the radio but can't name, when from beneath me comes a rustling. A whimper follows, and the rustling intensifies to scrabbling. I start—thoughts of rodents, nothing like the library's mice, more like rats, maybe raccoons or skunks, given the volume of the scrabbling—and the heel of my left shoe, *Helen's* shoe, a fancy blue-and-white spectator pump about one size too big for me, catches on the riser beneath my feet. The shoe drops down into darkness below. There's a thud as the shoe makes contact, another whimper, and then more scrabbling.

"No," I say, as if the shoe will hear and obey, magically reverse its fall and slip itself back onto my foot. These spectator pumps cost more, I'm sure, than all the shoes that I've ever owned put together. They're supple, finely stitched leather fit for a debutante, which is exactly what Helen was. If only I'd resisted borrowing them. Vanity, vanity. Now I'm going to have to climb down into the dark and deal with whatever is there. Let this be a lesson to me.

I hoist the hem of Helen's dress and kneel where my feet should be, take a deep breath, ready myself for the drop. Then, as my eyes adjust to the dim, the sun shifts, emerging from behind a cloud to filter in thin planks between the risers.

Children. Children, not rats. A boy in particular, holding Helen's blue and white shoe. He tips his head up to meet my eyes, and the sunlight glances off his black hair, illuminates his round, brown face. He wears small wire-rimmed spectacles, and behind these, his eyes are black and almond-shaped, with lashes so long they're noticeable even from this distance, in this dusty light. He wears a short-sleeved shirt, buttoned to the throat, and belted trousers; the sunlight glints on his shined shoes and on the lenses of the spectacles, momentarily obliterating his eyes. He looks to be about nine or ten years old.

The other children gather closer around the boy. I do a quick head count. All together, there are six kids of various ages. There's even a toddler, cradled in the arms of an older girl. They look to be Mexican. They watch me warily. Even the toddler appears guarded and anxious.

"I accidentally dropped my shoe." I keep my voice light, trying to put them at ease.

"We weren't going to take it." The boy goes up on the balls of his feet and lifts the shoe as high as he can. "Are you able to reach it?" There's not a trace of an accent in his voice. He sounds more Californian than I do, with my Oklahoma drawl.

"I'll try." I'd lie down on the riser, but there's the problem of Helen's beautiful dress. So I bend over and reach down as far as I'm able. The boy stretches his arm, too, but there's still a good twelve inches between us.

"I'll throw it to you," he says.

"Gently."

He nods. "Underhand."

We smile at each other like conspirators.

Then the rustling starts again. The children murmur and mill around the boy; the older girl clasps the toddler in one arm, points at something off to the side. They are not smiling now, not one of them, not the boy holding Helen's shoe, either. "Run," I hear one of them say. They tug at one another and at the boy, and now they cry out, yanking at his shirt so that it comes untucked, pulling and pulling until he drops Helen's shoe. In a scramble of limbs, they are gone. There is Helen's shoe, lying below me among the litter. The stands quiver with the weight of the returning crowd.

"What are you doing?"

It's Helen, standing over me, a steaming paper cup in each hand. Cider. I can smell it from here. The fellow behind her carries a grease-stained bag that must hold donuts.

I force a smile. "I'm having a bit of an adventure."

Feet slap hard against the ground beneath me, and there is the boy again. In a single swift gesture, he grabs Helen's shoe and tosses it up, underhand.

I catch it. "Bravo!" I shout, delighted.

"Hey, you! Kid!"

This is a man's voice, loud and angry down below. A yelp escapes the boy, and he whirls around to bolt. But he makes it only a few steps before the man, hunched low, scuttling crablike beneath the bleachers, grabs him by the tail of his untucked shirt. It's the barrel-chested, mustachioed campus guard who checked our identification cards at the gate. He grabs the boy by the collar, too, and the boy claws at his thin, brown throat.

"You're choking him!" I cry, but the guard doesn't release his hold. As he drags the boy out of sight, I realize that choking is not the boy's worry. "Papa's cross!" he gasps.

"You broke Papa's cross!" And there it is, small and silver, gleaming on the littered ground. A cross and, threaded through it, a torn cord. The boy must have worn it around his neck.

Helen is saying something, but for once I'm ignoring her. I slip off the other blue-and-white spectator pump, tuck both shoes under my arm, swing my legs around, hang perilously from the waist for a moment, the riser cutting into the blue belt of Helen's dress, and then I push myself off and drop. My knees buckle when I hit the ground, and I sit down hard, wincing. "Ruth! You okay?" Helen cries. I think I say something reassuring as I shove my feet into her shoes, snatch up the silver cross, and then, following the guard's lead, head toward the back wall of the bleachers. There's a gap that opens out into the parking lot. They must have gone through it. I do, too.

In the open air, I look around for the boy and the other children. But there are only adults walking to their cars, and not one of them is the guard. I look down at the little silver cross and then at my wedding band. Certain things should not be lost or removed. Certain things should never, ever be abandoned.

It seems imperative now that I find the boy and return his cross. I begin to search the grounds around the stadium, the streets to either side. In the distance, boat horns blow and shrill whistles sound as points are gained and lost. Minutes turn into an hour; the game surely is drawing to an end. But still, no sign of the boy or any of the children. Like Charlie, they seem to have vanished from this earth.

A timer buzzes faintly, reminding me of a bee trapped under a glass. The cheer that follows suggests the Fighting Spartans have won.

Helen has better luck finding people than I do. She locates me on the front lawn of the campus, where I'm having one last look in case the boy is hiding there among the trees—palm trees with their great leaves drooping from the drought, orange trees with their ripening fruit. Navel oranges, I've been told these are. In the late-afternoon light they gleam like lanterns among the branches. Come November, when they're at their tastiest, students will be allowed to pick and eat them. This year, given the drought, the oranges may need to be picked and eaten earlier than usual; the drought will shorten their season. Helen, mingling with our peers, learns things like this and relays them to me.

Now she runs to where I stand, beneath what would be an abundance of fruit back home. She catches hold of my arm. "Your hair's a mess! And thanks to you, Ruth, we're late for our own party!"

She leads me from the trees to Garland Hall.

WE ENTER OUR dorm room to find college students and older alumni decked out in blue and yellow, talking and laughing, lounging about. Barely do I recognize a few faces, let alone names. The few I do recognize are girls from the floor, the closest among Helen's many friends, who are busy dishing up generous slices of blue-frosted yellow cake, popping caps from soda bottles, and distributing such victuals to the many ready takers. Four young men have commandeered one corner of the room; in perfect harmony, they perform a comically languid rendition of the school song. As always, the only words that stay with me are also the title: "All Hail Valient Spartans." The way this quartet articulates *hail*, the word sounds suspiciously like *hell*; they're singing in what I now know is "an Okie drawl," as disdainfully mimicked by those who aren't Okie at all. That's exactly what the young men are doing, I realize as the song goes on: They're making fun of people who talk more like Helen and me than not. Helen stiffens; she's heard it, too. In a flash, she's left my side and cut through the crowd. Next moment, the singing stops. With a flick of her hand, Helen disperses the foursome.

Our dorm room has always seemed good-sized to me, especially compared to the bedroom I shared with Charlie or the one I had at Mother and Daddy's house. Tonight it's tight quarters, packed to the gills, and so noisy I can barely hear myself think. A number of young women sprawl across my bed—across the quilt Charlie and I shared; young men sprawl across Helen's. People sit two to each of our desk chairs. Other girls from our floor have lugged in chairs to share, and these are occupied by multiple people as well. Our turret's three wide windows have been flung open; far too many folks perch shoulder to shoulder on the sills. Here's hoping no one takes flight and falls to the ground.

The thought of our little bathroom crosses my mind: Me inside with the door closed, collecting myself in the relative quiet, maybe tucking the boy's silver cross into the medicine cabinet for safekeeping. I manage to maneuver my way there only to find the bathroom crowded as well. Three fellows sit in the tub, pretending to row, row, row their boat, while several girls sit on the tub's rim, simultaneously calling out conflicting commands: "Hold water!" "Check it down!" "Power ten!" Another fellow sits cross-legged in the sink, and three girls have plunked themselves down on the closed lid of the toilet.

I turn away from the bathroom, my fists clenched. Everyone, everywhere, seems at ease with the chaos and closeness; even the resident director and the resident assistant have made themselves comfortable, sitting, respectively, on Helen's desk and mine. Their presence means this party is being monitored for contraband—the liquor and cigarettes of which Helen has told me some people partake, both off campus and on. The resident director, name of Miss Myrtle Voyle, sports a steely helmet of hair and the sharp eyes of a commanding officer. Her assistant, willowy Jane Something-or-other, leaps up now to scrutinize the contents of every cup, the room's every nook and cranny. I want nothing more than to escape, grab my books, and go to the library, a nearby café, anyplace quiet where I can get some work done. But when she claimed my desk for a seat, Jane removed my books and notes and put them who knows where. I'll have to find my things before I slip away. I tuck the silver cross into the pocket of Helen's blue dress and start weaving through the crowd. I'll check the closets first.

But Helen blocks my way, shoves a burlap sack of peanuts into my hands. Her eyes blaze with excitement: Hel Fire is in her element. "Mind putting these into bowls and setting them artfully about?" She foists blue-rimmed bowls upon me—crockery from the dining hall, no doubt snitched for this event. I'd chide her, but she's already back in the fray. Probably best to placate her a bit—do my duty, then disappear when the party really gets going, which, given the early hour, it probably has yet to do. By then Helen will be too preoccupied to notice my absence.

I move from peanut duty to pretzel duty. Within twenty minutes, I have learned more names than I can remember, and have been invited to more upcoming parties than I can ever attend. I've been asked out for coffee, walks, car rides around the city, and drives up into the mountains, where the view, apparently, can't be beat. Young men do the asking; boys, they seem to me. Mere children. To each and every one of them, I politely say, "Thank you, but no." Then I make sure each and every one of them sees my wedding band. To a man, they flash awkward smiles and edge away from me, until—*alakazam!*—they're absorbed in asking some other girl for her company. Someone whose left ring finger is bare.

Pretzel duty finished, I find myself standing in a raucous corner, picking away at a plate of cake. And that's when I spot my books and papers piled unceremoniously on a nearby radiator. I scoop them up, set the plate of cake in their place. Out the door I go.

It's only eight o'clock. The library stays open until ten. I take myself there. It is blissfully quiet, empty but for a few glum-looking students overseeing the place. I go to my favorite desk, hidden away in the farthest corner of the top floor, behind a shelf of old books about military history, rarely sought out by students or professors. With a relieved sigh, I open my textbook. I bow over it, try to pick up where I left off this morning. But words seem to jump and rearrange themselves before me. Why can't I concentrate? I'm always able to concentrate, even when there's no pressing need. Monday there's an exam, so tonight there's a need, especially since tomorrow is Sunday, and I try not to study on Sundays or do anything that might be construed as work. If I read, it's the Bible. Or—true confessions—one of Helen's fashion magazines.

I sit back in the chair, trying to clear my head. My hands find their way into the pockets of Helen's dress. The boy's cross. I grip it.

And like that, I'm up and heading downstairs to the card catalog. What was it the Friend of FDR by Proxy, Hollywood Movie Star man, said the night of my arrival here? Something about sending the Mexicans back where they belong. Those people at the train station seemed willing to go; they weren't strong-armed like the boy beneath the bleachers. Probably the boy beneath the bleachers was strong-armed because he didn't have a ticket to the game. But still. There's something about these two incidents. I should have looked up the word *repatriation* the first chance I had. *These are the kinds of questions you need to ask*, Miss Berger said. If nothing else, I should have done a little research for her.

I flip through the *R*s, searching for *repatriation*. There's nothing. From what the card catalog suggests, the word doesn't even exist in the English language. I shut the drawer.

How do you say *repatriation* in Spanish? I wonder. When I check, I see the library doesn't have newspapers for Spanish speakers. I couldn't read Spanish, anyway, and I know no one who can translate for me. So what does that leave me with? What other words should I find in the card catalog? *California? Mexico? Mother country?* Perhaps. But how do I find *little boy, lost?*

FIVE

Next morning, I wake tucked deep down under the quilt, trying to ward off the chill that leaked in through windows accidentally left open all night. I returned to Garland Hall soon before the party dissipated. By that time, Helen and I were both so tired, we dropped right into our respective beds. Now we face the party's aftermath. The furniture and floor, even our bedcovers, are covered with litter: smears of cake and icing, peanut shells and pretzel bits, dirty plates and crumpled napkins, soda bottles and caps.

"Ugh," Helen grumbles into her pillow. A puddle of sunlight pools on her bed; she stretches like a cat in its warmth. Her movements send a soda bottle clattering to the floor.

I close my eyes again. "Guess we better get to it."

"You don't have to help. You didn't stick around to enjoy the festivities, after all, which, honestly, Ruth . . . we played a whacky game of charades. You—yes, even you—would have had fun." She sighs. "It's a bit odd, don't you think? Ducking out of your own party?"

I open my eyes, give her a look. "*Your* party, you mean."

"Oh, I suppose." She rolls over in bed, blearily rubs her face. "Don't bother helping to clean up."

"One for all, all for one." Kicking off my covers, I bolt to the windows and close them. "Besides, then you can't hold a grudge."

"I never hold grudges!"

I hustle into my robe, wrap a scarf around my neck for good measure. "Then you'll never force me into another party again. That's a fair exchange."

Helen yawns. "I'll think on that."

It takes us nearly an hour and a half to get our domain in order. Then we dress as quickly as we're able and manage to make the last church service of the day, held in the little white chapel across the quad from Garland Hall. It's a sweet, simple service, very different from those I attended growing up, with hymns to sing and a fair portion of time for prayer. I try to pray for the boy from yesterday—for his safety and for the safety of his friends. I pray they are at their own church services this morning, sitting with their families, singing and praying, too.

On the way back to Garland Hall, I tell Helen about the children's swift disappearance from the game.

She shrugs. "Kids were where they weren't supposed to be. That's all it was."

"Maybe."

Helen gives her hair an impatient toss. "If you're going to worry about anything today, Ruth, I'd say worry about tomorrow's midterm. Even I'm a little anxious. I'd think *you'd* be overwrought."

Turns out, Helen has no qualms about the Sabbath. She tells me such notions are old-fashioned and that God would far rather she study than fritter away time and money by failing the class, which she just might do if she doesn't get at least a B on this exam. Once we're back in our room, she proceeds to pore over her textbook through the afternoon and into the evening. I can't help myself: I break the Sabbath, too, scouring one chapter after the next, refreshing my memory, and then some.

PROFESSOR TOBIAS IS "holding forth," as Helen likes to say. Midterms collected, the bell about to ring, he sits jauntily on the edge of his desk, and regales us with a description of what we'll study next. "Progressive education, based in a commitment to experiential and hands-on learning, as described in *Democracy and Education* and other works by John Dewey." Professor Tobias crosses one leg over the other, as at ease being the center of attention as someone else might be in a hammock. "I happen to have interviewed John Dewey, which will be the basis for my next scholarly article." He runs a hand through his carefully groomed dark hair. His fingers are long and graceful, his clipped nails buffed to gleaming. He wears a sapphire pinky ring. Sapphire cuff links adorn his shirt cuffs, and there's a sapphire on his tie clip, too. He loosens his tie, smiling. "I promise, if you continue to be a very good class, I'll reward you with a few particularly delectable tidbits from my conversation with Dewey. Who knows? Perhaps I'll share portions of my article. You could be my first readers—you might be able to put that on a résumé someday! But only if you're very, *very* good."

Laughter bubbles throughout the room, and inside me, too, a giddy release after so much focused concentration— directed toward a mediocre end, I'm afraid. So many questions, so little time, and me a bit sketchy on some answers, although I did anything but rest yesterday afternoon. I grimace, guiltily recalling this, as someone tugs smartly at a lock of my hair. Helen, who sits just behind me. I turn to find her dramatically batting her eyelashes. "Swoon," she breathily whispers. I scowl; she scowls back. Then she winks. "Not you, silly," she mouths. "Look around."

Some of the young women in the class do seem to be swooning. They incline themselves toward Professor Tobias, elbows on desks, chins balanced on open palms or backs of hands, eyes either wide or drowsily half-mast. There are more than a few parted lips and flushed cheeks. I sink down in my chair, embarrassed for us all, and study my desktop, sticky with old varnish and who knows what else. And there, scratched into the wood: *Prof T + Me.* I didn't notice this before. Too busy taking notes and exams, I guess. Too much, in my own way, in his thrall. Charisma and charm, couldn't care less. Looks, the last thing on my mind. But intelligence— that's another thing altogether. Surely he knows that. Surely he knows that's why I hang on his every word. I'm not swooning. I'm absorbing ideas.

The bell rings. In a rush, students stand and, chattering, gather their things. Young women surge around Professor Tobias, still lounging on his desk, exchanging pleasantries. "Thank you!" "Till next time!" That kind of thing. The lone young man in the class lingers longer; he leans against the desk like he, too, if invited, would take a seat there. Pilot, co-pilot. Captain, first mate. They have a brusque yet jovial exchange that ends in a manly guffaw. Never mind that they've taken up residence in what is typically a woman's world: a classroom for would-be elementary school teachers. They're men's men, these two. Don't anyone forget it.

"Are you coming?" Helen stands over me, textbook balanced on her hip.

"In a minute."

She nods knowingly. "Politely waiting your turn to kiss his ring?"

"Will you *stop!*"

Helen shrugs. "Maybe. When I've sufficiently goaded you to expand your horizons. There are other fish in the sea, Ruth." She saunters away.

Fuming, I clumsily collect my things. The male student slouches toward the door, only to hesitate at the threshold. "Tonight, then?"

Professor Tobias replies with a salute. General, lieutenant.

And now it's just plain old me approaching him. I've raised my hand to ask questions or give answers in class, but otherwise we haven't spoken.

"Yes?" His gaze is disconcertingly intense.

I clear my throat. "I wanted to apologize for the quality of my work on the midterm."

"Really, Mrs. Warren?" His tone is droll and dry. "Surely you jest."

My cheeks go hot. "It's true, sir."

"Well, if it's true, I ask only one thing. *Do not* make another student disclaimer in my presence. Nothing is more humiliating to either of us. Not to mention predictable to the point of boring. And you can do better than that, Mrs. Warren."

"Understood." I start to the door.

"Wait."

I glance back. Professor Tobias pulls the stack of exams onto his lap and begins rifling through them. He withdraws one and sets the others aside. I recognize my handwriting on the back page. Suddenly breathless, I watch as he scans my responses. Long minutes pass while he flips through all four pages. Then he turns back to the third page and begins to read aloud.

"'Whenever the standard of education is low, the standard of living is low, and it is for our own preservation in order that our whole country may live up to the ideals and to the intentions which brought our forefathers to this country, that we are interested today in seeing that education is really universal throughout this country.'" He drops my exam atop the others and gives me an appraising look. "Word for word, a direct quotation from the address delivered by Eleanor Roosevelt to the National Conference on the Fundamental Problems on the Education of Negroes."

"Yes, but—" I swallow hard. "I cited her as the source and mentioned the conference as well, didn't I? I intended to do so."

"You did indeed, Mrs. Warren."

"Good." My shoulders sag with relief, then tighten again. "But did the quote dominate too much? Did it overwhelm my own ideas? Sometimes I get so caught up in what I'm reading that I can't see the forest for the trees."

"I know exactly what you mean by that." His eyes glint with amusement. "But don't worry. I'm sure you made your thoughts perfectly clear, and Mrs. Roosevelt merely substantiated them."

"I hope so!"

At my fervency, Professor Tobias smiles and stands. He glances at his watch, then, almost as an afterthought, strolls over to me. His cologne smells like nothing I've ever smelled, like something out of a book by Rudyard Kipling.

"Mrs. Warren, you're an interesting woman."

I blink at him. "Thank you, sir."

"I well remember your application to Union. I was the head of the committee that offered you the scholarship. Your answers to the essay questions took my breath away. Your thoughts were sometimes a bit rough, other times downright raw. But most applicants' essay statements can be summed up as: 'I want to teach because I like children.' You, on the other hand, articulated ideas that I believe even Eleanor Roosevelt would have appreciated. So in spite of the fact that I was concerned your marriage duties might stand in the way of your advancement, I insisted we award you that sum of money. I wanted you on this campus and in my classroom. The fact that your husband is no dimwit, either—well, that sealed the deal. I felt fairly confident that he was too smart a man to stand in your way. And then I heard through the grapevine that he was awarded a scholarship by the Science Department, which confirmed my assessment of his intelligence. So I was doubly reassured."

First the surprising compliment, then the horrible reminder.

"Was," I hear myself say.

"Pardon?"

"My husband *was* no dimwit."

"I understand his gifts are—"

"My husband is dead."

Professor Tobias draws back a bit. People often respond like this when they learn of Charlie's death—as if my misfortune is contagious. "I had no idea." He clasps and unclasps his hands, then shoves them into his pants pockets. "I'm sorry."

"I'm late for my next class." I turn again toward the door.

Professor Tobias catches hold of my elbow, and with a thud, my books and papers drop to the floor. In an instant, we kneel to collect my things. Standing, arms laden, we smack foreheads. He apologizes. I apologize. And then, smoothly, as if this were his intention all along, he tells me he's in need of a teacher's assistant. The one who was assigned last spring dropped out of school two weeks into the term—a problem of funds. He doesn't want to invest more time and energy in training someone who is going to slip through the cracks before any work gets done. Or in someone who's less than devoted to the field. Or in someone who's going to give up teaching as soon as she feathers her nest.

"How about you, Ruth? Given your scholarship, I imagine you're not going anywhere any time soon. You're intelligent. You're mature. You're an experienced woman, not a giddy college girl. Are you interested in the job?"

When I hesitate, Professor Tobias goes on to say that I'll be paid, "not much but something." I'll be welcome to engage in any of his work projects or field studies that prove interesting to me—"and believe me, there are waiting lists for these." Important research, access to scholarly journals and lectures, he'll share these with me as well.

"Do well, and you'll receive a glowing recommendation from me upon your graduation—*prior* to your graduation, should you choose to seek an internship or a summer job. I don't write just anyone a letter, Mrs. Warren. You'll find my opinion carries a lot of weight in professional circles."

The clock ticks on the wall. Next class is well under way. But work projects, field studies, recommendation letters . . .

"I'll do it."

"Brava!" Professor Tobias claps his hands, cuff links flashing. "Let's meet together tonight or tomorrow evening. We've got a lot to figure out. Working with me is highly rewarding and highly demanding, the best of my assistants always say. Rewarding *because* it's demanding, demanding *because* it's rewarding. Bear that in mind as we begin."

I nod. "Tonight?"

"Six o'clock sharp, in my office. Until then, Mrs. Warren."

"Please," I say. "Call me Ruth."

His eyebrows arch, and then he nods. "I'll do that."

THE FALL TERM flies now, and my assistantship proves to be as Professor Tobias promised: equal parts rewarding and demanding. Each night I stay up late, juggling his work with mine. For each quiz I take, I grade close to one hundred. I type up his research notes, dashed off on scraps of paper. I mimeograph handouts and am his second reader for most student papers, checking for grammatical errors after he has scored the overall content and structure. Reading his scrawled remarks and criticisms, I feel for the first time that I am really learning how to write and think critically. When I'm able, I sit in on his other classes, the better to inform my efforts. I assess the multiple choice and short-answer sections of his exams, too. I record all final grades in his grade book. I repeatedly organize his cluttered office. I come to understand his quirks, habits, and preferences better than I understand Helen's; almost better than I understood Charlie's; perhaps better than I understand my own—no, *better* than I understand my own, given the way I'm changing. I feel like some kind of creature shedding its skin—not an easy process, but a necessary one. My single regret as Thanksgiving break approaches is that Helen and I aren't as close as we once were. Still, I'm never lonely. Even when I'm alone, I experience the almost palpable presence of Professor Tobias—his mentorship and demands.

"You're by far the best assistant I've ever had, Ruth," he says one night in his office. He waves his hand at the student work I've finished evaluating, stacked in neat piles on his desk. "If you ever decide teaching isn't for you, I'll take you on permanently." He stretches his arms above his head, flexing his fingers. "I merely need to determine in what capacity."

A knock sounds at his office door. I start to rise from my chair, but he holds up his hand in warning. "Let me. God knows who's here at this hour." He appears more distressed than surprised, bumping his leg hard on the edge of the desk as he bolts to the door in an uncharacteristically awkward manner. He cracks the door and peers through it into the hallway.

"Are you with someone, John?"

An older woman's quavering voice, and rising like a cloud above Professor Tobias's shoulder, a crest of soft white hair. Otherwise, his broad back blocks my view.

Professor Tobias murmurs a swift, polite response; I catch only *assistant*. Then for a moment, he and the woman in the hallway stand in silence.

"You said Patrick O'Brien would be your assistant after Nora left." Her voice is sharp, the quaver all but dissipated. Patrick O'Brien is the young man in my class. The copilot. The lieutenant.

Professor Tobias responds in a mannerly fashion, although this time his voice is so low that I'm unable to make out a word. My name, I suppose he says, and perhaps how it was a good thing he chose me over Patrick O'Brien, for I'm the best assistant he's ever had. I can't help but smile. It's exhilarating to be affirmed; only Charlie, Miss Berger, and Helen have done so in the past.

Professor Tobias firmly closes the door. He tugs his jacket into place and then, his sophisticated self again, moves easily through the close quarters of his office to sit behind his desk. He rolls his eyes heavenward; we seem to be sharing a joke. I smile encouragingly. "Who was that?"

He kicks his shoes up on his desk. The heels land squarely on student papers. "You don't know?"

"No. Should I?"

"Oh, you most definitely should. That was only Union University's finest antique. Some know her as the Old Battleax, but the Right Reverend Florence Windberry is my preferred nomenclature."

I don't know whether to chuckle knowingly or shape my expression into one of utmost respect. I hesitate, and then: "She's a minister?"

Professor Tobias throws back his head and howls with laughter. "A minister! Florence? That's rich." Tears brim in his eyes. He tugs a handkerchief from his lapel pocket and swipes them away. "I'll have to tell the other faculty you said that. It'll make their collective week."

I wince, embarrassed. "Please don't."

"No doubt Florence would love to be a minister, I'll give you that." Composed now, Professor Tobias folds his handkerchief and tucks it back in his pocket. "Heck, she'd boss God around if she could."

"Who is she?"

I sound more than a little snippish, and Professor Tobias's merriment abates. Levelly, he says that Florence Windberry is the former chair of the Education Department and faculty emeritus. When I give him a questioning look, his voice grows taut with impatience.

"She's long retired. But she haunts these halls like a specter, keeping perpetual watch and poking her nose into other people's business."

"My goodness, you're hard on her."

I intend this as easy banter, but Professor Tobias does not receive it that way. He steeples his fingers beneath his chin. Over their tips, he gives me a long look.

"Have you never encountered someone who seemed intent on questioning your aspirations and inhibiting your actions? Someone who challenged your very worth?"

Images flood my mind. There sits Daddy with the other Elders, lecturing me on my behavior; there he stands, snatching up my books—the ones he deems questionable; there he goes, carting my books away. There he is time and again, saying I'm not good enough, saying I'm in the wrong. Telling me no.

I nod.

"Who?"

"I prefer not to say."

"Tell me, Ruth." His voice is gentle but firm.

I hesitate, the words clotting in my throat. But then I blurt them out. "My father."

"Your father!" Professor Tobias draws in a sharp breath. "I loathe people like that—men like him, women like Florence." He shakes his head. "You brave thing. I applaud you for getting this far."

I study my hands, clenched in my lap. If I could, I'd take back my words. I'm not a gossip or disloyal. Despite what Daddy may think, I do try to follow the Fifth Commandment. "He wasn't—isn't—that hard on me. He's always done his best, I'm sure. He's a man of his time and place. That's all."

"A sorry excuse."

I look up at Professor Tobias, who scowls.

"You don't know him."

"But I know you."

"As well as you know Florence Windberry?" I sense that

my frustration is out of proportion to the situation, but I can't suppress it. "You act like a gentleman with her, but then you speak ill of her when she's not present. I wonder what you really think of me."

Professor Tobias regards me coldly. "I think you are a naive woman with a fair amount of potential who's received an enviable opportunity, which, if you're not careful, you might jeopardize." He spreads his hands flat on his desk, as if, in measuring their span, he will remember himself. "Now, if you don't mind, I have work to do tonight."

Clearly, I am dismissed. Flustered, I blindly stumble over a book on the floor as I make my exit. Only by catching hold of the doorknob do I keep my balance. I open the door and turn back to him, mustering myself to make things right.

"Tomorrow, then, as always? During your Friday office hours? I'll collect whatever work you have for me?"

He's shuffling through papers now. He doesn't look up. "If you like, Mrs. Warren."

It hits me then. All may be vanity—I know it is—but that by no means inhibits my desire for affirmation. Especially from authority. Especially when that authority is a man.

HE IS NOT there during his office hours the next day. A folder stuffed full of student papers awaits me instead. The grading takes up much of my weekend, to Helen's annoyance and, for the first time, mine. I have my own work to do, yet I spend three times as long evaluating that of other students', trying to be exacting and accurate in my comments, trying to surpass expectations. As a result, I neglect the two papers that loom for me between Monday and Wednesday of this week—the few days left before Thanksgiving break. I'll hand the papers in late, receive the obligatory lower grade, in order to get back in Professor Tobias's good graces.

And so it is that I spend most of Thanksgiving break alone in my room at Garland Hall or in the library, catching up. Helen has gone to meet her parents, who are spending the holiday in Santa Barbara so she can be with them. Most everyone else has places to go, leaving Union a veritable ghost town. I expected this; I wasn't planning to go anywhere. There isn't time to return to Alba, and even with the money I received from the oil company, I really can't afford the trip. I'll be lucky if I'm able to return to Alba at all over the course of the next four years, and even then I'll probably go only if there's an emergency—serious illness or (unthinkable) another death.

As far as I know, Mother, Daddy, and Miss Berger are doing just fine. Miss Berger is my primary source of information. In spite of my many letters to Mother, I've heard from her only once—a postcard with a picture of a buffalo on the front.

Dear Ruth,

I'm glad you are good. I like hearing all your news. But from now on, send mail care of the library. Miss Berger says she will put it aside for me. I got to your last letter, but the one before that, he burned it in the stove. Otherwise, everything is the same.

Your Mother

Miss Berger reassures me that Mother appears healthy: *No sign of real distress, I promise you, Ruth.* And then she surprises me by writing that Mother has begun to spend time at the library. *She visits when your father is occupied elsewhere. I quite enjoy our discussions about the books I give her to read.*

On Thanksgiving Day, Miss Myrtle Voyle invites me and a few other "Thanksgiving orphans" to dinner. We eat roast chicken, potatoes, stuffing, and gravy, balancing plates in our laps in the sitting room of the resident director's apartment. Miss Voyle, her helmet of hair freshly styled and lacquered to a metallic sheen, polices the conversation, determinedly asking each member of the small circle about our interests. The other young women, two freshmen and one sophomore, speak of field hockey, nature walks, sightseeing adventures in beautiful Pasadena. I am at a loss. Interests? I find myself talking about my assistantship and Professor Tobias.

Miss Myrtle frowns. "But what do you do for *leisure*?"

"I don't have much time—"

Miss Voyle clucks her tongue. "All work and no play make Ruth a dull girl." The other young women simper at this, and the conversation continues from there, still commandeered by Miss Voyle, who, to my relief, asks about our favorite classes. *This* I am able to discuss. Soon enough, our dinner winds down. We thank Miss Voyle profusely; indeed, it's comforting to be full of home-cooked food. If only I weren't so tired, craving a nap. I'll have to make a cup of strong tea in the dormitory kitchen. No, I will make a whole pot. I have that much work to do. One paper down, one to go. That's what I'm thinking, following the others out into the hallway, when Miss Voyle draws me aside.

"Professor Tobias is . . . compelling, wouldn't you say, Ruth?"

I watch the others escape around a corner. "He's a terrific teacher." *Terrific.* I sound like Helen talking about the latest millinery style.

Miss Voyle manages a dour smile. "He's quite the taskmaster, too."

"Yes." There's an innuendo to her tone that I don't understand. "But I knew the nature of the assistantship when I took it on. He warned me."

"I suppose he did." Her smile fades. "Well, I will be sure and let Professor Tobias know."

I blink. "Know what?"

"I'll let him know that I'm aware of his influence on you—on all my girls. Professors like Tobias don't reflect on their influence enough."

She releases me with a nod, and I return to my room. I'm no longer drowsy—I suppose that's one benefit of the exchange. I'm jittery, fidgeting at my desk. It's dark outside; I can see my reflection in the window. I'm struck by how drawn I look, a thin ghost of my former self. I shouldn't be surprised. Helen has pestered me with her concern. "Stop skipping meals, Ruth! Let's have lunch and dinner together again, as we used to. I'd like that, and you need a reminder to eat!" And then she pointed out how my wedding ring keeps slipping off my finger. She suggested I wear it as a necklace. "Otherwise, skinny as you are getting, you're going to lose it!"

For the first time in a long time, I remember the boy at the football game, the little silver cross he wore around his neck. For the life of me, I can't remember where I put the thing. Abruptly I get up from my desk and begin to search the room. It takes me over an hour, but I finally find the cross tucked in a safe place I'd never forget—which I promptly forgot—deep beneath my mattress, where I also hid my money and Charlie's life insurance check.

Suddenly terribly lonely, tears sting my eyes. Last Thanksgiving, Charlie and I ate two dinners, one with his mother, one with my parents. We took a long walk in the evening and talked about our future. It stretched before us, golden and sure. Loss and grief were other people's problems. We'd only ever start over together.

Clutching the boy's cross, I rush downstairs to the lobby, where a wooden booth holds a telephone I've yet to use. I go inside, lift the mouthpiece from the cradle.

"Number, please," the campus operator says.

I say the number.

"You do realize you'll be charged for this call? You'll receive a bill in your mailbox?"

"That's fine." I've saved most of the money I've earned from my assistantship. If that's not enough, I'll use my earnings from the library, or cash the insurance check.

The operator puts the call through. I listen to the ringing, half a country away. Like others in Alba who were once able to invest in a telephone, my parents share a party line. There's a click, then another and another, as several people pick up telephones. This is the way it always goes, along with the inevitable eavesdropping.

"Hello?" Mrs. Dennis, who lives down the road from Mother and Daddy.

"Hello?" Mr. Schneider, from next door.

"Hello?" Finally. Mother.

"It's me." I'm crying now, no doubt about it.

"Ruth? Ruth!"

A flurried exchange in faraway Alba follows, and at least one person hangs up the telephone. Mother starts asking questions, never mind the inadequately stifled breathing of whoever is listening in. Again and again, I try to reassure her that I'm all right. I miss her, that's all. Yes, I had a nice Thanksgiving. Yes, it's the warmest November I've known. Yes, I'm doing well in school. Yes, I'm enjoying my assistantship.

"What about you?" I roughly brush the tears from my cheeks. "How are you?"

Mother answers vaguely, "Fit as a fiddle." Daddy must be standing close at hand. I'd like to ask about her visits to the library and the books she's reading. But it's too risky.

"Listen to yourself, alone on Thanksgiving night!" Mother blurts. "You promised me a favor, Ruth. Don't you dare wait any longer. Call the Everlys."

For a moment, I can't think what Mother means. Then I remember: her childhood friend, the woman who, with her family, moved from Oklahoma to California when times got bad.

"Ruth? You have the number and address still? I wrote it down for you, remember?"

"I do. I carry it in my pocketbook, in case." I think it's

still there. I haven't used my pocketbook since my arrival—there's been no need. But I don't mention that.

"Hang up now and call them."

"But I'm fine—"

"They'll invite you for Christmas. Now, Ruth. Call them. You promised me."

"I did. And I will. But—"

"Now."

"Can't I talk to Daddy first?"

Silence.

I swallow hard. "He prefers not to talk to me?"

"That's right."

I hear a little gasp from the eavesdropper on the line. "Oh!" Mother yelps like she's been slapped. "Is that you, Bud Schneider?"

There's a click. Mother and I listen to the silence. Then she tells me she's hanging up, too, because I've got another call to make.

I retrieve Alice Everly's number from my pocketbook, talk to the campus operator again. She puts the call through, and this time, a man picks up. "Pride of California Canning." He sounds like he'd like to bite my head off—clearly, he'd rather be spending his holiday elsewhere. Readying myself for his ire unleashed, I give him my message: *Daughter of Mary Steele. Lives in California now, too. Hopes to visit, maybe over Christmas? Please call this number and leave a message with the Union University operator saying when you might be able to receive my call next time.* The man speaks more kindly to me now; perhaps he hears sadness in my voice. Alice Everly will be in for her shift tomorrow, he says. He'll make sure she hears every word of what I had to say.

In due time Alice Everly returns my call and leaves her own message: *No need to ring me back. We'll expect you for Christmas. Come as soon as you're able. Stay as long as you want.*

SIX

Forgive and forget. Apparently, that's Professor Tobias's motto. After Thanksgiving break, we resume our familiar working relationship, and the semester draws swiftly to an end.

On the final day of exam week, I meet Professor Tobias in his office to collect the last of the work for the semester. We are intent upon getting his grades in by the twenty-third of December. Just in time for the holiday break, when we will each, in our respective ways, be able to rest.

Professor Tobias shuts his office door against the noise of the giddy, exhausted students who are causing a general ruckus in the hallway. And then without further ado, he invites me to his home on Christmas Day.

"Who wants to be alone on the holidays? Not me. Not you, I'd venture. I'm having a New Year's Eve party, and you're welcome to that as well. I've invited a few other students and some of the faculty—only those who are up for a little fun, of course."

I thank him and decline, explaining about the Everlys.

He laughs. "You're spending your vacation working the farm with Okies?"

I force a smile. He's joking, surely. "You forget: *I'm* an Okie."

"You're absolutely not, not like that, Ruth. You're lovely, educated. You've overcome your origins—" He hesitates as my smile fades. "I apologize. What an idiotic thing to say! I'm originally from the Middle West, too, you know. Des Moines area. I simply can't stand the thought of you doing hard labor after the extraordinary effort you've given this semester. I think you deserve a little rest, that's all."

"I doubt I'll be working, except to help Mrs. Everly around the house. At any rate, they're not farmers. They work in a factory."

"Oh," Professor Tobias says wryly. "Well, that's a big difference." I stare at him, and he shakes his head, waving away his words. "Again, my apologies. Unnecessary and idiotic. I'm protective of your interests, that's all, Ruth. I truly care about you. Sometimes my feelings get in the way of my judgment, I suppose. You are special. I've never met anyone like you—more my equal than my student. Occasionally I'm unsure what to say or how to act. You leave me unsettled, and sometimes, I fear, behaving for the worst. I hope you understand."

"I understand." I don't, but I'm not sure how to express this without offending him. He's had his own kind of effect on me, and it's not purely intellectual. It's emotional as well. Like Miss Berger, he has believed in me, and so helped me believe in myself again.

Professor Tobias is watching me closely, his eyes flicking over my features. I feel the flush rising warm on my face. He reaches out and takes my hand in his. He lifts my hand carefully, like it is something precious and delicate. His fingers and palm are smooth, dry, and warm; mine, all torn cuticles and gnawed nails, have gone clammy. With his thumb, he traces the blue veins that branch across the back of my hand; my skin prickles with discomfort and I withdraw it.

Professor Tobias gruffly clears his throat. "Go easy on yourself with the grading, Ruth. It will get done. I've asked too much of you, I fear, these last months. Next semester, we must work on taking better care of you."

He opens his office door. Dazed, I turn to go. As I step into the hallway, he murmurs softly into my ear. Unsteady on my feet, I make my way back to Garland Hall. It's only when I'm in my room again that it sinks in.

"You're a fine woman. And a scholar." That's what he said.

TWO DAYS BEFORE Christmas, I walk from Garland Hall to the bus station, lugging my suitcase, which holds a few changes of clothing and some books. I buy a round-trip ticket, open-ended from Pasadena to San Jose, where the Everly family now lives.

The first bus leaves in an hour. I find a seat in a corner of the station's nearly empty waiting room and prepare to bide my time. I am out of practice when it comes to doing nothing. The last few days, I've by no means gone easy on myself. I've graded exams and papers nearly around the clock, and somehow managed to write to Mother and Miss

Berger, summing up the end of the semester and confirming my Christmas plans. Driven as I've been, I haven't been able to think about Professor Tobias. When I do, confusion overcomes me, and I find myself wasting time I don't have. So I don't think. I do, and I do, and I do some more.

Here in the station now, simply sitting seems a lost art and a luxury, and also a very risky business indeed. Dangerous, more like, with the black fog threatening again, now that there's no work to keep it at bay. I will myself to stay in one place, quiet and still. I close my eyes and try to slow my breath.

The station grows noisier with the gathering crowd, the waiting room, stuffy and hot. I've not slept much since I don't know when. *We have to take better care of you.* A nice thing for Professor Tobias to say. Gentlemanly. A comfort. Such drowsy comfort, like a sedative.

There's a throaty cry, and I open my eyes with a start. I glance at my watch. I must have drifted off—a little over half an hour has passed. Thank goodness I awakened in time to board my bus. I look toward the noise: the station entrance. There's movement there, people, and another cry. Blinking, trying to clear my head, I get to my feet, the better to see, as do a few others around me. Two men in military uniforms— the drab green of the U.S. Army, with turtle shell–like helmets on their heads and guns in their holsters—stand just outside the entrance. They hold a struggling man. I glimpse the man's brown skin and black hair, his face contorted with anger and fear. He's spitting mad—literally, he spits on the floor. Then he's dragged out of sight.

"Wetback." That's the verdict of a grizzled man who stands behind me.

"Illegal. That's what he is. That's what they all are."

This comes from a woman sitting a few seats away, who speaks with a soft, slow drawl very much like my own. She catches my eye, shakes her head—*What can you do?* Reflexively, my response mirrors hers.

"*Roaches*, these illegals, infesting this country, stealing our jobs—*my* job," mutters another woman a few rows ahead. From the look of her clothes, grubby face, and lank hair, this woman has fallen on hard times. A burlap bag and a bedroll sit on the floor beside her. She doesn't look like she can afford a bus ticket. Perhaps the station is the best place she can find to take a rest.

I tucked an orange into my pocket this morning, plucked from one of the campus trees. I take it out now and hand it to the woman, tell her I hope she has another job soon.

Better find my bus, I decide then, particularly if there are going to be any other episodes like the one we've just witnessed, which may complicate matters even for those who aren't involved. Carrying my things, I walk quickly outside to where the buses are lined up, waiting to depart. I spot mine, number seventy-three, and hand my suitcase to the attendant, who slings it into a storage compartment. My suitcase lands with the other luggage already stowed in the bus's belly. In spite of his rough carelessness, I thank the attendant. At least this time I know that my things and I are aboard the same vehicle.

I'm about to board when I hear another shout. I glance

down the block to see a line of school buses parked across the street and a long line of people—all of whom appear to be of Mexican descent—stretching around the corner to who knows where. What they carry varies by person: trunks, suitcases, boxes, bags; one man carries a crate of chickens, another, a small orange tree in a pot. But to a person they are herded forward by more men in army uniforms and turtle-shell hats—ten, at least—who pace along the line, keeping watch. As on my first night in Pasadena, police officers also bark directions, and several men dressed in business suits carry clipboards and check paperwork.

These repatriates are not nearly as docile as those on my first night here, however. Like the spitting-mad man, many are cantankerous, even contentious; others are anxious and distressed. Women and children along with some of the men weep. Others glower. Two young men break away from the line to yell heatedly at one of the suited officials. A soldier steps in, and another, and a third; ultimately, it takes four soldiers to subdue the young men. The soldiers stay with them, monitoring their actions. Another brief flare-up of anger and the soldiers restrain them both. A police officer stalks over, jangling two pairs of handcuffs as a threat, and I realize I'm glad for the soldiers' presence. *We must take better care of you.* Comforting. These officials will take care of us all.

That's what I'm thinking when someone's weeping rises to a wail. There's the sound of a fist striking flesh, and now I don't want to see or hear any more. I board the bus and throw myself into a seat by a window that faces away from the dispute.

The whole winding way from Pasadena to San Jose, I stare out the window. I should be taking in the landscape, seeing more of California. But I might as well be gazing into a haze. I keep hearing that sound—the sound of one person striking another, of fist on flesh—a sound I'd never heard before but recognized instantly. The sound makes me think of raw meat thrown on a butcher's block. As if this is what it ultimately boils down to, our human condition: Any one of us could be pummeled into submission, cast aside, or shunted off to who knows where. The mother country, I guess. Pray only those who deserve it are treated this way. The illegals.

ALICE EVERLY AWAITS me at the San Jose bus depot, a straw hat on her head, a black rubber apron tied around her neck and thick waist, a pair of dirty work gloves clasped in her hands. "I took a late lunch break and hurried over," she explains, hugging me, pushing me away to get a better look, hugging me again. "Oh, you're the spitting image of your mama, with that neat little chin of yours and that lovely mouth. But those eyes are all your daddy's." Her smile holds a tinge of sadness, because she's missing Mother or troubled by the thought of Daddy, I'm not sure. "Sorry, honey, but we've got to hurry," Alice continues. "A fellow brought me in his truck—owed me a favor—but he won't be happy at a delay. Can't be late, the job won't wait," she explains in a singsong.

Alice leads me to a rusted pickup. She helps me heave my suitcase into its bed, and then we clamber into the dusty front seat. The driver, Alice's friend, proves to be a hard-muscled, flinty-eyed man named Hank who also works at the factory. He doesn't say a word the whole ride, and I don't, either, though Alice rambles on, reciting the names of the farms we pass, as well as the crops harvested there. Asparagus, melon, and beets, she says over and over again.

Hank drops us off outside a wood-frame duplex that stands in a tight row with similar duplexes on either side. "We live in a very different neighborhood from our place back home," Alice says, gesturing at the dirt road beneath our feet. As we walk to her front door, she removes her hat, and a tumble of gray hair escapes from the bun pinned low at the back of her head. She shakes out her hair and a sharp, metallic smell fills the air—the smell of tin from the factory, it seems to be. "Least we have somewhere to live." Alice opens the door. "Shouldn't complain. Talmadge—my husband—hates it when I complain. But sometimes I can't help myself."

The duplex proves sparsely furnished, but clean and tidy, with oddly elegant accents here and there—a thick red rug, an ornately carved wooden rocking chair, and a stained glass reading lamp in the front room; in the small, crowded kitchen, a fancy dining room table and four large chairs. There's a bathroom with a shower and toilet, and two bedrooms. One bedroom can't hold much besides a big four-poster bed; the other has a narrow Murphy bed, already unlatched from the wall and neatly made. There's a little desk and chair tucked into a corner here, too. Alice gestures for me to put my suitcase in the space beside that. "Consider this your room," she says. As I start to thank her, she puts her finger to her lips: "Hush, now. We know how it is."

She explains how her family—she, Talmadge, and their two children—came to live in this place; she explains the toll it took on them, getting here. After the Everlys left Oklahoma, they traveled for nearly three years, moving from ditch-bank camp to farm camp to ditch-bank camp again, on and on, always changing location with the changing season, migrating to the next harvest. Only about five months ago she and Talmadge wound up getting jobs at the local canning factory. "Back home we used to have everything we wanted, or we could get it easy as pie, but we still didn't have enough. By the time we came here, we found ourselves wanting only steady jobs, and we had to fight for them, don't you know, prove ourselves superior to the younger employees. It wasn't easy. But by this time we had the muscle, the calluses, and most important, the determination. The desperation, more like." She shuffles sideways between dining room table and kitchen counter to reach the block of ice in the icebox, then chips ice into two glasses and edges over to the sink to pour us some water. "After a few months, we scraped together enough money to rent this place. We're only just settled, but here we plan to stay."

We drain our glasses in silence. I'd hoped the cold would refresh me, but my eyelids are drooping. I can hardly keep my eyes open.

"You're exhausted," Alice confirms. "Take a nice, long nap, why don't you? Talmadge and I get off work around seven o'clock. We'll have dinner then."

She steers me back to my little room, makes sure I sit down on the bed. As soon as I hear the front door close behind her, I fall back on the mattress, too tired to crawl under the covers.

After a series of dreams that tangle and unravel like a

skein of knotted yarn (Professor Tobias figures in many), I dream of the boy beneath the bleachers, only this time, horribly, he has the face of the spitting-mad man.

I awake to the sound of footsteps. Sweaty yet chilled, I sit bolt upright, expecting a boy turned man or a man turned boy—I'm not sure which, doesn't really matter which, either will be spitting mad. But it's Alice and a silvery-haired fellow who must be Talmadge, standing there, at the bedroom door, smiling.

TWO QUIET DAYS pass, during which I often find myself nodding off and dreaming strange dreams. Suddenly, it is Christmas Eve—sunny and pleasant, like spring in Oklahoma. Alice and Talmadge return from work at seven o'clock, as usual, only tonight they're giddy with the fact that the holiday will span a long weekend. Today is Friday. Tomorrow, Saturday, they won't have to work. Not on Sunday, either. "A two-day weekend," Talmadge says with a sigh, dropping into an easy chair, kicking off his beaten-down work boots. "Almost like old times."

We've talked a lot about old times, these past evenings together. Alice and Talmadge miss everything about Alba. To keep things simple, I say that I do, too. When they ask what happened to Charlie, I spare myself some pain and give an abridged version of the truth: killed in an accident. They knew Charlie; they knew his mother, Margaret, too. They've had their own grief, they tell me. Their daughter, Grace, died about two years after their arrival in California. She was so young, only fourteen, but she got typhus and there was nothing they could do.

At this revelation, Alice abruptly leaves the room. Talmadge and I sit in awkward silence for a few moments until she returns carrying a mottled cardboard frame, the kind used by portrait studios. Inside there's a hand-tinted photograph of a pretty young girl. Her hair is thick and curly, pinned back by a blue velvet bow to reveal a striking widow's peak that perfectly accents her heart-shaped face. Her round hazel eyes hold bright pinpoints of light. She is smiling—a kind smile, a smile wise beyond her years. The narrow gap between her front teeth only adds to her charm.

"Grace." Talmadge sounds like he's calling out to his daughter, calling her home.

Alice sets the photograph where we can easily see it, on the orange crate that serves as a coffee table. "Losing her about killed us." Then Talmadge drapes his arm around Alice and holds her steady. "About killed our boy. Her big brother, Thomas. Not the typhus. The loss."

"Did kill Thomas," Talmadge mutters. "Our son—the boy we raised—is gone for good."

Alice presses a restraining hand to her husband's chest. "Thomas thinks differently now. Different than us, that's all."

"He thinks like one of them Commies."

"He's not a Communist." Alice draws away from her husband. "Don't you dare say so. Especially in front of our company."

"Might as well be. All those meetings and demonstrations. Remember that fellow Guthrie we heard sing over at the Bakersfield camp? Thomas can't keep a tune, but if he could, he'd be singing that kind of song. Heck, I don't believe he considers us family anymore. He considers those other people family. And those people are nothing like us."

"Hush." Alice yanks a pocket watch from Talmadge's vest and draws in a sharp breath. "He'll be here any minute." She turns to me. "Please don't hold our boy's opinions against us or him. He's still the good man we raised him to be. This is just a hard season in his life. It's got everything to do with Grace's passing. You understand, Ruth, don't you?"

I nod. "I do."

"Grace's passing, sure," Talmadge mutters. "But there's more to what's gotten Thomas all stirred up."

"Bear in mind what's important, will you?" Alice snaps. Talmadge starts as she drops the pocket watch in his lap. "Our son is coming home for the first time in a long time. Don't you dare ruin his visit or you might find me at odds with you, too. Permanently."

"Not half likely," Talmadge mutters, tucking his watch back in his vest pocket.

"I'm going to bring in the Christmas tree." Alice stands abruptly. "It'll be good to be decorating when Thomas arrives. He can join right in."

I move to help her, but Talmadge pushes past us both and goes outside. He returns in a moment, dragging a scrawny pine that he cut down this morning. He anchors the tree in an old paint can filled with stones, then tips it this way and that. No matter his efforts, the tree stays at a tilt. Alice finally determines that the trunk is too crooked for it to stay upright on its own, so Talmadge drags it to a corner of the front room and braces it between the walls there. Meanwhile, Alice pops popcorn, then sets me to work with a needle and thread, stringing garlands. She applies herself similarly to a bowl of bright cranberries. Talmadge sits on the floor, looking—never mind his silvery hair—like a little boy as he cuts snowflakes, hearts, and paper chains from old newspaper. All seems peaceful again. Over the course of the evening, we complete our simple decorations. By bedtime, they festoon the thin branches.

"Good enough," Alice says, topping the tree with a paper star.

Still no sign of Thomas, though. By some unspoken agreement, we don't mention this. We head to bed, Alice lingering to unlock the front door.

HOURS LATER, I am dreaming uneasy dreams when the mattress gives beneath me. I open my eyes to see in the darkness the darker shadow of a man. He sits on the bed beside me. Next instant, he's up and backing away.

"Who's there?" the man gasps.

Thomas Everly. Let it be Thomas Everly.

"Ruth Warren. From Oklahoma." My heart bangs in my chest. "Your folks—they invited me to stay. I'm visiting just for Christmas—"

"Oh." His breathing begins to quiet. "I'm sorry to wake you."

"You're Thomas?"

He barks out a humorless laugh. "They've told you about me already, have they?"

"They'll be relieved to know you've arrived safely." I sit up, clutching the blanket to my shoulders. "I've done my share of sleeping these last days." I try to smile, hoping he can hear warmth in my words. I swing my feet to the floor and stand, dragging the blanket with me. "You have the bed. I'll take the couch."

But he's already at the door, blocking my way. I can't make out much about him beyond the fact that he's not much taller than I am—smaller in stature than most men. After a moment of confusion—*What's he got? Some kind of stand or tool?*—I realize that he supports himself on crutches.

"The couch is fine for me. I'll probably be more comfortable there." Again his laugh, only kinder this time. "Easier access to the front door and my escape, if need be."

Thomas turns agilely on his crutches and heads off down the dark hallway. I stand there for a moment, waiting, but there's not a peep from Alice or Talmadge, and not another peep from their son. So I take myself back to bed.

SEVEN

I awake to the sound of singing. A young child unaccompanied by other instruments, with a voice like clear, clean crystal, ringing high and bright.

> I wonder as I wander out under the sky
> How Jesus the Savior did come for to die . . .

The Christmas carol unfolds, stately and haunting in its slow time. The child sings of Jesus' birth and of the people— wise men, farmers, shepherds—who gathered around him beneath the star's light. Wanderers under the sky, that's who Jesus died for, the child sings, poor people, like you, like me.

When the song ends, a man's sonorous voice fills the air. "That was 'I Wonder as I Wander,' sung by a member of the Vienna Boys' Choir . . ."

My bedroom door opens a crack as the announcer relays more about the choir and the carol. Alice peeks in at me, her round face beaming. She's wearing what must have been a very nice dress—perhaps her nicest back home, red with jeweled buttons. "Merry Christmas, Ruth!"

"And to you! The music was beautiful."

"It's our Christmas gift from Talmadge to me, and me to Talmadge, and our birthday gifts, and every gift for many years to come, as it took us so long to save up for it. A radio! Our old one broke some time back. Now we can listen to our shows again. It's secondhand, but it sounds fine." Alice presses her hands to her breast, barely able to contain her excitement. "And Thomas arrived late last night."

"Yes?" It wasn't a dream after all.

"He said he'd come to church with us this morning." She smooths her hair now, and pins her bun more securely into place. "We have to hurry or we'll be late for the service. But don't worry—there will be more music to enjoy, both at church and back here afterward. I can assure you of that!"

Alone again, I quickly get ready, then go to the kitchen, hoping to down a cup of coffee and gobble a piece of toast. Thomas already sits at the table, crutches propped against the back of his chair. As I hesitate in the doorway, he regards me over the rim of his coffee cup. From behind the rising steam, his gaze is steady and serious, his eyes more golden than brown. A lion's eyes, wide-set, heavy-lidded, with eyelashes and brows that are noticeably dark against the amber irises. His brown hair, still wet from his washing up, tips to a widow's peak that recalls his sister's in the photograph. Thomas has rigorously raked his bangs back into place—the marks left by the comb's teeth are distinct—but already, waves and cowlicks have sprung up to thwart his efforts.

"Good morning," I say.

He sets his cup down on the table, revealing a strong jaw and a wide mouth. He nods at me. Then in one, fluid movement, he pushes himself up from the table and, crutches beneath his arms, propels himself to the coffeepot on the stove. He pours a cup, hands it to me without a word. I thank him.

Still standing, Thomas slathers a piece of toast with jelly, wolfs it down, and drains the coffee from his cup. Next moment, he brushes past me on his crutches, his broad shoulders and muscled arms straining against the thin white cotton of his shirt. He bears weight only on his left leg; he keeps his right leg slightly bent so that his foot skims the floor. As he moves, the cuff of his right trouser leg hitches up an inch or so, and I see the reason for the crutches. Where Thomas's ankle should be, there's a narrow column of smooth, pale wood; bolts secure his black shoe in place. I'd never have guessed he wore a prosthetic. Broken bone— that's what I assumed from his bold, unencumbered movements. A missing limb hasn't slowed him down in any way; rather, it seems to have encouraged inhibition, lending a madcap quality to his otherwise graceful movements. Crutches pounding against the floor in a fast, uneven clip, Thomas swings himself through the kitchen doorway and into the front room.

I quickly eat, and in a matter of minutes, the Everlys and I are on our way to church. Thomas leads the way;

Talmadge, Alice, and I have to hurry to keep up with him. Alice is, as usual, talkative—so much so that it's hard to get a word in edgewise. Then again, I'm the only one who makes an attempt, my manners kicking in as I try to respond to what she says. "Oh, my," I manage at one point. And "Really?" at another. Otherwise Alice chatters on, filling Thomas in on the canning factory, the acquaintances she and his father have made there, the nature of their work, and their plans for the future (in a nutshell: put every extra penny aside and retire one day with just enough to live out their lives and pay for their funerals). "You could get a job at the canning factory, too, Thomas!" Alice exclaims, only to be met with grim silence from her son and husband. Thomas and Talmadge stay a good distance from each other and avoid eye contact altogether. Complete strangers, that's what they appear to be. If it weren't for the fact that their expressions are set to the same degree of stubbornness, and that Talmadge, too, has a widow's peak, silvery though it may be, I might assume these two men had never met. Without Alice's verbosity, this walk would be strained to the point of excruciating.

Church is a small white clapboard building with a narrow bell tower that reverberates with clanging as we approach. There are steps up to the sanctuary door, and Thomas takes them two at a time. Only at the entrance does he finally come to a full stop. He follows me inside, the last of us to enter, and as he does, he sucks in a long breath, as if storing up oxygen for a deep dive.

The church is crowded and warm. Alice manages to find enough space for us to sit together in a pew near the back.

Alice sits down first, then Talmadge, then me, and finally, Thomas, who occupies the aisle seat, carefully laying his crutches on the floor, well out of the way of any passersby. While Thomas seems uncomfortable, constantly shifting in his seat, I relax into the wooden pew. This is familiar. I know what I have to do, or if I don't, I will be told. I can listen, and if the sermon proves dull, who knows? I might hear a word from God.

The white-haired pastor preaches on Luke 2:1–20, that beautiful passage about Jesus' birth and the shepherds' arrival at the stable. I anticipated the baby wrapped in swaddling cloth and laid in a manger, the angel's message on the hillside, the things that Mary treasured, and pondered in her heart. But the pastor never gets to that. Instead, he focuses on the first two verses of the chapter—the description of Caesar Augustus, his decree of a census, and Joseph's willingness to take Mary from Nazareth to Bethlehem to be registered as a member of the house and line of David.

"Here is yet another biblical example in which governmental orders are followed by godly people," the pastor says. "We must take this as our model. If we are asked to obey, we must do so, especially in such difficult times. Pay your taxes. Give your landlords, farm owners, and bosses their due. Report those who do otherwise. We've elected our political leaders. Now let's help them keep the peace."

Talmadge sits straight, shoulders back, fists clenched on thighs. Except for the fact that he's nodding in agreement, he might as well be carved from stone. On the other side of him, Alice shifts uneasily, her expression tight with anxiety.

As for Thomas, his nervous system might as well be constructed of frayed electrical wires; sitting close to him like
this, I believe I can feel his fury emanating in sharp jolts.
Though he's given to silence, it's clear he wants to speak; his
mouth works as he bites back words.

"Are you all right?" I whisper as Alice leans over, trying to
reach her son. "Your mother," I whisper when Alice fails to
catch hold of his sleeve. "She wants you."

At this, Thomas grabs his crutches and rises from the
pew. The pastor looks up from his notes and the congregation turns to see the cause of the commotion. Thomas
doesn't linger. He launches himself down the aisle and out
the door.

"Well." The pastor nods knowingly. "Guess someone
doesn't see things the way I do."

He continues with his sermon. Though I try to listen, I
find I can't. I bow my head slightly, so no one will notice, and
begin to pray. Mother, Daddy, Miss Berger, Edna Faye, the boy
beneath the bleachers—this litany of names comes to me as
always. But now I lift up Alice, Talmadge, and Thomas, too.

AS SOON AS the service ends, Alice prods Talmadge and
me to leave the sanctuary, and quickly. Outside, where few
have yet to gather, there's no sign of Thomas.

Without a word, Talmadge and Alice start home. The
whole way, they don't exchange a word, so I am quiet as
well. The walk seems longer now, and I yearn for Alice's
banter. Clouds scud across the sun, casting a pall over the
slapped-together duplexes. Any illusion of Christmas in
paradise—blue sky, warm temperature, palm trees and

poinsettias basking in the sun—has vanished. There's a raw chill in the air. A burst of wind spits down cold rain, and soon enough, we are drenched. When we finally arrive at the Everlys' home, we find Thomas sitting on the couch in the living room, reading a tattered newspaper. He doesn't look up at our entrance.

"So it's going to be like this," Talmadge says.

Thomas turns a page. Talmadge swoops down on his son, yanks the paper from his hands, and throws it to the floor. The pages scatter.

"Please," Alice says.

Neither of the men looks at her. Thomas trains his gaze on his father, who is shouting. "In my house, my church, you show some respect. You can have your opinions. I can't stop you. But you keep them to yourself, you hear me, or you can damn well leave."

Alice claps her hands over her ears. I go to her and slip my arm around her shoulders. She is shivering in her wet clothes. As I draw her into the hallway, she begins a strangled apology.

"Hush, now," I say. Though Mother would blanch, I tell Alice that I'm more than a little familiar with family disagreements. A flicker of relief passes over her pained expression. "Why don't you go put on some dry clothes," I say. "I'll make some hot coffee. We can sip it while we cook Christmas dinner."

Alice nods and stumbles off to change. My own dress, I've realized, clings wetly to my every curve. I make a few adjustments, pulling at the fabric here and there. Then, before I can reconsider, I march into the living room and suggest that Talmadge, who fell silent soon after our retreat to the kitchen, find us a good radio station. Now I turn to Thomas, who is holding that blamed newspaper again. I place my hands squarely on my hips. If only briefly, I once ran my own little household. I know how to set things straight. I set Professor Tobias's office straight time and again, and I set straight students who ask smart-mouthed questions, and foolish ones, too, and, come to think of it, long before I shared a home with Charlie, I set straight entire sections of the Alba Public Library. I can set this situation straight. I can also delegate chores.

"There are potatoes to be peeled." When Thomas doesn't lower the newspaper—an act of further resistance, I suppose—I stride over to him and flick the pages down so he has to meet my eyes. "Out on the back porch might be a good place to do the peeling, if it's not raining too hard." I lift my chin and frown down at him. "*Tempus fugit.*"

Am I seeing correctly? Do the corners of his eyes faintly crinkle with humor? Do I strike him as funny?

Before I have time to decide whether I've offended him or not, Thomas hoists himself from the couch and maneuvers his way into the kitchen. Talmadge busies himself at the radio. He finds a bright Christmas carol, and then he, too, leaves the room—to change, I presume. I steal away as well. In the bedroom, I shed my wet dress, strip off my underthings and put on dry ones, then consider the skirts and blouses I have left to wear. Though it might be deemed inappropriate, I slip into my well-worn, comfortable housedress, yellow accented with violets and green leaves. I would have worn it to cook Christmas dinner with Charlie. Talmadge,

Alice, and Thomas have revealed their less than decorous selves. I might as well do the same.

As an afterthought, I turn to the mirror and brush out my wet hair.

JACK BENNY IS joking on the radio.

I start toward the kitchen, but on second thought, I retrieve Thomas's newspaper. Out of sight, out of mind. I'll return it to him when I'm sure things have settled down.

The little desk in my bedroom seems the best place to hide the newspaper. I open the top drawer and start to tuck it inside. It's only then that I notice the headline.

Mexicans Leave for Home—
Another Lot of About 1200 Repatriates
Accept Offer of L.A. County

I read on.

In light of the concern expressed in a recent editorial in these pages, this reporter has interviewed both local and state government authorities to determine the willingness of members of the Mexican population to be repatriated to their original home. Also interviewed are leaders of Los Angeles's Mexican community, who work to maintain a decent and law-abiding district in the area north of the Olvera Street Plaza. Below are their collected statements.

A string of quotes follows the introduction. I skim them. It is no surprise that I don't recognize the names of those quoted—I know nothing about California politics—but each person confirms, in various ways, that the repatriates, all citizens of Mexico, are relief recipients or charity cases who are taking a further toll on the already struggling economy, and putting the larger community at risk due to their tendency toward contagious disease. All those quoted confirm that the illegals are more than willing to return to their home across the border.

Home. The word is repeated time and again, as is the fact that the people are being *offered* their return to Mexico and *rewarded* for it in the form of transportation payment, be it by train, bus, or truck. The United States government both supports and funds repatriation, as it is the result of a federal act put in place by the Hoover administration in 1930, and supported by the Roosevelt administration today.

Repatriation appears to be exactly as I've been told it is: necessary and justifiable, with positive repercussions for all. The article concludes:

> The ongoing rumor that forced raids have been conducted without due process in public settings, including that which was purported to occur in the Plaza at Olvera Street, also known as La Placita, in February 1931, is simply that: a rumor, insidious and destructive in its intent. This particular incident of repatriation, like every other, was in fact a government-sponsored undertaking, duly enacted by the Immigration and Naturalization Service.

No surprises here, really. Things are as I've been told. I fold the newspaper and shut it away in the desk drawer.

The kitchen is warm; Alice, also in dry clothes, has gotten the oven going. She's poured us two cups. Already, she's preparing the chicken. She may be a little more subdued than usual, but with tasks at hand, she seems fairly steady. I take a sip of coffee, then set to work mixing up a batch of dumplings. The sack of potatoes has gone missing from its place on the counter; Alice confirms that Thomas is peeling away on the porch. We don't mention the rain, still falling hard, but as soon as Alice sees I've finished the dough, she snatches an umbrella from the line of coat hooks on the wall and presses it into my hands. "There's an eave and gutters, so he won't drown. But will you see how he's doing?" She wants to know more than the number of potatoes peeled, it's clear from her furrowed brow.

I slip out the back door, letting it close behind me. Thomas sits on the top step, his upper half sheltered, as I am, by the eave. But his legs—he's carelessly stretched them out on the steps below. They're soaked, his trousers clinging below his knees as my dress recently did. The difference between his legs is so clear now that he might as well have his trousers rolled up. His left calf is lean and strong, the shinbone and muscles clearly defined; his right, while shaped like its counterpart, is noticeably thinner, with unnaturally smooth contours.

I open the umbrella. Stretching out my arm, I shield his legs from the rain as much as I'm able. "You're going to catch a cold if you're not careful."

He shrugs. He has yet to look up at me. He holds a half-peeled potato in one hand; the peeler rests in the palm of the other. Only two potatoes of the entire large sack lie peeled in the bowl beside him.

I prop the umbrella on the porch railing so that it continues to provide partial shelter for his legs, and then, taking the peeler from his hand and a potato from the sack, I sit down beside him, careful to keep my legs tucked in close. At least one of us will stay dry. Thomas acknowledges my new perch by shifting slightly away from me. Otherwise he stares out at the narrow, weed-ridden backyard, which serves both the Everly family and the people who inhabit the other half of the duplex. There's an overturned tricycle beside the dilapidated picket fence, and a wooden sandbox. Any hollows in the sand and yard are now puddles, rapidly expanding.

"We need this rain," I say, for something to say. "It's a godsend, really."

A man of few words, now as ever, apparently. I start peeling the potato.

The neighbors' back door bangs open, and a man carrying an umbrella and a wailing baby hurries into the yard. The baby is swaddled in a red blanket, and is red faced, too, from the crying. The man wears a brown suit. He joggles the baby up and down, trying to soothe it.

"We have to go!" the man yells at his back door. "My parents are waiting dinner!" He sees Thomas and me then, makes a sheepish face, and nods at the baby. "She won't quiet down. Colic, we think. Thought some fresh air might help."

A woman appears on the porch, holding a brimming spoon and a glass filled with amber-colored liquid. "Whiskey and honey," she calls to the man. "Tilda across the street said to try it." She dashes through the rain to join her little family beneath the umbrella and, there, mixes the spoonful of honey into the glass. Together, fumbling and cooing, the man and woman spoon the solution into the baby's mouth. The wails crescendo to howls. "It'll calm her, Tilda promised. Just give it a minute." The woman raises her voice to be heard.

It takes a few minutes, but the baby's wails do diminish to fretful squalls. "See?" the woman says, taking the baby from the man's arms. The family goes back inside, woman and child first, then the man, who hesitates at the door to apologize for the noise. "Didn't mean to disrupt your peace and quiet." His smile is rueful. "But don't worry. We'll be on the road momentarily. You know how it is. *Babies.*" And with that, he goes inside.

A knot forms in my throat as I stare at the empty backyard. Charlie and I had hoped for our own version of this. If our baby had been colicky, my Tilda might have been Edna Faye's mother. I might have asked her for a remedy if things had been different.

"My mother told me about your husband."

I look at Thomas, startled. With his thumbnail, he digs at a potato eye, then flicks it to the patchy grass at the bottom of the porch steps. "I'm sorry. I lost someone, too." He nods to where the woman and man just stood with their baby. "I loved the girl who used to live next door. Sounds like a song, doesn't it? I guess it's kind of your song, too, as Ma said you all but grew up with your husband."

I swallow hard against the lump rising in my throat. There are black-eyed Susans I hadn't noticed before, planted in a patch at the back of the yard. The storm has stripped away their yellow petals, leaving only the brown, brittle centers. "No *all but* about it," I say. "Charlie and I did grow up together."

Thomas nods. "The girl I loved was—*is*—named Guadalupe. She had to leave with her family." He is soft-spoken, but the words tumble from him as if pent up too long. "This is the first time I've been home since she left, so her ghost is everywhere. Yes, she's alive, but the living can haunt the people they leave behind, too. Losing a person—" He glances disdainfully at his prosthesis. "It's worse than losing a limb. Phantom limb, that's what it's called when you feel like your leg is still there. There's a tingling sometimes, or a feeling of—I don't know—*wholeness*, like I'm the person I used to be. Then I remember I'm not. Sometimes the pain of the injury returns, too. I lost my leg in a so-called farming accident, but you want to know what really happened? What really happened was the boss didn't want to pay to have a tractor blade repaired. And when the phantom limb hurts like it's still flesh, well, God help me, sometimes I have to bite on something, a stick or a rag, to keep from making a ruckus. But being haunted by Lupe is worse than any of that, I promise you. A dark-haired woman will pass me by, wearing a dress Lupe might have worn, and for a moment I'll think she's returned. Once I ran after such a woman. I caught her by the arm and spun her around only to see that she was a stranger. I frightened her. I frightened myself."

The rain drums on the eave that covers our heads, on the umbrella and the weed-ridden grass, and what's left of the black-eyed Susans.

"Lupe and her family had to leave." I keep my voice soft, almost a whisper. If he doesn't want to respond, he can pretend he didn't hear me. "Were they repatriated?"

"Did my parents tell you?" His jaw goes so tight that the little muscles ripple there. "What was their version of what happened? No, don't tell me. I can just imagine."

"It wasn't them," I quickly say. "They haven't said anything about her. It was her name. It's not *any* name. And your newspaper—the story on the front page. I wasn't sure, but the way you were absorbed in that article, it seemed a logical conclusion."

"Like that newspaper, my parents would have told you the official story. The unofficial story—that's the one you should hear."

"Well, they didn't tell me anything, if that's any comfort."

We both start as the door opens behind us. Alice peers out. "Why don't the two of you come inside and do that?" She flicks her eyebrows at Thomas, trying to make light. "If you're in a better mood, that is."

Thomas nods. Clearly pleased, Alice turns back inside. We start to get up, but Thomas's crutches slip on the slick porch. I catch his arm to keep him from falling.

"Thanks." His voice is sharp. "But I don't need any help."

I quickly release his arm. "Well, I do."

He cuts me a look. "What help can I give you?"

"Tell me the unofficial story when you have a chance."

CHRISTMAS DINNER—CHICKEN and dumplings, carrots, mashed potatoes, and cornbread—starts out a subdued affair. Alice raises up a strained prayer, emphasizing her gratitude for my presence and Thomas's. We *please pass* this and that for a while, and then we dig into our food. Poor Alice. Her gaze darts nervously between her husband and son, who keep their eyes on their plates and eat with forced dedication. "The food is delicious," I finally say; I don't want this fact to go unnoticed. Alice casts me a look of gratitude, and then, her voice quavering with desperation, she asks me to tell Thomas about my college experience—how I came to be there, what it's like, and what I'm studying. I set down my fork, take a deep breath, and launch into the fullest summary I'm able to provide of these last few months. When I get to the part about my long-held desire to be a teacher, Thomas sits up a little straighter. "I know where they really need teachers. I teach a bit there myself." But after a sharp look from Talmadge, Thomas doesn't elaborate. So I carry on talking, going into more depth about what kind of teacher I aspire to be. In the whole of this rather lengthy monologue, I leave out only the information I most want to share with Thomas: my experiences at the train station and with the boy beneath the bleachers, and the small silver cross that lies hidden beneath my mattress at Garland Hall.

And so the meal passes. By the time Thomas and I are washing the dishes, the tension seems to have all but lifted. Alice hovers about us, drinking in the sight of her boy, I believe. Talmadge makes occasional appearances, refilling his coffee cup, collecting matches from a drawer. But mostly he's in the front room, busy with something that Alice says is a surprise. The radio plays; carols accompany the cleaning up. If I weren't missing Charlie so much, I'd say I was happy. But now that we've survived dinner, my thoughts turn to him.

Feels like my heart is breaking all over again. It's a physical sensation, a hollow ache in my breast. Even as I bow my head over the brimming sink and bury my hands in soapsuds, I sense a black fog coming on.

"You all right?" Thomas asks.

I glance over my shoulder. Alice has left the kitchen, so I feel free to I shake my head.

"Phantom limb?"

And like that, tears spring to my eyes and fall into the sink. One, two, three, four, parting the soapsuds, sinking into the water. Five, six, seven, eight, like the rain outside, which has lightened to scarcely a drizzle. Thomas drapes the wet dish towel over the counter, then tentatively puts his arm around my shoulder. Scrubbing my tears away with the back of my soapy hand, I look out the window before us. The darkness outside makes the glass a mirror. There I am reflected, with a man standing near, comforting me, a man who is not Charlie.

Footsteps sound. Thomas swiftly withdraws his arm, and we step apart. A chill settles where his arm was; I shiver. But Alice's approach—for these are her footsteps, heavy and brisk—has knocked the tears right out of me. I am dry-eyed as she enters the kitchen.

"You know what's up, don't you, son?" Alice wrings her hands, not in worry but in delight.

"I do." Thomas smiles stiffly.

"Don't spill the beans, all right? Let's surprise our guest!"

With that, Alice takes a clean dish towel from a drawer and, when I give her my surprised permission, wraps it like a blindfold around my eyes. "We're coming!" she calls. Then she takes me by one arm, and Thomas takes me by the other, and they lead me slowly from the kitchen to the front room. There, they sit me down on the couch. No sound from the radio now, but there's the sulfuric odor of matches recently struck, and the sizzle of freshly lit wicks.

"Ready?" Alice asks. She takes my hand in her plump one, and I realize she's talking to me. I nod, and she yanks the blindfold from my eyes.

The room is dark other than the soft light cast by the flames that flicker from slender cream-colored tapers anchored in the brass candleholders clipped to the tips of the Christmas tree's boughs. It's a holy glow, little tongues of fire licking the air. Talmadge begins to sing, his rough, husky voice perfectly on pitch.

O, Holy Night! The stars are brightly shining,
It is the night of our dear Savior's birth . . .

Talmadge sings only the first verse of the carol, and then quickly, lest the candles burn too low, he puts a long, thin tube to his lips and proceeds to blow out each flame. The room is shadowy for a long moment, a faint haze of smoke circling the tree. Then Alice turns on the lights.

"That was beautiful." The hollow ache is still there, but perhaps it is tempered.

"My mother was Swedish," Talmadge says. "This is the one tradition she passed down that we've kept alive all these years. Even on the road as we've been, we've managed it."

He turns on the radio again, and another carol fills the room—"Away in a Manger." Alice joins me on the couch; Talmadge takes the ornately carved rocker by the radio; Thomas pulls in a chair from the kitchen. There are no gifts tonight beyond the music, the meal, the candles on the tree. But as Alice darns socks, and Talmadge draws on his pipe, and Thomas pulls out a piece of wood and starts whittling away, there is something to which I can't quite put a name, and it is enough. It is enough for me to endure this Christmas. Enough for me to believe yet another Christmas will come. Enough to lighten the black fog to gray.

EIGHT

N ext morning, Sunday, there's no sign of Thomas in the front room or kitchen, so I assume it's just Talmadge, Alice, and me bound for church. But upon our departure, there Thomas is, waiting outside on the front porch. He grimly mumbles something about an early-morning walk down memory lane. Talmadge doesn't acknowledge this, but Alice, carrying a picnic basket, swiftly kisses her son's cheek.

"I'm so glad you returned in time," she says. "I'm glad we can try again."

I wait until Alice and Talmadge are a safe distance ahead, then I ask Thomas if he'll be all right, no matter what the preacher says.

Thomas cocks his head thoughtfully, as if trying to parse every element of my serious tone. "Yes, ma'am. I'll be good. I promise."

He's teasing me. I lift my chin and stride after Talmadge and Alice. Soon enough Thomas takes the lead as he did yesterday and keeps a quick pace all the way to church. Yesterday's storm has scrubbed the sky a cloudless, bright blue, washed the air clean, polished palm leaves to a high sheen. Dew-drenched blades of grass sparkle. Only the flowers seem to have suffered from the lashing rain and wind.

The church sanctuary is crowded, and again the four of us have to squeeze together in a pew: Thomas in his place by the aisle, then me, then Alice and Talmadge. In this sermon (to our shared relief, I am sure), the pastor emphasizes the importance of gratitude in times of both abundance and need. Can't really argue with that. Thomas stays the entire service and participates with the rest of us. Alice's whole demeanor softens; she can't stop smiling even as the pastor reads of Job's suffering. At one point, she reaches over me for Thomas's hands, and he responds, reaching for hers, and there the three of us sit, with their hands clasped above my lap. I have to press my lips together to keep down the laughter bubbling up inside me—not because I find this humorous but because it fills me with joy such as I haven't known in a long time. Here is a moment of grace in spite of everything, or because of it. Then I remember Daddy and Mother, and a pang of longing shoots through me. Will I ever experience something like this, no matter how fleeting, with both of them? With Mother, yes, maybe. But with Daddy? I doubt it.

After the service, Alice tugs the picnic basket from beneath the pew, and we walk to a nearby park. Talmadge spreads a blanket in the shade beneath a circle of trees, and we settle down to lunch. Stiff and ungainly, Alice and Talmadge occupy the majority of the blanket. I perch at the fringed edge. Thomas rolls over onto his belly in the grass, his legs stretched out behind him, his crutches within easy reach. Propped up on his elbows, he looks the most comfortable of any of us. We savor the food—what's left of yesterday's chicken, egg salad sandwiches, some oranges, and treats so rare they feel decadent: bottles of fizzy, warm Coca-Cola and a melting Hershey bar to share. The air warms to hot; the sun casts mottled shadows through the leaves, rustling overhead. Birds utter calls that are strange and exotic, at least to me. Our movements slow to languid. Even my eyes are drooping, and Alice and Talmadge, having worked hard at the factory all week, can't stop yawning as they finish up their chocolate and sip the last of their sodas.

"Remember Sunday afternoons before, in our backyard?" Alice murmurs, leaning in to her husband.

"Remember the screened-in porch." Talmadge smacks a drowsy fly and misses.

We are quiet for a moment. Then Alice sighs and turns to me with a rueful smile. "I wanted to show you the sights of San Jose. But, oh, for a nap first! Can't think of the last time I took one."

"Can't think, either." Talmadge stretches his arms above his head, and his joints give a loud crack. Wincing, he reclines on the blanket, turns on his side, settles his hand beneath his cheek for a pillow, and closes his eyes.

I glance at Thomas. He is watching his father, his steady gaze gone soft with emotion. Grace. Here it is again: the love a son can have for his dad, when times are simple and peaceful and shadows of blame and hurt retreat. I've never seen a man look at another man as Thomas is looking at Talmadge now. So tender is Thomas's expression, I have to look away.

"Do you mind, Ruth?" Full cheeks flushed, Alice speaks apologetically. "An hour or so, and then we'll take a look around? I'm feeling awful guilty, as you are a guest. And Thomas, it's been so long—" She hesitates, perhaps afraid of saying too much. "But a little rest would make me a better companion. And we'd still have time to see the most important places."

"Of course you should rest," I whisper, so as not to rouse Talmadge. "You, too, Thomas, if you like. I'll go ahead and take the picnic basket home." I smile, trying to reassure Alice. "That way we won't have to carry it later, when you're raring to go."

Alice nods gratefully and lies down beside her husband. As she spoons her wide back against his narrow chest, her dress strains against her thighs, and the dingy lace of her slip peeks out from beneath her hem. If I could, I'd cover them with something soft, tuck them in for sweet dreams. But it's too hot for that anyway, and they look perfectly content, babes in the woods—or rather, beneath a small circle of trees.

"I'll go with you, Ruth. I could use a walk." Thomas squares a crutch on the ground and hops up, then snags the other crutch and the picnic basket. He frowns, noticing, as I do, Alice's expression: Tired as she is, she manages to give us a knowing look.

"You two have fun, now," she says.

Thomas turns abruptly away from his mother. "Back soon," he casts over his shoulder. And then, carelessly: "Come on, Ruth, if you're coming."

Only when we're out of Alice's sight does Thomas allow me to catch up to him. "I don't want her getting her hopes up," he says.

I nod. "Me, either."

Without a word, Thomas starts off again, and—no surprise—I have to walk briskly to keep up. At his parents' house, he doesn't bother to go inside; he simply drops the picnic basket on the porch and turns to me.

"You said you wanted to know the other side of the story?"

"I did."

"If that's still true, then let's go."

THOMAS LEADS ME to the outskirts of town, where the duplexes and small bungalows dwindle to overgrown, empty lots. A low, uneven line of green spans the horizon.

"One of the bigger citrus groves in this area." Pointing, Thomas breaks our quick pace. "But what's between here and there—that's what you need to see." He nods at a ramshackle tumble of glinting metal and bleached wood only a half mile or so farther down the road.

"A Hooverville?"

"Not exactly."

Without explanation, Thomas sets off again. When we

reach our destination, I have to bend over, plant my hands on my knees. It takes some moments for me to catch my breath. Only then can I see what's right before us: a ditch filled with stinking standing water over which gnats and flies swarm. Scum and algae slick the water's surface; long-legged spiders skitter across brilliant clots of green. From somewhere close at hand, bullfrogs bellow.

"Look there." Thomas nods toward the opposite bank, where sludge steadily bubbles. Could be a spring gushing up from below. But the reek tells me it's not. It's some poisonous combination of refuse churning up from the sediment.

On the other side of the ditch stands—or rather, *lists*—the ramshackle tumble. A sorry excuse for shelter, it's a patchwork mess of shacks, sheds, and lean-tos cobbled together from tin, wood, tarp, and palm fronds, long gone dry and brittle. No doors to be seen. No windows. No privies. Stranger still, no sound. This so-called camp is dead silent, which makes all the more noticeable the disturbance in the muck, the occasional pop of air bubbles.

I clear my throat, which has gone dry; I've been trying to breathe only through my mouth to reduce the stink. "Ghost town?"

"You could say that."

Thomas propels himself toward the fetid ditch. Pushing off with his crutches, he vaults it. He lands hard on the other side, a tangle of limbs and wood. For a long moment, he doesn't move. Got the wind knocked out of him, I bet. He sits up then, hitches up the left leg of his trousers, and, grimacing, adjusts his prosthesis. "Come on." He can barely speak; he's still breathless.

"I'm no athlete."

"If I can do it, you can do it."

"I don't want to fall in."

"Then don't."

The gray clouds of yesterday are scudding across the sky again, obliterating the sun. Thomas glances up, and when he looks at me again, his expression has turned cool. "You don't really want to know it, do you?"

"What?"

"The truth."

At this, I kick off my shoes, hoist my skirt above my knees, run as fast as I can toward the ditch, and jump. I fall flat on my face on the ground near Thomas, my feet dangling over the side of the bank, my toes digging into the thick, sticky mess below. "Guess again," I gasp. I pull myself up and rub my feet in the grass, trying to clean them.

A grin flashes across Thomas's face. It's the first time I've seen him really smile. Dimples cut into his cheeks, deep and long—more weathered lines than dimples. Deep lines radiate from the corners of his eyes, too, nearly reaching his temples. This is the face of a man who likes to laugh. But then his smile fades, erased by another grimace, and he seems another kind of man altogether. He's hurt, I realize.

"A fool, that's what I am." He strikes his fist against his thigh. "Should have taken more time getting across. I've done it now." He rubs his shin where flesh and bone must meet the prosthesis. His pained expression is also sheepish. "I could use some help, Ruth, if you don't mind."

"Of course." I go to him, and he tells me to put my hands where the crutches usually go, and help him up, if I can.

I hunker down to use the muscles in my legs. With a grunt, I try to lift him; with a groan, he tries to help me. Together we get him to his feet. I retrieve his crutches, and he leans on them, his mouth tight against the pain. But he doesn't complain. He looks toward the ghost town. "Shall we?"

Faltering now in his movements, Thomas leads me into what seems a senseless maze. There are no roads; we follow overgrown, meandering footpaths. In more out-of-the-way places, the paths are punctuated by deep holes, which once served as toilets. A vision of Edna Faye, weeping at my departure from East Texas, flashes through my mind. Did she know about places like this? Had she *lived* in places like this? Was her sadness laced with dread?

"It's worse than I imagined," I say.

"This is where the Mexican farmworkers had to live after the Dust Bowl refugees took over their original camp. It was a dump prior to that." Thomas's voice is sharp with anger. "The people who lived here did the best they could with what they were given. Lupe had friends who lived here. She brought me to visit them just before she and her family got taken away. Right after, the people who lived here were deported, too."

"I'm sorry." My words sound empty and flat, and Thomas doesn't reply.

We do a thorough investigation of the camp. It takes us some time to navigate the abandoned structures; we peer inside most of them. There are things there—belongings left behind during what must have been a chaotic departure. Luggage, opened and unopened, scattered clothing, books, and toys, overturned furniture, broken dishes, pots and pans, paintings and photographs hanging at haphazard angles on shack walls. Food was left behind, too. Dirt and cobwebs cover everything else. Thomas tells me that this is a fraction of what was here when he visited this place soon after the deportation. "There's been looting," he says. "So who are the real criminals—the people who lived here? That's what the government says. But you tell me."

We have come to a shack made almost entirely from rusted license plates nailed together to form walls and roof shingles. Most of the plates are from Mexico; a few are from Texas, Arizona, and California. I am stunned by the workmanship, and I tell Thomas so.

He gestures at the low, narrow opening that serves as the doorway. "Go inside for a better look."

Ducking my head, I enter. Thomas follows. The roof proves so low that neither of us can stand up straight. I turn in a hunched, slow circle to see one room, a dirt floor, no windows, although daylight—and the elements, insects, and animals, I imagine—streams through chinks between the license plates. There's a potbellied stove in one corner, with a tin chimney that extends through a hole in the roof. A mattress on the floor. Clothesline hanging from the ceiling. And there's a cedar chest so big that I wonder if the people who lived here built their shelter around it. Above the cedar chest hangs a tin crucifix and two mildewed photographs. One photograph shows a bride and groom. Though their clothing is from the last century, their postures and expressions are reminiscent of Charlie's and mine in our wedding portrait—proud and joyful. The other photograph shows several generations of what looks to be an extended family— all dark-haired and dark-eyed and wearing fancy if antiquated clothes. They stand before a fine house, the columns of which are festooned with lush flowering vines. *Una hacienda*—yet another Spanish word I've learned since coming to California.

"This was the home of Lupe's friends," Thomas says. "They came here after the Mexican revolution. They would have been killed if they'd stayed in Mexico. The United States greeted those fleeing the revolutionaries with open arms." From his pocket, he draws a brass key and, with it, gestures at the chest. "Open it, if you like. I have."

I turn the key in the chest's lock and slowly lift the lid. It rises creakily, emitting the spicy scent of cedar. First thing I see is a thick book, leather-bound, its title in Spanish, the engraved letters printed in gold. I pick up the book; beneath it is another leather-bound volume. The stack of books continues down from there. I carefully leaf through the volume in my hands. The colorful, glossy illustrations suggest that it is some sort of Arthurian romance.

Page after page I turn until I come to the last page and carefully set it back on the stack. Along with the books, there are toys nestled inside the chest—china dolls dressed as flamenco dancers, wooden alphabet blocks, a ball. There is a cream-colored afghan, delicately crocheted, and a black fringed shawl embroidered with bright flowers. A set of sterling silver candlesticks wrapped in clean rags, and a number of china bowls and crystal goblets, similarly stored. Last but by no means least, at the very bottom: a photograph album filled with more images of the people in the photographs on the wall. Other people appear in the pictures as well—babies wearing baptismal gowns, young boys and girls holding white Bibles and dressed in lacy white confirmation clothes, men and women resting in woven chairs, surrounded by beds of blooming flowers, and a few people, quite elderly, lying in state in funeral caskets.

"Why didn't they at least take this?" What I'm looking at should not have been abandoned.

Thomas shoves his hands in his pockets, kicks at the dirt floor. "I came here right after the authorities had 'swept the camp.' That's the official terminology." His mouth twists in disgust. "'Cleaned it.' That's what others say, as if the people living here were dirty on purpose. Didn't matter that prison and death might be waiting for them if they once were rich. Didn't matter that this family, as well as many others, had legal documents and work permits. Didn't matter that nothing was waiting for them back in Mexico if they were poor. Didn't matter if families got separated." He taps the photo album in my hands. "Didn't matter what they left behind. They were herded up and sent off like cattle. What had they done wrong? They'd lived in a place nobody else wanted, because they *had* to. That's what they did."

"How did you come to have this key?"

He shrugs impatiently; apparently I've asked the obvious. "Before Lupe was taken away, her friends suspected there might be a raid, so they gave her the key to the chest. She and I were hoping to find a way to get it out of here and back to her place, and from there, back to Mexico and its rightful owners. Lupe managed to pass the key on to me when the authorities came for her."

I lay the photograph album back in its spot, close the chest, and turn the key to lock it. I give the key back to Thomas. "So what do we do?"

"We." There it is—the hint of his smile. "I was hoping you'd say that. Because I need help, and I'm not getting it from my folks, I can tell you that. They didn't like Lupe. They don't like Mexicans as a rule." He stares darkly at the key in his hands. "I'm glad I didn't have to come here today by myself, and I'm glad I won't have to figure this out by myself, either. Thank you, Ruth."

"Alone is not easy."

"Alone is all right sometimes. But lonely, that's another kind of thing altogether."

As we leave the camp, he asks if I can get a truck. The best way, he thinks, is to ask his mother. She'll be suspicious if he makes the request, and she doesn't want him driving. "'With that leg,' she says." With a truck we will be able to get the family's belongings out of the camp, Thomas explains. He has friends who will meet us here and help. A man named Ezra, another man named Ray. They will have some idea what to do next. They make runs to Mexico, trying to restore belongings and documents to deportees. People left behind—family members—they transport as well. "Sometimes they are able to reunite families," Thomas says. "Other times the search only gets started. They're far and few between, the people who do this work. And there's a reason why. If they get caught, they're put on government watch as Mexican sympathizers and Communists."

"Are you . . . that?" I ask.

He stops walking, looks at me. "That's what my parents told you."

"Not exactly. They argued about it, though."

"I sympathize with people who are being deported without due process. I sympathize with those, like Lupe and her family, who are U.S. citizens. So maybe I'm a sympathizer. But I'm no Communist. Are you?"

I have to smile at this. "I hardly know what a Communist is."

"Well, read up."

At this, I bristle. "I will."

"Good." Thomas starts walking again, and after a moment, I catch up to him. He resumes our conversation as if in midsentence. "But you have to ask my mother soon. Today, if possible. Left and right, Mexican camps are getting torched. The reason is the filth, the fear that disease might spread.

Also, white migrant farmworkers are demanding better living quarters, and they've caught the government's ear. The Farm Security Administration is starting to build halfway decent compounds." Thomas shifts his weight on his crutches, trying to ease the pain of his injury. "I'll be here until New Year's Day. I'm leaving then. Gotta get back to work. How about you?"

"The semester starts on the second. As long as your folks don't mind me staying, I don't have anywhere else to go until then."

"So we have six days. That's not long, since we're at the mercy of other people's plans." He glances at me. "I'm sure my parents will want you to stay, Ruth. You make the house feel less empty, now that Grace is gone."

We've reached the ditch. This time Thomas plans more carefully for his jump, and I do, too; still, he falls flat on his face, and I do, too, and again we barely get him to his feet. To judge from Thomas's expression, he would find the walk back to San Jose unbearable. We decide he should forgo the extra blocks it will take to get to the park. We just manage to get him to his parents' house. There, I insist he take the bed in which I've been sleeping. He doesn't protest. When I ask what else I can do for him, he tells me to go. His folks are waiting. Rest is what he needs for now.

Alice and Talmadge are disappointed but not surprised that their son is not with me. We take in a few of San Jose's sights—pretty buildings and churches, shops, a particularly lovely park. Though I feign interest, my thoughts are elsewhere. My thoughts are somewhere I've never been, with people I've never met, whose photographs are growing moldy in a cedar chest. My thoughts are far, far away.

THAT NIGHT AFTER dinner, Thomas and I join his parents in the front room, where they are listening to the *Fleischmann's Yeast Hour* variety show, featuring tonight's special guest, Eddie Cantor. I force myself to pay attention to his jumping-jack delivery and madcap gags. Soon I am laughing along with Alice and Talmadge; Thomas joins in, too, now and then. I find myself wondering what Mother and Daddy are doing tonight. Why, they could be listening to this very show on their radio. The three of us have listened to it in the past, though I never laughed like this with them. I've laughed like this only with Charlie.

It hits me then. New Year's and before that, New Year's Eve, which is the day of our wedding anniversary. In five more days, Charlie and I would have been married a year.

I go to the kitchen, pour a glass of water, and force myself to drink it down in one gulp. But the water fails to wash the knot from my throat.

"You all right?"

Thomas stands beside me. There is our reflection again in the dark window. I watch myself shrug.

"They'll go to bed soon," he says.

"I know what I need to do." My tone is biting. I try and soften it. "Waiting for the right moment, that's all."

Thomas nods. "Nothing to be nervous about."

"I don't like lying, and I'm going to have to lie."

"Withhold a portion of the truth. That's different."

"Semantics." I cut him a look. Thomas is nothing like Charlie, my one true love. He's nothing like Professor Tobias, my teacher and guide. He's not above withholding a portion of the truth.

"What do you do, exactly, for work?" I ask.

He sways a little, probably uncomfortable standing this long. He's tended to his injured leg as best as he could. At least that's what he said. But he won't let me see it, so who knows what's really going on where wood meets skin and bone.

"I work for the WPA. You know it?"

I snort, truly offended this time. "I haven't been living with my head in the sand. Of course I know it—the Works Project Administration. Relief, recovery, and reform. I'm surprised that you're working for the same government that's pushing for repatriation, though. Isn't that a conflict of interest? Which of the R's does the government pay you for, exactly?"

I glare at our reflection. Though Thomas is a bit taller, he's slouching into his crutches, so we are the same height. He's studying the window, too, so he must see the look in my eyes. Do I know the WPA, indeed. I may not know much about Communism, but I have read up on other things. Roosevelt's laws and domestic programs are growing ever more liberal and controversial—Daddy doesn't approve—but many say the WPA is making it possible for poor people to survive, providing hope for economic restoration.

If Charlie ever erred in his assessment of the extent of my knowledge and understanding, it would be to presume I knew *more* than I actually did.

The reflection in the window alters and dims as my vision clouds with tears. I miss my husband something terrible, and no one, no wealth of knowledge and understanding, *nothing*, not even time will ever change that.

"You're upset."

Again I'm at the sink wiping away tears. "What gave you that idea?"

"Why?"

"You're taking money from the very government with which you disagree."

"You sound like my father. And to him I always say: That's democracy. You get to disagree and still be a citizen." Thomas sighs. "What is this really about, Ruth?"

I step away from the sink, the window, and our reflection there. "I won't ever love another man."

Thomas goes still. To judge from his stunned expression, I might as well have struck him. "I never said you would."

"I want this to be clear."

"It is."

"I love Charlie."

He runs a hand through his hair, flattening the shock that springs from his widow's peak, which stands out darker than usual against his tanned skin. The color has drained from his face, I realize.

"I love Lupe," he says.

"Do you have a picture of her?" I blurt.

He gapes at me for a moment, and then he nods.

"Show me."

Thomas fumbles in the back pocket of his trousers, pulls out a worn brown wallet, and draws from it a photograph not much bigger than a stamp. He holds it up for me to see. When I reach for it, he pulls back his hand. "I'll hold it."

I lean forward to peer at the little square, the corner of which is obscured by his ragged thumbnail. So this is Lupe, in black and white, Lupe from her shoulders on up, this little bit of her, salvaged from a larger photograph. A man's arm is around her shoulders. I could swear the arm is Thomas's. Her dark hair falls in waves against her delicate jaw; her black, almond-shaped eyes shine beneath thin, arching brows; her cupid's-bow lips are parted in laughter.

"She's radiant," I say.

"She is."

I turn away from the two of them—him and her—suddenly embarrassed. "I'll talk to your mother now."

"Wait."

I hesitate in the doorway. "There's no right moment. Now's as good a time as any."

"You asked what I do for work." He speaks gruffly, his voice thick with emotion. "How I can accept money from the government when I feel the way I do about the deportations." He presses Lupe's photograph to his chest, as if she might feel his heart beating and know he still loves her. "I think our government is about as good as it gets. I want you to believe me when I say this."

"Democracy. I know."

He nods. "So here's what I do, exactly. By day, I oversee a Mexican migrant camp, Kirk Camp, located in Puebla, a *barrio* east of Los Angeles. By day, I'm the person most Mexicans in most camps would call the bad guy. *Chico malo*. Except it's not like that in Kirk Camp. I fill a necessary position, help when I'm needed—which is pretty often, I have to say, since mediators play an important role between those working the farms and those who own the farms. But Kirk Camp is unique in its self-sufficiency. They need me, but they don't *need* me, you could say. And we all like it that way."

"And by night?"

His smile flickers. "Remember we have something in common? By night I'm a teacher. I don't have my certification, understand. I'm probably not as much of a teacher as you are after one semester at college. I've never even been to college. But I'm able to teach basic math, reading, and science to the Kirk Camp kids after they've returned from the fields and had their supper. By night I do the work I like best."

In the front room, the radio clicks off. We evaluate each other, Thomas and I, taking the measure of our new understanding. Then I turn away from him and go straight to Alice.

"Do you think your friend Hank might let me borrow his

truck? I need to run some errands. It won't take more than a few hours. I'll bring it back safe and sound, I promise."

All in a rush: The truth but not the whole truth. A portion of the truth.

Alice looks surprised, but promises to ask Hank first thing tomorrow morning.

NINE

Next morning, the thick, heavy sunlight informs me I've slept later than usual. It was a restless night, filled with troubling dreams I can't remember. Half awake, I get dressed. When I emerge from my room, I find a note from Alice on the kitchen table. I should help myself to whatever I'd like to eat or drink. They'll look forward to seeing me early this evening when they get home from the factory, unless she hears yes or no from Hank. Then she'll try to get home at lunch to tell me.

I find Thomas at work on garden beds. Talmadge has been trying to build these for a while—he's dug the trenches into which the bed walls will be set. But he hasn't had the time or the energy to complete the task. So Thomas's Christmas gift to his parents was a promise that the beds will be up and ready for planting before he says goodbye.

While I slept this morning, Thomas nestled the first layer of four-by-four planks into the trenches. Now he sits cramped in a little red wagon that I assume belongs to the family next door, slathering thick glue along the tops of the planks. He nods good morning, then pushes himself along the bed's perimeter and applies more glue. When he reaches the end of this tier, he pulls himself up out of the wagon, hops to the dwindling stack of planks, picks up another, and carefully sets it atop the adhesive. "Your timing is perfect," he says. "Hand me a clamp?" He point at a metal device that looks something like the letter *C*, with a long screw extending through its base. I hand it to him, and he twists the screw, securing the two pieces of wood. He thanks me, then arches his back and rolls his shoulders, stretching his muscles. Then he retrieves another piece of wood, I hand him another clamp, and he does the same thing all over again.

In this way, over the next half hour or so, I help him set up the walls of one garden bed. There are two more beds to go, but Thomas is sweating, and he looks about as tired as I feel. I suggest he take a break. I haven't had breakfast yet, and it turns out neither has he.

As it's nearly lunchtime, we have that instead. Brunch, Helen would call it. I make two fried egg sandwiches, and we eat these on the back porch. It is nice out here in the sun. Thomas, leaning against the porch railing, looks more relaxed than I've yet seen him. As I tear a crispy edge from the fried egg white, I find myself telling him that Charlie liked his eggs cooked this way. "We called it bacon," I say, and Thomas nods, smiling, and tells me that makes sense. At this, I catch my breath. I've never shared a sweet memory of Charlie, I realize. I've shared only sad ones.

Guilt hunches my shoulders. Quickly, I ask Thomas what's next with the garden beds.

"Not sure." He frowns, eyeing the project, then downs the rest of his sandwich, leverages himself up, takes his dish to the kitchen, and returns to drag the wagon to the second bed. "Might as well do this one," he says. He hunkers down on the wagon and sets to work. Finished eating now, I help him. This time I clamp the pieces of wood together while he applies the glue.

We finish the walls to the second bed in half the time it took us to finish the first. I'm clamping the last piece of wood into place just as a pack of kids storms out of the duplex next door and into the backyard. At their laughter, Thomas looks up. He watches them for a few moments. "Cousins, visiting until New Year's Day," he says. "I met them this morning when I borrowed the wagon."

"They'll probably want it back now. I'll go ahead and return it."

"Thank them for me, okay?" He smiles sadly. "They remind me so much of Lupe's brothers and sisters."

I trundle the wagon over to the children, who immediately incorporate it into their play. When I return to Thomas, I find Alice standing beside him, wearing her work apron, as she was the day I arrived.

"This is wonderful! I was never a gardener back home." Alice grimaces, laughing. "Heck, I wouldn't have wanted to get my hands dirty back then. But take away the hardship, and gardening can feel good. That's one nice thing I learned from all that's happened. I believe I earned myself a green thumb, too."

I smile. "'Homegrown tomatoes. A little taste of heaven.' That's what Mother always says."

"Mama's always right." Alice raps Thomas lightly on his head. "Now. Good news. Hank says you can borrow his truck, long as you fill it with gasoline before you return it. Mind, it's almost on empty, so it will cost a pretty penny. You should decide if you can afford it before you go."

My pocketbook holds a twenty-dollar bill, which I've been saving to buy a thank-you gift for Alice and Talmadge. I imagine I'll have enough left to buy something worthwhile after I replenish the tank. "That's fine," I say.

Alice smiles, holds out a set of keys. "You mind giving me a ride back to the factory before you run your errands?"

I let Alice lead the way to the truck. Before I follow, I whisper to Thomas that I'll be right back. We'll do what we need to do then.

THOMAS AND I rattle in Hank's truck to the outskirts of town, then turn down the road that leads to the ditch-bank camp. Black smoke billows before that uneven horizon line of green, obliterating much of the citrus groves beyond. At the sight, Thomas slams his fists against the dashboard. "God, no!" he shouts. "Drive, Ruth! Drive faster!"

I accelerate until the steering wheel shakes, just shy of uncontrollable in my hands. Soon enough, Thomas's *no* reveals itself as the worst kind of *yes*. The ditch-bank camp is all but burned to the ground. Even inside the truck, the shimmering heat from the fire hits us like a wall.

The Tulsa race riots, Minah, Susan, and Jubilant, the wolf at the door—the memory of all this flashes through my mind. Thirty-five city blocks were destroyed in Tulsa. This, though a very different situation, seems like more of the same.

There's another pickup truck parked near the ditch-bank camp. Two men sit inside, watching the dying fire. Straw cowboy hats shadow their faces, but even with the truck windows rolled up tight against the smoke, I can see that one man's skin is brown, the other man's white.

"Ezra and Ray, here to help," Thomas says.

The white man springs out of the truck and runs through the heat and smoke to where we're parked. Thomas rolls down his window, and instantly, the air in the cab is hazy and gray. I cough, my eyes stinging, as the man peers inside. The man is older than I thought, given the speed at which he ran. He has wire-rimmed glasses, a thick white mustache, and thinning white hair. He is swearing a blue streak. Noticing me, he stops midexpletive. "Sorry," he says, though he doesn't sound sorry at all. He sounds livid.

Thomas introduces the man as Ray. My eyes are streaming now. I swipe at my tears and give a nod of greeting, but he ignores me. "We would have gone on in if there was anything left to save," he says.

Thomas groans. "Nothing? Not even on the far side?"

"Nothing."

"You're sure?"

Ray scowls, his mustache bristling. "We could make absolutely sure. We could crawl through there, digging our way. And we could die. What good would that do anyone, really?"

Thomas doesn't say anything to this. He's holding the key to the cedar chest, I realize. Ray turns and heads back to the truck where Ezra sits, and in one swift movement, Thomas pitches the key out the window. It lands in the ditch's polluted water. The algae and scum are so thick, it doesn't make a ripple. Thomas looks at me, and his eyes, red and swollen from the smoke, are teary. "You go on, Ruth. I'll catch a ride with them. The three of us need to talk."

And then he's out the door, running to join his friends.

They're still watching the fire as I turn the truck around and head back to San Jose. I roll down the windows, trying to air out the cab. Don't want to return the truck to Hank smelling like this. I have to *do* something first. Fill it up. Clean it out. Make something better.

I drive into the center of town, fill the tank at a gas station, and then park the truck in a nearby vacant lot. There's a rag shoved under my seat; I use it to wipe away the ashy grime, revealing again the rust-spattered paint. The wind comes in gusts: good. I leave the windows open. There's also the faint scent of smoke on the air. That might be good, too. Maybe I can fudge the truth a little and say I drove past the fire. Actually, that is the truth, isn't it? It was a fire unlike any I've seen.

I've got hours before seven o'clock, the end of the day shift, when I need to have the truck parked where Hank can find it. I'll leave the windows open every last one of those hours while I walk the streets of San Jose, looking into the windows of shops that were closed yesterday for the Sabbath. Looking, but still too dazed to see much, although I swear I'm going to find a gift for Alice and Talmadge.

Finally, something catches my eye—an empty picture frame, beautifully carved with scrolling flourishes and lilies. It's a frame worthy of Grace's photograph. It's the gift I've been looking for.

IN THE FEW remaining days, Thomas and I work on the garden beds. The work helps me stave off the black fog; perhaps, to gauge from the intensity of his focus, it serves a similar purpose for Thomas. We don't say much. We don't need to say much. There doesn't seem to be much to say anymore. Dispirited but for the work before us, we finish the beds, prepare the ground. Dirt gets beneath my nails, covers my hands. It feels good to get my hands dirty. It is good to break up the ground so the ground can become a garden.

Thomas and I finish the job the day before New Year's Eve, to the delight of Alice and Talmadge. The next day, New Year's Eve, my one-year wedding anniversary, I wake to find that Thomas is gone.

Smiling, Alice hands me a slip of paper. "He left this for you. His address. In case you ever have need, he said."

I go to the bedroom and stuff the slip of paper inside my pocketbook. When I return to Alice, I tell her what day this would be for Charlie and me, and she doesn't mention Thomas again.

That night I give the picture frame to Alice and Talmadge. Alice weeps, thanking me, and for the first time, Talmadge draws me close in a hug. We have our last dinner together, and I thank them for their hospitality so repeatedly that they finally beg me to stop. Next morning, New Year's Day, I pack my things and board the bus back to Pasadena.

On the ride, I write to Mother and Miss Berger. I expand on the good things about this holiday—the kindness of strangers who are strangers no more, the sights of San Jose, the garden beds. I omit the bad things. Mother never wants to know the bad if she can help it. And though Miss Berger would want to know, I choose not to tell her. I don't want to write it down. I don't want to live it all over again—the abandoned camp, the fire, and Thomas's grief, coupled with mine.

TEN

I open the door to my room in Garland Hall to find Helen standing before the big bay window. She whirls around to greet me, a chain of red hearts draped around her neck, a heart pinned in her blond hair. In one hand, she holds a silver foil Cupid, arrow set in bow, ready to fly; in the other hand, she holds a ball of red twine. She casts these things on her bed and makes for me, the chain of hearts dragging on the floor behind her. She throws her arms around me and squeezes the breath from my lungs.

"I don't think I've ever been happier to see anyone, Ruth!" Helen grabs my suitcase only to drop it on the floor, then helps me out of my coat and shoves a bowl of colorful candy hearts into my hands. "Take one. Take as many as you like! Only you have to read the message printed on every one you eat. That's our new tradition."

Hel Fire, feisty as ever. Dutifully, I choose a lavender-tinted heart. *"Be Mine."*

Helen laughs. "But I am! You should know that by now."

And then: "In all seriousness, I missed you terribly. It was lovely with Mama and Papa. But I'm a different person now, I realized that. I know we were ships in the night the last half of fall semester. You were so busy with your work. I was so busy having fun. But I want to change that, Ruth. I want us to see more of each other this spring. I want to do more work and have a little less fun, and I hope you'll have more fun and do a little less work. What do you say?"

"Sounds wise."

"Well, I've never been called that before!" Flushed with happiness and conviction, Helen plucks a pink heart from the bowl. "*Always and Forever,*" she reads. Solemnly, she taps the little heart against mine in a kind of toast, then pops the candy in her mouth. "Now you, Ruth."

I eat the candy heart. It tastes like sugared chalk, but I don't say so to Helen. Her words have worked some good in me. I'm glad to be back at college, back here with her. I'm glad—and relieved—to start in again on my chance at another life.

Before I unpack, I offer to help Helen decorate our room.

"It can be such a dull time of year, January into February," she explains when I ask if we aren't jumping the gun a little on Valentine's Day. "It's much prettier here than in Oklahoma in the winter, of course. But these are the days when I strive to live up to my New Year's resolutions and inevitably fail. A bit of color and a few decorations lift my spirits, times like this. They probably do the same for most everyone." Helen catches her breath, and her green eyes widen. "Unless— Oh, Ruth, I didn't think! With Charlie and everything, maybe all this lovey-dovey stuff isn't a good idea?"

I look quickly away from her, trying to hide my expression. I focus on tacking a cupid to the wall. "It's Saint Valentine's Day, after all. Valentine didn't live his life and lose it for romance. From what I've read, he ministered to persecuted Christians." I manage to flash her a wry smile. "Until he got himself decapitated, that is."

Helen wrinkles her nose in disgust. "I didn't know that part of the story. I didn't *want* to know that part! You can be such a know-it-all sometimes, Ruth!"

She's not angry at me, not really. And by the time another hour has passed, our entire room looks like one big Valentine. She's nothing but happy then.

In the weeks that follow, Helen and I eat dinner together in the dining hall two nights a week. We go for weekend walks. Rising in the morning, we tell each other the plan for our respective days; readying ourselves for bed, we summarize the reality. In short, we become the best of friends. This is college as it should be, I tell myself. This is the best life can be without Charlie.

All the while, I am who I've always been: studious to an extreme—though thanks to Helen, a slightly lesser extreme than last semester. I remain devoted to my job as Professor Tobias's assistant. "He's a taskmaster," Helen complains. She can't seem to understand how much I need and want each task. It's still true: As much as I'm learning in my classes, I believe I'm learning far more from the assistantship. "Who knows? Maybe someday I'll get my master's in education," I tell Helen. "If I do, I bet it will be a breeze, given all the information I'm gaining now."

It is Valentine's Day. We are sitting at a large, noisy table in the dining hall. Outside, the sun, a fiery red ball, is slowly disappearing behind a line of palm trees.

Suddenly, Helen's fork clatters against the table, and she glares at me, her hands clasped in furious appeal.

"What is it?" I balance my fork on the edge of my plate.

"I can't bear it anymore. I was talking with some seniors the other day, Ruth. And I— Well, I've been waiting for a time to tell you. They won't tell you. Nobody will, because you keep your distance with everyone but me."

"Helen." I push my plate away. "Tell me."

Helen looks miserable now, her fury having dissolved into distress. "When I mentioned you were Tobias's assistant, Ruth, they had some pretty strong things to say. That man has a reputation. That's what I'm trying to say."

"I'm not sure what you're getting at." I clear my throat, trying to steady my voice. "He does have a reputation. He's renowned in academic circles."

"Oh, he's renowned, all right." Helen laughs without humor. "He's renowned for having his way with this girl and that."

The rooms seems to dim. I press my napkin to my lips, then fold it and carefully—too carefully, I realize as I'm doing it—tuck it under my plate. "He's been a gentleman to me. He cares about his students, yes. But he's never crossed the line. Not with anyone I know. Not with me. I'm not going to give up this opportunity because of a few rumors. My friendship with you, my studies, and this assistantship . . . Believe me when I tell you these are what keep me going. Please don't . . . complicate things."

We stare at each other across the table until we become

aware that the people on either side of us—couples; it is Valentine's Day, after all—are listening in. Helen stares at one couple, and I do the same to the other. Only when they resume their conversations do we finish ours, speaking in quieter voices.

"I'll do anything for you. You know that." Helen picks up her fork again, pokes at her food.

"Thank you. And I'll do anything for *you*."

"Except quit your assistantship," Helen says.

"Except that."

That night I try to grade Professor Tobias's quizzes in the library. I try to write my own paper, "The Montessori System: A Recent Alternative to the Traditional Student/Teacher Relationship." But after my conversation with Helen, I find myself distracted, discontent. I find myself thinking of Thomas, the quiet, easy way we worked together on the garden beds—a hard task that could be accomplished. We accomplished it. We finished something together, and we could stand back and look at it, wood frames, readied earth, and know we'd done well. I miss Thomas, I realize to my surprise. My other friend. Thomas. This thought makes me restless. I leave my desk and roam the library stacks—which is typically a familiar, comforting activity that reminds me of Miss Berger. But though the act feels familiar, tonight there's no comfort in it. Now I'm searching through recent newspapers and magazines, I'm looking for something, I just can't think what. And then I realize: I'm looking for any reference to repatriation. But once again there is nothing mentioned in the press.

On the other side of the periodicals department, a man is

at work: the library janitor, methodically sweeping the floor. In the past, I've heard him speaking Spanish with a coworker. He appears to be from Mexico originally. But for the two of us, this part of the library is empty. Why not ask him what he knows?

I am making my way over to him when a reference librarian blocks my path.

"The library has been closed for half an hour." She smiles sympathetically. "It's far past time for you to go." When I press for a few more minutes, her smile fades. "Now," she says. "Rules are rules."

I RETURN TO Garland Hall to find two pieces of mail in my mailbox. One is a brightly colored valentine from Helen. It shows two little girls, one with blond hair, one with brown. Both ride prancing ponies. Scrolling words ring the picture, the familiar nursery rhyme:

> *The rose is red, the violet's blue,*
> *The honey's sweet, and so are you.*

And in Helen's hasty scrawl: *Love you, Roomie.*

The other letter is enclosed in a small, thin envelope. I recognize the handwriting: Mother's stiff, careful script, each letter pinched and constrained. Right there in the little mailroom, with other girls chattering, laughing, sharing Valentine's greetings and grumblings, I tear open the envelope. Here is Mother's handwriting again, only this time smeared with her efforts. And here is a ten-dollar bill. Tears sting my eyes. It's the most money Mother has ever given me—a real sacrifice on her part. I can't imagine how she got it past Daddy.

> *Ruth,*
> *Captain died. Daddy was stricken until he brought home another rooster and named him General. What will be next? President?*

I laugh right out loud; it is rare when Mother jokes. A good sign, I hope.

Other girls glance my way, surprised at my outburst. It's as rare that I laugh as that Mother jokes, apparently. I smile, embarrassed, and head to the lobby for more privacy. But the lobby, too, is packed to the gills with Garland Hall residents—young women talking and studying together, or gathered around the piano, listening as a conservatory student improvises wildly on "Twinkle, Twinkle, Little Star." A few others work on a large puzzle spread across the coffee table, which shows a nighttime view of the Hollywoodland sign rolling unevenly below the crest of an arid hilltop. The puzzle's full moon punches a white hole in the dark sky above. Only a small portion of sky and land is yet to be completed; as I watch, a girl cries out and snaps a puzzle piece into place to the exuberant cheers of her friends. I look toward the stairs. Since Helen isn't down here, she'll be up in our room, unless she's sneaked out again. After our dinner conversation, I won't take the risk of going up. I doubt she's put aside her worries about my assistantship, and I'm not ready for another discussion. Not yet.

I go to the front door, where Miss Voyle waits, watching

for stragglers after curfew. If I know our Never Failing Bulwark of a Resident Director, she'll stand guard for at least another hour. I show her my letter and ask permission to read it outside on the front steps. "You can keep your eyes on me the whole while," I say.

Miss Myrtle gives a queenly wave of her hand.

I sit on the bottommost porch step. The chapel bells sound ten-forty-five as I again begin to read.

> Alice wrote me last week. You weren't alone in enjoying the holiday. The Everlys were glad for your visit. She said you got along real well with her boy.
>
> I'm doing fine. Your daddy's doing fine. But we miss you. Not just me but your daddy, too.
>
> Please write when you are able and tell me all your goings-on.
>
> Your Mother

I fold the letter and slip it back in the envelope. I sit on the bottom step, missing them—not just Mother but Daddy, too—until Miss Voyle demands that I come inside.

ELEVEN

At the end of nearly every day now, I write to Mother. Sometimes just a postcard. Other times longer notes and full-fledged letters. I write to Mother the way I might keep a diary if I were the kind of person who kept diaries. I tell her most everything. Most of most everything wouldn't interest other people—the details of what I'm learning in my classes and through my assistantship. But for the first time in my life, I choose to assume that Mother will care. She will care as much as Miss Berger, if not more.

Of course, I write Miss Berger as well. A few weeks after Valentine's Day, I write her in more detail about my trip to San Jose and my experiences with Thomas. (These things I still keep from Mother. And any description of Thomas might pointlessly intrigue her, as it did Alice.) For Miss Berger, I describe the deportation I witnessed at the bus stop, the abandoned camp, and the torching—all this and a bit about Thomas, too. And so the Repatriation Act becomes Miss Berger's concern as well. Through her library connections, she gains access to Spanish-language newspapers and, utilizing a Spanish/English dictionary, tells me what she gathers from these articles. They are replete with descriptions of farmworker strikes and union meetings, which are frequently raided, as are the Mexican migrant workers' camps. The journalists cover the ongoing harassment and segregation of Mexican people, along with Filipino people, they report, and Japanese. *If we're not careful,* Miss Berger writes, *we'll be living the Indian Removal Act all over again, only with a different population made to suffer. "We must eliminate the alien horde!" That's one of the many troubling refrains intoned by the supporters and sycophants of Labor Secretary William S. Doak. Honestly, some of these raids and sweeps are reminiscent of those perpetuated by the KKK, only these perpetrators wear suits and uniforms instead of white robes.*

At moments like this, Miss Berger's fervency leaves me unsettled. If she's correct, then to whom and what do I pledge my allegiance? I consider writing Thomas to ask him what he thinks about all this, but he'll only confirm Miss Berger's opinion, I'm sure, and where would that leave me? Overwhelmed, most likely. Entirely swayed by the force of their arguments. Unable to make up my own mind. So I save my letter-writing for Miss Berger and Mother, and otherwise escape into academic pursuits. The Ivory Tower is an apt term, I realize. Up here, Rapunzel can plait her hair and live an ordered life of the mind, with everything viewed at a reasonable distance. Down there in the fray of the real world, things quickly unravel and come undone, and when they do, Rapunzel can't see or think straight for the tangled mess.

* * *

I MARK THE day of Charlie's passing alone in my dorm room. It is not a Saturday. It is not a Sunday. It is a Tuesday, and for the first time—the only time, I vow—I skip classes, appointments, all work. I make no excuses. I turn my face to the wall when Helen tries to rouse me. She knows what day it is; she finally gives up and leaves me alone. I stay in bed, blanketed by black fog, for much of the morning.

Helen returns at lunchtime, carrying a carton of tomato soup. "If you won't eat, I'll force-feed you," she announces. So I sit up and take a few dutiful spoonfuls, then a few more. I'm hungry, I realize. I finish the entire carton of soup, and as I do, Helen starts to question me. To my astonishment, she asks me about Charlie—more about him and our life together than she's ever asked. "What was he like as a little boy?" "When did you know you loved him?" I hesitate, wary of what such talk will do to me, but then I find myself telling her the story of the snowfall. The one and only miracle of my life. And as I describe this and other memories of Charlie, the black fog begins to lift. I *remember* him. I put my memories of him back together, and he is not entirely lost. When Helen heads off to her afternoon classes, I lay the photographs of Charlie and me on my desk. I look at them for a long while. I thank God for him. Then I get dressed, open the curtains and the windows, and start to study. I have work to catch up on now. And Professor Tobias expects a stack of quizzes graded and returned to him tomorrow.

The following Sunday is Easter. Given the short break,

most people stay on campus, so for this holiday, at least, I'm not alone. Helen and I attend the service at the campus chapel and a lavish Easter Day luncheon in a meeting room off the dining hall, hosted by the Education Department. The luncheon is open to all majors, as well as faculty, staff, and their families. The meeting room proves packed, and noisy with talk and laughter. *This* feels like a real celebration, even to me, and enjoying myself as I am, that must make me a true college coed. I wouldn't claim to be the poster girl Helen is. But for the first time, I feel like I fit in.

Before we sit down to eat, Helen hands me a narrow black velvet box topped with a silver bow. For her, every holiday entails gift-giving—and not just a token, like the chocolate bunny I bought her at the last minute and set in a little pink woven basket atop her pillow while she showered for church—but a Present with a capital *P*. For Christmas, for instance, she gave me a complete edition of Shakespeare's plays. I gave her a new umbrella because, around and about as she always is at all hours, in all weather, hers kept turning inside out. So it is with some trepidation that I open the velvet box. What's inside is as beautiful and perfect as I assumed it would be: a delicate gold chain, wound around a white satin pillow, and beside the chain, a tiny embossed tag that reads *24 Karats*. Besides my wedding band, it's the nicest piece of jewelry I've ever received. The nicest thing I own. I start to say something inane—*Oh! You shouldn't have!*—but Helen holds up her hand.

"I wanted to, and for good reason." Helen takes the box

from my hand and the necklace from the pillow and holds it out so I can see its full length. "You've shed a few pounds since you've been here, you know—too much work and not enough food. You're going to lose Charlie's ring. It keeps slipping off—you know it does. You'll be wearing it on your thumb soon, Ruth, and that would look plain silly. So I got you this. It will look lovely on you, and your ring will be safe. You'll be able to keep it close to your heart. What do you say?"

For a moment I hesitate, but then, unable to say anything, I nod.

Smiling, satisfied, Helen watches as I thread the necklace through my wedding band. She latches the necklace at the back of my neck and spins me around to take a look.

"Lovely," she pronounces. "And loyal as ever."

STUFFED TO THE gills with glazed ham, scalloped potatoes, asparagus, and lemon chiffon pie, we students profusely thank the faculty and staff, and then, after helping clear and wash the dishes in the dining hall kitchen, we head out into a gloriously sunny afternoon. For once, it's not me solo, or me completing the duo that is Helen and me. It's me, part of a happy group. Helen has suggested a game of capture the flag, which will occur on the football field in twenty minutes, after we've all changed out of our church clothes and into, as Helen says, "our play clothes." I can't think what she means by play clothes. All I have are skirts or dresses. But she has several pairs of the latest in women's trousers—high-waisted, easy and comfortable to wear—stored away for times like this. "I'll dress you right," she promises.

We are leaving the meeting room, Helen's arm linked through mine, about to step out on the porch flanked with early-blooming lilac bushes when Professor Tobias calls my name from across the room.

Helen's grip on my arm tightens. "No. Not today."

"A moment of your time, please. That's all I ask." Professor Tobias's tone is cheery but firm. In spite of Helen's resistance, I turn to him. He stands beside the crystal punch bowl, which I washed clean in the kitchen only a few minutes ago. On the table, clustered around the punch bowl, are a host of matching cups, and on the floor, two good-sized boxes filled with crumpled balls of paper. Professor Tobias smiles at me. "We'll just pack all this up and carry it back to my office, Ruth, and then you're free to capture any flag you want."

"He's positively *mellifluous*, and he knows it," Helen often says. "He uses that voice of his to get his way." If I look at her, I know she'll make a similar scornful remark now. I don't look at her.

"I'll be right there," I tell Professor Tobias.

"I'll help, too. We'll finish the job all the faster," Helen says.

Professor Tobias tugs his light blue suit jacket into place. Next moment, he's crossed the room to stand before us.

"I pay Ruth to help me with things like this. I don't pay you, Miss St. Pierre." He speaks quietly, but the look he gives Helen is a forceful one.

Helen juts out her chin, defiant. "But it's Sunday. It's Easter, for heaven's sake."

Professor Tobias frowns. Audacious Helen has no real

sense of what it means to need a job as I do; if I'm not careful, she could cost me it. I dearly love her, but there are times—times like this—when the division of class seems to widen between us, and we stand on opposite sides.

I withdraw my arm from her grip. "Lay out what you think I should wear for Capture the Flag, Helen. I'll be changed and at the field before you know it."

Professor Tobias thanks me, turns on his heel, and strides back to what needs to be done.

"*Hurry*," Helen hisses.

"*I will*," I hiss back.

As Professor Tobias and I swaddle china cups in packing paper and settle them carefully into their boxes, our conversation turns from the success of the luncheon to the academic progress of the other students in attendance. This is what I most appreciate about my assistantship, I realize: No matter what Helen thinks, Professor Tobias makes me feel more like a colleague than a worker bee—which is Helen's opinion of me.

"The punch bowl isn't terribly heavy, empty," he says now. "If you carry it and I carry the glasses, we'll be able to make it to my office in one trip."

As we cross the empty quad to the academic building, Professor Tobias tells me that the punch bowl and glasses originally belonged to his mother. "She died when I was very young, which left my father to care for five boys. To say he failed at the task is an understatement. So you see, Ruth . . ." He sets the boxes carefully on the ground by the building's entrance, pulls a ring of keys from his trouser pocket, and unlocks the large wooden door. "I've known hard

times, too. I've come to believe that's what draws me to people, and people to me—that kind of understanding, based
on personal experience. People like Miss St. Pierre . . . they
may be decent people, but they don't really understand.
Maybe one day. But not until they've passed through the
dark wood."

"Dark wood?"

"From Dante's *Inferno*. You know."

I don't know. I'll have to find out.

We make our way down the dim hallway to the wide,
curving staircase that leads to Professor Tobias's office on the
third floor. In the thick silence, our footsteps sound loudly
against the creaky steps. There appears to be no one else in
the building, which is not surprising. Any given Sunday, let
alone Easter Sunday, is supposed to be a day of rest. No one
is supposed to be in the academic building at all.

Professor Tobias leads the way down the third-floor hall.
"In terms of the dark wood, we're more alike than not, don't
you think? I cherish this about you, Ruth. You're not like any
of the other students here, male or female, and you're certainly not like any of the assistants I've worked with before.
Your loss makes you special. Not that pain is something for
which you or any person should strive, but there should be
some reward for surviving it and carrying on. And in your
case, the reward is distinction."

This compliment doesn't settle well. But still I mumble
my thanks. I'd prefer not to extend the discussion. The
punch bowl is weighing heavily; its cut-glass edges bite into
my fingers and palms. But finally, here we are at the door to
the Education Department. Again Professor Tobias sets

down the boxes, pulls out his ring of keys. He unlocks the door, we step inside, and he closes the door behind us. The main office is windowless, so it's instantly dark. Professor Tobias grunts, bumping into something. "Stay put, Ruth. Not the easiest going here. Don't want you to hurt yourself."

Again the thunk on the floor; again the jangle of keys and an opened door. Then soft light flares from Professor Tobias's office—the familiar glow of the little lamp on his desk.

"Come on in," he calls. And when I do: "Put the bowl down—carefully, take your time—just over there." He nods at the chair in front of his desk, the one in which students sit during his office hours, the one in which I've sat innumerable times, early in the morning, during my lunch hour, late into the night. I carefully lower the punch bowl onto the seat of the chair.

I feel him then, his muscled arms around my waist, pulling me up and against him. Tie clip, belt buckle, the length of his body, pressing against the length of me.

"Ruth." He breathes my name into the bare skin at the back of my neck, and the downy hairs there prickle and rise. My jaw locks, my throat closes. I can't make a sound. Not a scream, or a word, or a growl of resistance.

"Ruth."

He's strong. He twists me around, and again the whole length of him presses against the whole length of me—the other side, the front of me, which, like the back of me, has only ever been touched by Charlie, my husband, my dead husband, whose ring I now wear on a thin gold necklace around my throat, whose ring nestles in the hollow between my collarbones, whose ring Professor Tobias regards, gazing down at the neckline of my dress and below that, where, breathless as I am, my chest rises and falls. And now he presses his lips against the hollow between my collarbones, and his tongue touches my skin ringed by Charlie's gold.

I maneuver my right knee between his legs, and he moans. He likes this—my leg between his. Let him like it. For one moment, let him like it, let him like it just long enough to let down his guard, so I can ready myself, steady myself, steel myself. There. Now. I lift my thigh, and my knee slides where I want, between his legs, near his groin. And then with one sharp, fast movement, my knee jabs him there.

But not hard enough.

"What the—" Professor Tobias's face twists. He throws me down on the desktop. Papers crackle beneath me, and tests, a metal roll of tape, a stapler, pencils, and pens. From the corner of my eye, I glimpse the brass trophy he earned some years ago: *Teacher of the Year*. It's shaped like an apple, and there is his name, engraved on the white marble base. And he's on top of me now, straddling me like a horse he wants to ride. Except for our ragged breathing, it is quiet—the silence of a nightmare. There should be sound. I should scream. But I can't. There's a weight on my chest, his hand pressing down, pinky ring and cuff link flashing silver in the lamp's glow. Pressing down. "The easy way or the hard way. Which way do you want?" He says this. The blood rushes in my ears, loud as a passing train.

The easy way or the hard way? The hard way. But unable to catch my breath, his weight on me like this, I can't fight like I want to fight—like Daddy's two roosters fought the one time he was foolish enough to have two roosters, Private and Corporal, who pecked and clawed each other to a bloody pulp.

Suddenly, he freezes. The high color drains from his face, and still astride me, he looks toward the door. And then like that, he drags me upright and pulls me to him again, yanking my arms around his shoulders.

"What's going on here?"

Quavering voice, crest of white hair. Hunched and frail in a pink suit and a feathered Easter hat, Florence Windberry, professor emeritus, stands in the office doorway. And Professor Tobias cowers—*cowers*—in my arms, then shoves me back and away. I trip over my own feet and fall. My head strikes the base of the wooden stand that supports a world globe. The stand teeters, tips—sharp, penetrating pain, specks of white light flashing—and the globe cracks as it strikes the floor. The world is in pieces. I see this through specks of light, and then my dress, hiked up near the top of my thighs, my legs spread in an ungainly fashion, and Professor Tobias towering over me, eyes smoldering. "You want to know what's going on, Florence? Ask her."

I close my legs, yank down my dress. I try to sit up. Head spinning, I make it only halfway.

"Not again." Florence Windberry is clenching the door frame for support.

"It happens, Florence. It's like they can't control themselves. One minute they're demure girls. Next minute they're sluts." He shakes his head, weary and wronged.

"The last one made an attempt on Suicide Bridge after she got expelled. A police officer stopped her just in time." Florence Windberry's voice no longer quavers. It is strong and hard as steel.

I lurch forward, woozy and nauseated. I have to lean against the desk to stay upright. I know Suicide Bridge. Like the train trestle that brought me to this place, it spans the deep canyon that is the Arroyo Seco.

"I'll contest your accusation once again. You know that, don't you, Tobias?" Florence Windberry says. "I'll go to the department, the administration, the university president, the students if I have to. I'll tell them the truth."

"You do that, Florence. Your female hysteria has worked so well for you in the past." Professor Tobias manages to sound both relaxed and disdainful. "Now it's time for both of you to leave. Go on. Get out of here."

He nudges my thigh with the toe of his shoe. When I fail to move, he grabs my arm and pulls me to my feet. I nearly fall into Florence Windberry as he pushes me toward the door. Somehow I make my way out into the hallway. Hand pressed against the wall, I keep myself upright, if not steady.

"I'll do what I can, Mrs. Warren." Florence Windberry's voice follows me down the hall; even in my distress, I'm comforted that she knows my name. "But prepare yourself for the worst. If a miracle happens, then all will be well, and we will be glad. But expect otherwise."

I've had my one and only miracle, the one and only of my life. It's come and gone. I would tell her that, but it takes all my concentration to continue walking.

WHAT HAPPENS NEXT happens fast, in a blur of distorted sensation. I am in my room again. I fall, limbs aching and askew, on my bed. It is dark. I am cold. Now it is bright and someone shakes me. Tobias? I flail my limbs and someone shouts in pain. The someone is a girl, a woman. A young woman. The someone is Helen. I see her through half-open eyes. I see her blond hair. "Wake," she says. "Up," she says. "Ruth," she says. My eyes close against the bright light, and Helen's voice, too loud. She shakes me again. Make her stop. The smallest movement and my head splits open like a world globe. Her movements are anything but small.

The shaking finally stops. Darkness again, and cold.

When I next open my eyes, Helen sits cross-legged at the end of my bed. Now there are two of her, her many fingernails to her two mouths, her many teeth tearing at her cuticles. Now there are three of her. Now she is one whole person, not duplicated or broken to pieces. She and everything around her—dresser, chocolate Easter bunny in pink basket, desk, desk lamp—go in and out of focus, multiply and divide. The entire room turns kaleidoscopic, with no predictable pattern.

"What happened to you?" Helen spits out a shred of cuticle. "You've been out for twelve hours. You were here when I got back yesterday evening—I couldn't wake you— and you've been dead to the world ever since. It's Monday morning now, after nine o'clock, Ruth. This isn't like you at all."

"Tobias." My voice sounds very far away.

"Yes, we missed his class this morning. Sorry. I tried to wake you. I really tried. And then since *you* were sleeping in, I decided why shouldn't I."

I strain to lift my head from the pillow. Pain stabs my skull. I sink back down again. "Hurts."

"What hurts? What *happened* to you?"

A sharp knock sounds. Helen looks toward the door. I'm unable to do so.

"Open up." Miss Voyle, her voice as sharp as her knock. "Open this door now, please."

Helen shoots me a questioning glance, but when Miss Voyle raises her voice and repeats the command, she goes to the door and opens it. Miss Voyle pushes past her, stopping only when she stands by my bed. To my surprise, she kneels stiffly beside me.

"The dean is expecting you in his office in half an hour, Ruth. It will bode worse for you than it already does if you are late, I can promise you that." She evaluates my state, her hawklike gaze sweeping my body. "Are you able to dress yourself? From the look on your face, I think not. Helen?"

She oversees while Helen does what she does so well—gets me dressed. "Careful! Oh, be careful!" I beg as she starts to comb my hair. Helen touches the lump on the back of my skull and gasps, compelling Miss Voyle to prod it, too. My vision goes black with the pain, and now Helen is crying. Miss

Voyle says something to her. There follows some kind of exchange. Gently, as if the strands of my hair were as fragile as spiderwebs, Helen resumes work with her comb. Then she dabs my face clean with a warm, damp cloth, slips shoes on my feet, and helps me stand.

"We'll get you to the infirmary right after the meeting," Miss Voyle says quietly. "I promise you, Ruth, we won't let you go untended."

"I'm coming with you," Helen says.

Miss Voyle doesn't protest. Holding me upright, they guide me from the room and down the stairs, out of the dorm, and across the quad to the administration building, where they have to plead with me to walk through that door again. Finally inside, we climb the single flight of stairs to the dean's office.

In the waiting room, I find myself swaying from dizziness. "Why are we here?"

"Tobias," Miss Voyle says.

I lean against Helen.

"Hush, now." Helen strokes my cheek. "We'll be right here. We won't leave without you."

Another door opens. I take a few steps, and the door shuts behind me.

The dean's office feels cavernous, with shadows that huddle in corners and only a few lamps lit—one on the desk behind which the dean sits, and a standing lamp that illuminates three men sitting in wingback chairs. My head still throbs, but the fresh air has cleared my vision: I can see one of everything relatively clearly. The shadowy room is made all the more shadowy by walnut-paneled walls, which, even in this light, appear dusty. Oriental rugs strew the floor, and these look dusty, too. Dust filters through the thin line of sunlight that has managed to squeeze between all-but-closed blue velvet curtains. The room smells of dust and moldering books.

The dean sits with the light behind him, so I'm unable to make out his features. But when I enter, he stands, revealing himself to be a tall, wide man. He moves silently on the thick carpet around the desk to shake my hand. His hand is warm and dry; he releases mine quickly, as if it's something he doesn't want to touch. Now I can see his thick blond hair, his long blond sideburns that tip up to join in a mustache. "Good morning, Mrs. Warren," the dean says. His wide mouth stretches into a smile, but his small eyes are as dull as the flat heads of nails. He gestures to the hard-backed chair before his desk. "Sit. Please."

Legs trembling, obedient as a well-trained dog, I sink into the chair.

Two of the other three men in the room introduce themselves as administrators of this and that. They are both older than the dean, nearly bald. The other man is Tobias (I will never call him *Professor* again). No introduction needed there. I do everything in my power not to look at him.

I am told by the dean that I have attempted to seduce the chairman of the Education Department, the very man who advocated for my scholarship to this university. I have abused his goodwill, used my womanly wiles to seek further favor.

One of the balding men regards me over tented fingers. "What have you to say for yourself, Mrs. Warren?"

I'm woozy again. I close my eyes. In the dark, I find I can think clearly. For the moment, at least, things have stopped spinning. I open my eyes. "I want a lawyer."

A long silence and then, to my horror, restrained laughter on the part of the balding men and the dean. Tobias remains silent. I tell myself that my eyes must be playing tricks on me again, but I can't deny that my hearing is perfectly fine.

"What do you think this is, Mrs. Warren? Where do you think you are? A court of law?" Again the dean stands, only this time he turns toward the window. What he sees through the narrow gap in the curtains, I can't imagine, but he stands perfectly still, hands clasped behind his back. "There's no question to be resolved here, no court to appear before. Professor Tobias has made clear what happened. Several other members of his department support his complaint. We've withdrawn your scholarship. If you'd like to pay your own tuition bill, you may reapply for next year. For now, we ask that you take some time away from our institution. You must leave Union University. Not next week, not tomorrow." He turns to face me again. "Today."

I stare at the dean, unable to think clearly for my throbbing head. *Pink suit. Feathered hat, crest of white hair.* And then her name comes to me. "Have you spoken with Florence Windberry?"

One of the other men—not Tobias—speaks from the depths of a wingback. "She's had her say. As she always does."

"Miss Voyle? Other students? My roommate? Will you speak with them?"

"No need, Mrs. Warren. You've made your mistake. Our minds are made up."

WHEN I EMERGE from the dean's office, Helen and Miss Voyle guide me out of the building and across the quad to the infirmary. There, the boyish-looking campus doctor confirms it. I have a concussion, a bad one. I need to take particular care.

"At all costs, stay awake today, but don't do anything but rest. Get a good night's sleep tonight, too, but make sure to wake up every few hours or so." He speaks rapidly and too loudly; I long to curl up on the exam table and put my hands over my ears to muffle his voice. "Take it easy in the days to come, both cognitively and physically. You've suffered head trauma, and you need to recuperate. So don't work too hard. Don't think too much. Don't do any vigorous exercise. For that matter, don't move around any more than is necessary." The doctor scribbles something down on a piece of paper, then tucks the paper into a folder that bears my name. "And don't be afraid to take aspirin when the pain flares."

"That's a lot of don'ts," Helen mutters. She's standing at my side, her hand at my elbow. Her hand alone keeps me upright.

The doctor shrugs. "Her brain got shaken. It needs to settle down. When people maintain their typical to-do lists, that doesn't happen."

The doctor produces another piece of paper from somewhere and hands it to me. "Don't read it!" he says. "I'll tell you what it says. It asks you to confirm that you understand your diagnosis and its treatment, and you'll take all necessary precautions. Sign your name at the bottom."

Yet another "don't." I don't bother to say that it will be impossible to take it easy in the days to come. Impossible not to move when I've been ordered by the administration to do exactly that.

I sign the paper.

Only when we have returned to Garland Hall do I tell Helen and Miss Voyle exactly what happened between Professor Tobias and me, and, as a fitting postscript, what happened in the dean's office. They don't rant and rail. They don't say *I warned you*. Helen wraps her arms around me. Miss Voyle pats my back. They are waiting for me to cry. But I can't. I won't. Crying will make my head hurt worse. I have to get out of here.

"You can go live with my folks," Helen says. "They'll take you in. They'll take good care of you."

"No. Thank you, though."

"Your folks, then?" Helen asks.

I could do that. I could live with my parents again. I could work in the Alba Public Library again. I could forever feel defeated. "No."

"Where, then?" Helen asks.

In case you ever have need. He said that, his mother said.

"I have friends here in California. I'll go to them." I turn to Miss Voyle then. "I'm going to come back here. I'm going to find a way. I'm going to reapply, and if they won't take me back, I'm going to appeal."

"You can try, Ruth." But the slump in Miss Voyle's typically ramrod-straight shoulders tells me she thinks it's likely I won't succeed.

It's Helen who packs my things. She's the one who, upon my request, locates Thomas's information in my address book, then goes downstairs to the telephone booth, telephones Thomas and confirms that he will indeed receive me, then telephones the bus station to determine the bus that will take me to where he is, Kirk Camp, just east of Los Angeles. While she's gone, I pull the boy's silver cross from beneath my mattress. Thank God I remembered it, because now I remember the insurance check and the money I have left from my work at the library. I tuck all this into my pocketbook, then take it out again. There's a little tear in the lining of my coat. I fold the money and the check and slip them into the lining. They will be safer in this hiding place—the kind of hiding place an Okie on the road might use, or a migrant worker, the kind of hiding place that helps keep a body safer. The cross, I will wear beside my wedding band. I slip the cross onto the gold chain and secure the necklace's brittle clasp. Suddenly I'm dizzy again. I sit down on my bed and rest my pounding head in my hands.

After only a few minutes, Helen returns. "The earliest bus isn't until seven o'clock tonight. But we should leave soon. It's already four o'clock, and I want to give us plenty of time to eat supper and get you to the station."

Helen helps me stand. Carrying my luggage and my pocketbook, she walks me out the campus gates, hails a taxicab, and then slips into the backseat beside me. We drive to the bus station. From here, we can see Suicide Bridge. The Colorado Street Bridge, it's actually called. I learned this during the city tour we freshmen took during orientation. It's a majestic, curving structure, its walkway brightly lit by elegant, ornate lamps. And it's a long, long way down to the dry riverbed at the bottom of the Arroyo Seco that the bridge spans. That other young woman, Tobias's other assistant—what must she have endured to take herself there? I think perhaps something worse than myself.

I tug on Helen's arm. "I want to see the canyon one last time. Do we have time to walk out onto the bridge? We don't have to go far."

Helen was beside me when the freshman class crossed the bridge, only to return again in some kind of orientation ritual. Cars stirred the air as they passed us, lifting the hems of dresses, messing hair. We looked over the parapet, one hundred and fifty feet down, to see the riverbed, sinuous as a snake below. A maze of smaller bridges and roads was down there, too, and a smattering of tin shacks. Our guide told us that rumor had it the place is haunted. During the bridge's construction, a worker fell over the side into the wet concrete that would become his tomb. Ghosts are said to walk the riverbed—"The place is thick with specters," the guide said—and there are cries and echoes in the night. Come here after dark, and you might see a man with a cane, a woman in a long, flowing robe. You might see them stand on the parapet wall. You might see them jump and vanish.

"Not a chance we're walking out there," Helen says now. "Not you, or me, or both of us together. Not now. Not ever again."

She turns me right around and steers me into the bus station. There's a café there. She finds us a table, orders food. I eat some of what's on my plate. Then I stagger to the restroom, crouch over a toilet, and throw up. The doctor said this might happen with a concussion as bad as mine. When I emerge from the stall, Helen is leaning against the sink. She steps aside so I can wash my face and rinse water through the messy ends of my hair. Clean as I can get again, I take the handkerchief Helen offers, dry my face, and force myself to look at her. "I must look like the girl Tobias and the others say I am."

"Don't even think thoughts like that! They're beneath you, Ruth." Helen waves the handkerchief, indicating I should keep it. "Now come on. Your bus is leaving soon."

We're standing before the open bus door when Helen's face contorts, mottling, until a body might think she were homely if a body didn't know better. She's sobbing. I take her face in my hands, draw her close until our foreheads touch.

"We'll find a way to get you back here," Helen manages to say. "I'll help you."

Bile rises in my throat again, and I swallow it. "College is the only thing I've ever really wanted, besides Charlie. I won't let them take it from me. If I have to, I'll find another place to study, a better place. I'll go there."

"I'll join you." Helen sniffs, swipes at her nose with the

back of her hand. "As it is, I'm dropping Tobias's class. I'll never take another from him. And whoever his next assistant is, you can be sure that I'll give her a talking-to. I'll warn her, best as I can. I'll be specific, if you don't mind me mentioning you. I'll protect her. Oh, Ruth! I'm so sorry I didn't protect you."

"You tried."

"This time I won't fail."

The bus is about to leave; Helen and I can say nothing much more now than goodbye. When I sit down in my seat, she's already lost in the crowd.

The trip to Puebla doesn't take nearly as long as I expected; the hour-and-a-half ride doesn't allow me to compose myself as I'd like. I'm working too hard to stay alert. My throbbing head doesn't help much with this, as I wish it did. It's the questions that prod me awake each time I nod off. Will there be a doctor in Kirk Camp? Will Thomas have an appropriate place for me to stay? How will I find him once I arrive? He promised to welcome me—that's what Helen said. But Tobias promised a lot of things, too.

A FAIR NUMBER of passengers get off with me at the Puebla bus stop. The sky is darkening quickly. There's only a single streetlamp to illuminate the wooden shelter that serves as the bus station here. I stand in its puddle of light while the other passengers greet friends and family. "Hello!" "Welcome." "*Hola.*" "*Bienvenidos!*" The two languages, English and Spanish, weave seamlessly together.

Soon I am the only person left waiting. At least there is a bench in the shelter. I drag my suitcase closer and sit down.

Before me stretches an empty two-lane road. The night is silent but for the hissing of the cars and trucks zooming past
on the distant highway, the occasional birdcall or cricket
chirp. Not twenty feet away, an animal's eyes gleam in the
shadows, and then something scuttles past me, low to the
ground. I swallow a yelp as the sweet, hopeful sound of whistling fills the air.

A man is approaching—a man in a uniform. A bus driver,
eager to head home for the night. He tips his cap to me. He
is a handsome man who, in his jaunty grace, instantly reminds me of Tobias. But what choice do I have? I push away
my apprehension, wave my hand in appeal. "Do you know
how I might get to Kirk Camp?" I barely get the words out.
Each word seems to ricochet around inside my head, bounc-
ing off the walls of my skull.

The bus driver gives me a look. "Why would you want to
go there?"

I have nowhere else to go. That wouldn't be a good answer, not alone, late at night, with a strange man, cheery
whistler though he may be. "My friend lives there."

"You one of them wetback lovers?"

"No! I mean—" For the life of me, I can't think what *wetback* means. From his expression, it's not something good.
"My friend is a teacher," I say.

The bus driver digs in his pocket for a pack of cigarettes,
shakes one out, lights it, and takes a drag. "I can drive you
there."

My heart sinks when it should rise. "It's not out of your
way?"

"Have to drive right past the place. No other way to go."

"Oh." I press my fingers to my temples. I can't think straight for the pain.

"Come on, then, if you're coming."

The bus driver walks to the lone car parked along the side of the road. Lugging my suitcase, I follow him. During the five-minute drive, he shares his opinion of Kirk Camp, though I don't ask for it. "It's its own little *communidad*, one big *familia*." His voice holds disgust. "A few hundred people live there, in their cardboard houses, walking their dirty streets, bathing in the Rio Hondo River. Most of them are Spics, but a few are Japs. They breed like rabbits—every kid that pops out is automatically a U.S. citizen. And Kirk Camp is just one of the stinking *barrios* springing up around East Los Angeles. Those people travel for the best picking, but hell if they don't usually come back here." The man stops the car by a field filled with the hulking shadows of other cars and trucks, some of which are long flatbeds. "Your teacher friend?" he says. "He's white?"

"Yes."

"Good. We don't need no more mixed kids running around."

I feel like I might vomit again, but there's nothing in my stomach. I swallow hard, look past parked cars and trucks to the edge of what must be Kirk Camp. There are no streetlights, but there is a moon that's nearly full, and it illuminates the shacks, cobbled together, as in all the other camps, from whatever is available. I can make out a few nicer homes, too—small and square, made of concrete and painted what in the daylight must be bright colors.

"You wanted Kirk Camp." The bus driver blows a stream of smoke at me from the corner of his mouth. "You got it."

I thank him for the ride and get out of his car. I drag my suitcase from the backseat and shut the door, trying not to slam it, trying to keep it quiet. He pulls away.

A dirt road takes me a few blocks into Kirk Camp. The road is flanked with little buildings—the shacks and small concrete homes I saw from the car, along with humble shops. All of the shops are dark and quiet, as are many residences. But a few of the homes are still lit from within. The glow of kerosene lamps and candlelight seeps through chinks in the walls, between curtains, beneath doors, and sometimes through gaps in the roofs, as do sounds of muffled conversation and laughter. In one shack, someone plays a simple tune, a melody I don't recognize, on a guitar. All in all, it feels peaceful enough, and I am grateful for the quiet. I come upon a gas station at one corner, and then a church, and the metal frames of a swing set, slide, and teeter-totter glint in the moonlight a few blocks down. There must be a park or a school yard. From all appearances, the community is, as Thomas said, self-sufficient.

Just past the church, weaving from the effort of walking and carrying the suitcase, I encounter a diminutive elderly woman. She wears a long black skirt, a tattered sweater, and a black shawl on her head. She draws back, startled. But before she can hurry away, I say Thomas's name and address. She eyes me warily, and I realize it's pointless to ask; she probably doesn't speak English. But then, without a word, she beckons and leads me down a side road to a dead end. There, a larger dwelling stands, cobbled together from scraps of tin and wood. She knocks once and then, as the door opens, steps behind me.

A man stands before me, and behind him sit other men gathered around a table, at the center of which are a cluster of candles. They are leaning toward each other, urgently discussing something in Spanish. There's the thick odor of men who've worked a long, hard day, and laced through that, traces of coffee, pan-fried onions, and meat. One by one, initially and then all at once, the group of men looks toward the open door and sees me: a foolish-looking, disheveled white woman carrying a large suitcase and a pocketbook, and, no doubt, wincing in pain.

"*Gringa,*" a man says, among other things, to someone I can't see. There's the sound of uneven footsteps—a slight hitch in the step. My heartbeat quickens. Sure enough, Thomas appears at the door. His eyes widen at the sight of me, and he takes a faltering step back.

"You're not using crutches." The words escape me, the first thing I can think of to say. A poor excuse for *Hello, I hope you don't mind, I couldn't think where else to go.* Thomas gives his head a slight shake, more to clear it, I think, than to signify yes or no. Then he hitches the leg of his trouser above the ankle to reveal a new prosthesis made of polished wood and shiny metal. A better leg in a sturdier boot, with a matching boot on his other foot.

"Courtesy of the WPA," Thomas says. "I'm forever in

their debt." He doesn't seem to be joking. But then, "What are you doing here already, Ruth? I never thought you'd arrive so quickly."

"I haven't had much control over anything this last little while. I didn't have much of a choice but to take the first bus."

To my horror, tears spring to my eyes. Admitting this, I'm shocked all over again; and the doctor was right: Talking does nothing good for my head.

There's a rustle behind me. I turn to see the elderly woman vanishing into the shadows. If Thomas wants me to leave, he'll have to show me the way back to the bus station.

I blink the tears away. "You said if I have need. Or your mother said you said. I have need, Thomas."

He hesitates a moment, then says something in Spanish to the men inside, and steps out onto the large flagstone that serves as a front step, closing the door behind him.

"Your roommate only said something had happened," he says. "She wouldn't tell me any more than that." He watches me closely. "What happened?"

You brought this on yourself. That's what some might say. *It's your fault. You acted a certain way, or dressed a certain way, or said a certain thing,* some might say—Thomas might say. *You're a young, naive, needy woman—a lost and lonely widow. He's a handsome, older man, a powerful man who was your mentor and employer and held your future in his hands.*

It all comes back to: *You brought this on yourself.*

"Ruth?" Thomas's hands are jammed in his pockets, his

shoulders hunched as if against the cold. In as few words as possible, I tell him what happened—my side of the story, the unofficial story. His eyes narrow as he listens. "Dear Lord," he says when I'm done. The words come from deep down inside him, a kind of prayer. And then: "You're ill, aren't you?"

My head weighs heavy. Swaying on my feet, I try not to close my eyes. I feel his hand on my arm before I see it, and then a weight lifted as he takes my suitcase.

"There's a place for you," he says. "I'll take you there."

PART III

May 1935–August 1935

TWELVE

Strong coffee percolates on the wood-burning stove, corn tortillas warm on a griddle, pinto beans stew in a pot. Breakfast awakens me, as it has every morning this past week. I turn on my cot to see, through the crack in the faded blue curtains that afford some privacy to the three of us who inhabit this place, Silvia Morales standing at the stove on the other side of the single room, her long black braid twisted into a crown at the top of her head. She wears a simple housedress, sack-like in appearance, given her small stature. The mismatched side panels of fabric reveal that the dress has been let out to allow for her pregnancy. Woven leather sandals protect her swollen feet, and even from here, I can smell the faint scent of the palm oil that her husband, Luis, rubs on her belly at night and in the morning, when the faded curtains entirely shield me from them and them from me. When their murmuring turns tender, I muffle my ears with my pillow and try not to hear. For their privacy, of course, and also because of the loneliness that tugs at me during those times—a loneliness that compels me to think I'm more alone than I actually am.

Thomas was right when he said there was a place for me here in Kirk Camp. The home of Silvia and Luis—this has proven itself the best place for me as the effects of my concussion continue to ebb and flow. Silvia comes from a long line of *curanderas,* female healers. She is as essential as a doctor back in Mexico, and she's essential in this community, too. With her herbs and methods, she's helped many here. She's helping me.

Her husband, Luis, is an artisan; ceramics was his particular interest before they came to California. Luis is also a gentle man, as his unflagging tenderness to his young wife reveals. If my time at Union University has made me sure of one thing, it's that I most value gentleness in men—in women, too. Honesty and compassion as well.

Silvia flips the tortillas. The gold of her wedding band glints in the sunlight. My hand goes to my throat; there is some small comfort in clasping my own ring and the boy's silver cross. Silvia turns at my stirring and catches my eye through the crack in the curtains.

"Good morning." Her low, soft voice holds faint traces of her original language.

"*Buenos días.*"

Silvia has been teaching me a bit of Spanish over the course of the few last days. This has allowed me to rest a lot—following doctor's orders, and Silvia's orders, too—and think a little, but not too much. We keep our lessons short. Typically, in our exchanges, she speaks English—she feels she needs the practice, though I've tried to reassure her that her English is very good. She speaks Spanish only when she needs to correct me, which, alas, is quite often. I know my numbers in Spanish now, up to a hundred. I know the correct Spanish pronunciation of the alphabet, basic phrases, and the words for the few household items that surround us in this one-room shack. Or, if I don't know all these things by heart, I have written them down in a little notebook, correctly spelled, phonetically spelled, and defined—my makeshift Spanish dictionary.

"Are you hungry?" Silvia asks.

"*Sí, tengo hambre.*"

She beams at me—a reward for my accuracy. "Luis and I ate before he left for the fields." She pats her swollen belly, grimaces. "But I am hungry again. Time for more."

I sit up, pushing aside the bright wedding quilt, and set my feet on the dirt floor. It must be later than I thought; the sunlight is dense, the heat oppressive. I run my finger under the collar of my nightgown, damp with sweat, hoping to let in some air. "I'll just be a minute, washing up."

For modesty, I throw a light gray shawl of Silvia's over my shoulders, then slip between the curtains and hurry outside to the privy. Then I clean myself as well as I'm able at the pump. The icy cold water stings my skin and makes the slowly shrinking lump on the back of my head flare painfully; the ache spans my skull and reaches my temples. I know from past mornings that my head will continue to hurt on and off throughout my waking hours. Sometimes the pain wakes me at night. But thanks to the rest Silvia has insisted I take, and the teas and poultices that she administers regularly, I'm feeling a little better each passing day. My nausea has abated. My vision is restored. I've got my balance back. Sooner than later, I'll be able to join Thomas in teaching the camp's children.

For this is what I decided my first night here, after Thomas walked me to Luis and Silvia's home and I shook her small hand, callused from the year and a half she spent working in the farm fields, until her pregnancy became complicated and she had to stop or put the baby at risk. Silvia's hand was still gripping mine when Thomas abruptly said that he had to go. If possible, he'd stop by to check on me tomorrow night, after he was done teaching. Those next long hours, sleepless and hurting, and all the next day, groggy and hurting, I decided to join him in his work. Not someday, somewhere. But here, now. I'll teach. Next night, I told Thomas of my desire. "Surely you could use some help. Assuming you'll take me on without a certificate," I added, knowing full well Thomas doesn't have a certificate himself. He rolled his eyes, said that was the least of his concerns. His biggest concern was my recuperation. "When you're better, you'll know where to find me, Ruth." He was terse; he's been terse with me all week. But he said yes, in so many words.

His yes, and all that I'm learning from Silvia, along with her ministrations, have provided a kind of balm, tempering, at least for now, the intractable reality of my expulsion from Union University and the reason behind it: Tobias's betrayal and, worse, far worse, my naïveté.

I go back inside. Still in my nightgown, I sit down at

the table with Silvia. My appetite has returned; my mouth waters at the sight and smell of the steaming food on our plates. Silvia says a brief prayer in Spanish. She's told me she only prays in Spanish; she only dreams in Spanish as well. "*Cristo, pan de vida, ven y bendice esta comida.*" Christ, the bread of life, come and bless this food. Each time she prays this prayer, in the language that is slowly revealing itself to me, I am struck by the expansiveness of God, who receives all languages, all people, as His own. I never fully understood this before I sat down at Silvia's table.

"Amen," we say in unison. In this word, only our different accents separate us.

IN THE EARLY afternoon, Silvia and I walk slowly to the shallow, rocky river that borders Kirk Camp. She carries a basket of dirty laundry; I carry a box of soap flakes and a washboard. This is my first real outing since my arrival. Silvia reluctantly agreed that I could join her for this chore; she'd much prefer I were resting on my cot. But I pleaded with her. "After seven days of rest, I'm going stir-crazy," I said. "That's a sign you've done me some good. I must be recovering or I wouldn't be champing at the bit like this."

I follow her up a hill. From here we can see much of Kirk Camp—nearly twenty acres, Silvia says, bordered on the other three sides by two-lane roads. Beyond, the San Gabriel Valley spreads.

Silvia points at sheets of tin glinting in the far distance. "That's Cooper Camp, another Mexican *barrio*.

There's competition between Kirk and Cooper. We think we are the best camp, both of us. We both have big festivals and concerts given by our musicians. Only *we* elect a May Day queen. They don't." Silvia smiles. "*They* elect a Harvest Moon queen. Otherwise we are much the same. Our roads are dirt, our houses made of scraps. We don't have sewers or streetlights or trash collection. We give a good portion of our wages back to the farmers who pay us and own the land on which we live. This binds us together more than the competition divides. Cooper Camp is part of our family. No matter what the Anglo newspapers say, we share with each other—food, money, whatever is needed—rather than go on relief. It's a matter of pride, a matter of dignity. *El oro y el moro.*"

"The gold. . ." That's as far as I can get.

"And the glory," Silvia translates. "That's what we were promised by the farm owners when we were invited to leave Mexico and work here. As you see, there's not any gold. There's not much glory. But we do the work no one else wants to do, and we are proud of our work. We are grateful to do it." She presses her hand to her belly. "For our children, if nothing else."

My head hurts again. The hike is taking its toll; I'm having a hard time keeping track of what Silvia is saying.

"You're out of breath, Ruth."

I try to smile. "I'm fine. I've been sitting at a desk these last months, that's all, and then resting like some fancy lady at your place. Look at you, the weight you're carrying! I have nothing to complain about."

We stand at the riverbank now. There are other people working here as well—elderly women doing wash, as the younger women of Kirk Camp are busy in the fields. Children too young to be picking fruit—it's strawberry season, Silvia has told me—play in the shallows. I'd venture none of these children is older than three or four. Some are new to walking, unsteady on their feet. There are babies, too, carried by the old women in slings on their backs. The women who notice me stare at me as if I'm a ghost. Indeed, I feel ghostly in my white skin. I'm the only white person here. But then they see Silvia, and her presence seems to relieve them. They turn back to their work.

Silvia swings the basket to the ground, lowers herself to sit on a fallen log, and wraps her arms around her middle. The sunlight glances harshly off the water. I shade my eyes with my hand. If I'm not careful, I'll get worse. Even more so, Silvia. The blood has drained from her face. The dark shadows lurking beneath her eyes look more like bruises now. I hadn't known she could look this spent. I hadn't known she could *be* this spent. I might get a bad headache, but if Silvia's not careful, she'll hurt herself and the baby.

"Your turn to rest," I say firmly.

Before Silvia can protest, I lug the basket to the riverbank, weaving my way carefully through the many articles of clothing spread on rocks to dry in the sun. I've never washed clothes in a river. I've used a washtub, yes. A wringer, yes. Clotheslines, yes. But none of these things is here. Only a sluggish river and the stony bank beside it. I glance furtively at the other women and follow their lead. Kicking off my shoes, hitching my skirt a little higher, I take an article of clothing from the basket—one of Luis's shirts, so dirty it's gone stiff, as Charlie's clothes used to do—wade out a bit into the river, and dunk the shirt under the water. The water is more tepid than cold, and I remember Thomas's sister, Grace, and the typhus she contracted. I won't think about that, as no one else seems to be. Even thinking about that is a luxury. I stir the shirt in the water, then lift it out, slosh back to the riverbank, and shake soap flakes from the box onto the wet fabric. The other women scrub and beat their wet things against the rocks in the river's shallows. Their work makes a steady, shushing sound as back and forth the garments go. When a piece of clothing comes down like a whip, drops of water fly, through which the little children purposefully run, their clothing clinging to their bodies like a wet second skin. They remind me of puppies, or more, river otters, in their play. I practice with Luis's shirt, cracking it down on the water's surface, and soon I'm sending out sprays of water, too. The children run my way, dashing through drops and the prisms cast by the sun. My heart lifts with their laughter. I've forgotten what it's like to make someone happy.

"Thank you!" Silvia calls from where she sits on the riverbank, resting her back against a fallen tree.

"*Es mi placer*," I say.

The longer I work at the washing, the more it does become my pleasure. I am clumsy compared to the other women, and I move much more slowly, trying to stay steady on my feet. But soon I realize this is a benefit. The children, seeing how much I'm sloshing about, gravitate to me. They seem to think I intend to get wet. Soon I am as drenched as they are; there's no reason why I should try to stay dry. I wade deeper and deeper into the water. It's not just fun; it feels good to boot—good to get really, truly clean. (Assuming the water is clean; I try not to swallow it.) Between dunking, scrubbing, and wringing out wet things, I cut my hand through the current so that arcs of water spew over the kids, who are soon splashing me in return. The women watch my antics, laughing and murmuring to one another. They might be laughing at me; they might be laughing with me. For the moment, I don't care.

I'm washing the last thing in the basket—one of Silvia's dresses—when my feet skid out from beneath me and I go down, bubbles and dress churning in the murk all around. The slow current prods me, its pull surprisingly strong, and I panic. I claw my way to the surface, gasping for air, to see the children doubled over, they're laughing so hard. The elderly women laugh, too, more openly this time, and two of them wade out to me and help me back to shore. "*Gracias,*" I say, and they laugh at this, too—at my clunky accent. I join in, not wanting them to think I'm offended.

I spread out Silvia's dress to dry, as I have all the other clothes, then go to sit beside her.

"Well done," she says.

"I hope so." I work on wringing out my dress.

"You made some friends, Ruth." I turn to see the children

edging toward us. With a suppressed groan, Silvia tries to get up. I stand to help her. "It will take some time for the things to dry. I think we should go back and rest while they do," she says. "I will tell the other women we will be back soon, or they will do our work for us."

"I don't mind waiting here." I catch Silvia frowning at me. "I'll take it easy, I promise! But perhaps I should walk you home and then return?"

"*If* you take it easy." She sighs, glances again at the children. "You want to teach? Maybe even these littlest can learn something, *claro*?"

"*Claro*."

BY THE TIME the clothes are dry—as dry as they're going to get, with the sun lowering in the sky—the children and I have made mud pies. I have been a very slow-moving horse to ride. We've all been horses in a herd, with me the oldest, most cautious one. We've pretended to be other animals, too—birds, cats, dogs. We don't have to speak each other's language or, as is true of some of the littlest ones, say much at all. We understand each other well enough.

Toward the end of our time, I sit down to take a rest. A few of the youngest children curl up next to me; soon they are asleep. The others continue to play. They cast frequent looks my way. It's all I can do to keep from joining them, but the throbbing at the back of my skull, and the little girl nestled in my lap, ensure that I stay put.

In the sun, resting with children all around, I find myself at ease for the first time since my expulsion. I consider writing Mother and Miss Berger, and it doesn't seem an impossible task. What will I tell them? The truth: where I am now, and how I came to be here, and how I hope to stay awhile. If college was all theory, then assisting at Kirk Camp could be considered practice. I could say that. I form sentences in my mind, transcribe them on imaginary pages, the letters I will send to Mother and Miss Berger: *Kirk Camp will be its own kind of education. In fact, my schooling here has already begun.*

When the other women begin to collect their laundry, I rouse the children and gather up Silvia and Luis's clothes. I join them, lugging and dragging laundry up the hill. Some of the children accompany me, chattering away, laughing and lending a hand. But once we reach the camp, they scatter to follow the other women down various streets and paths, heading toward the places they call home.

I find Silvia asleep on the narrow mattress she shares with Luis. She undid her braid; her hair spreads in loose black waves across her pillow. She stirs, made restless by the sound of the door opening and closing, but she doesn't wake. Quietly, I set the basket of folded clothes at the foot of her bed. The clock on the floor beside Silvia reads five. I want to lie down, too, especially as six o'clock, Thomas's dinner break, is fast approaching. I've been hoping that tonight I might watch him teach for the first time. A rest might make this possible.

I start toward my cot, but then I see Silvia's black book open on the table. This is the book she searched through for the proper herbs and methods to nurse my concussion. From it, she deduced what dried plant leaves would work best. She took me out to the garden she'd established behind the cabin; it grew in a carefully tended bed much like those Thomas and I built for his parents. Netting covered the plants—protection against birds, insects, and animals. Silvia lifted a swatch of the netting and picked a handful of leaves. Along with the growing things, dried herbs bound in tight bouquets hung upside down from the edge of the shack's roof, which is woven from palm fronds. Silvia took down a few of these as well, and then we went back inside. "I inherited my work," she told me as she ground the herbs, using a mortar and pestle. And then she revealed that the black book had originated with a long-deceased grandmother. The book had been supplemented with new discoveries and understanding acquired by later generations of women in the family. Silvia pointed out certain pages, written in an unfamiliar language. *"Nahuatl.* The old way of speaking," she explained. Descriptions and directions were written in the book in Latin and Spanish as well, on pages stiff and stained with age, and peppered with pressed leaves, flowers, and herbs, exacting drawings of trees and animals, and anatomical sketches—parts of the body, whole, sound, and vital; parts of the body, injured, diseased, or infirm. There were sketches of women ministering to other women and men—applying ointments or poultices, binding wounds and broken limbs, too.

With a start, I see that the book is open to a series of sketches of a woman giving birth.

I turn quickly to Silvia. She lies on her side, facing me, frowning in her sleep, eyebrows drawn together like the wings of a blackbird. She is sweating, her upper lip wet, her simple dress damp at the scooped neckline and beneath her breasts. Her strong brown arms hold her belly protectively. She's kicked off the blanket; below her knees, her bare calves and feet are exposed. I catch my breath at the sight of her ankles. They are terribly swollen, swollen as I've never seen before—skin straining, mottled red and purple with broken blood vessels. Her dusty feet are puffy, too, deeply marked by the straps of her woven sandals, toes ballooning around jagged nails. Silvia is a bird-boned woman turned bear-like at her ankles and feet. Two months until her due date. If this swelling isn't relieved, how will she endure it?

I choose not to lie down on my cot after all. I sit at the table, and squinting through my headache, try to understand the words and the pictures on the pages before me. This page was written in Spanish, but the language used is far more sophisticated than anything I know. I carefully turn the brittle pages, trying to find a sketch of a pregnant woman with swollen limbs, or a sketch of swollen ankles and feet— anything that might illuminate Silvia's condition. But there's nothing that I can decipher.

So I turn back to where Silvia left the book open, and I keep watch over her. I listen to her breathing, her occasional murmurs and moans.

Six o'clock comes and goes, then seven o'clock. But Luis doesn't return for dinner at his usual time; Thomas doesn't knock at the door. Thomas's absence doesn't surprise me; he's kept a distance since the night of my arrival. But Luis always comes home promptly. The three of us share whatever Silvia and I have prepared, and then the two of them slip away to go for a walk, or sit by the river, or gather with others around the bonfire where Thomas teaches each evening, and where, finally feeling well enough, I had hoped to go tonight. But tonight, no Luis. No Thomas. No scent of the bonfire drifting through the air. Silvia sleeps on. I can't leave her alone, not like this. So I stay by her side, watching and waiting, and growing ever more worried.

IT IS NEARLY ten o'clock when Luis barges in, Thomas just behind him. Their noisy entrance wakes Silvia, who lurches upright in surprise, and then moans, gripping her belly. Luis, a slight, strong man with a dapper mustache, is by her side in a moment, stroking her hair, whispering to her. I turn to Thomas. "What's going on?"

"Emergency meeting." Thomas is breathless. "Luis, a few other men and women from camp, and me. There was another raid today over at Cooper Camp—people deported, family members left behind, families separated. The remaining folks are going to protest. With their loved ones gone, they feel they have nothing to lose. They're planning a demonstration in the central plaza in Puebla. We met to decide whether to join them."

"*No!*" Silvia tries to stand, but her swollen ankles buckle; she drops back down on the mattress.

"*Sí.*" Luis's voice is quiet but firm, his hands still stroking her hair. "*Ten cuidado.*"

Despite Luis's request that Silvia be careful, she jerks away from him, uttering a rapid volley of words that I'm unable to translate.

"*No!*" Now it's Luis's turn to cry out.

Silvia reaches out a hand to me. One look at her passionate, determined expression, and I go to her and grip her hand. Pulling her up, I help her stand. Silvia leans on me, unable to bear her full weight, her belly firm and round against my hip. I shift my stance to keep both of us in balance, and something, a tiny elbow or heel—the baby!—jabs into my jutting hip bone. "Did you feel that?" I breathe the words.

"Our child is troubled, too." She stares her husband down. "*Juntos, no separados.*"

Juntos. Together. *No separados.* I can guess.

"The more witnesses, the better, far as I'm concerned." Thomas sinks down in a chair, rubs at his knee and then below, where the prosthesis latches on. His shoulders slump with exhaustion. But when he looks up, his gaze is as intent and earnest as ever. "Whatever you decide—whoever comes tomorrow—you must remember to bring your work permits and any other legal documents. If things get complicated, your papers will be your only hope."

Somewhere, in some bureaucratic office, I imagine, are stacks of United States citizenship papers, identification papers, and work permits left behind, when people were forced to leave. Or perhaps these documents never made it to an office. Perhaps they, like other material things—photographs, clothes, household goods, books, and family mementos—have been stolen or destroyed. Meaningful or necessary, meaningful *and* necessary, lost in an instant, like the seemingly certain opportunity of my college education. But worse, far worse, is what the deportees have lost and will lose in days to come.

"I'll be at the plaza, too," I say.

THIRTEEN

Next day, I climb into the bed of a pickup truck, and Luis and Thomas help Silvia, who carries her black book and the burlap bag she uses to hold herbs and medicines. Then, *juntos, no separados*, Thomas and Luis jump in beside Silvia and me. Three other Kirk Camp men have already taken their places here. Two more men sit with the driver. And so we are ten. We confirm that all have their work papers, and then we set off. It is not yet noon. Clear blue sky, birds, and flowers in abundance—it's a picture-postcard day. We rattle down the dirt road toward Puebla's central plaza. A far from sober group, the men seem invigorated, talking about this and that. Silvia sits on Luis's lap so she's at least slightly cushioned against the truck's jouncing. We're *doing* something—something peaceful, something of which Mahatma Gandhi himself would approve, Thomas tells me as we ride, as the farmworkers have shaped their protests after Gandhi's acts of civil disobedience in India. We'll meet with others, exchange information, and make plans. We have to figure out how to better help those who've been separated from their family members. We have to respond better to the local, state, and federal authorities when they make a sweep—as they may do today. "But we're not striking. We have to remember that. Not like we have in the last few years. Strikes are against the law now," Thomas says. "People were killed during those strikes. Many were injured or seriously wounded. Ultimately, the agricultural unions were dissolved. So we're *gathering* with others from Cooper Camp, that's all. We're doing nothing wrong. We've nothing to hide. These men are all here legally, by invitation of the farm owners, and Silvia is, too. If times were different, there'd be no risk in what we're doing today."

But I'm well aware every man present is taking a risk, Silvia is taking a risk, and maybe I am, too, who knows. Along with Luis, the hands of the three other farmworkers sitting here with us are stained red from the strawberries they started picking at sunup. These men walked away from their fieldwork. Most definitely, they will lose their few cents an hour. Possibly they will lose their jobs.

One of the men, Marco, holds a red-stained paper bag; he collected some of the bruised strawberries, not worthy of sale, that would otherwise be discarded at the end of the day. He shares these with us now. The strawberries hold the heat of the sun; they are the sweetest, most delicious things I've tasted in I don't know how long. We each get three. I eat mine slowly, finishing the last strawberry as we enter Puebla. Only now, nearing the central plaza, do we fall quiet and grow sober. There are squad cars everywhere, with policemen inside and posted at street corners, waiting.

The truck lurches to a stop beside the plaza—a wide cobblestone square accented by flowering bushes and palm trees, with a large burbling fountain at the center.

"*Estamos aquí.*" Luis squeezes Silvia's hand, then releases it. And then, "*Vámonos.*"

Luis, Thomas, and the other men clamber from the truck. Luis and Thomas help Silvia out, and I get out, too. People have already gathered near the plaza's central fountain—more people than I expected, nearly fifty, I'm guessing. Most look to be of Mexican heritage, though there are a few white people—I count five, all of them men. There are four Mexican women besides Silvia. A man is shouting something in Spanish through a bullhorn. His voice bounces off the buildings—some Spanish colonial edifices; others, the practical storefronts of today—that surround the plaza.

The ten of us start toward the fountain. Silvia slips one arm through Luis's and the other through mine. We walk slowly to help support her. She murmurs something in Spanish to Luis, and then to me: "Why would he do this? Is he a fool?"

I don't understand. Silvia and Luis are talking heatedly. I call to Thomas, who's walking just ahead of us. "What's the man saying?"

Thomas falls into step beside me, his expression tight with worry. "He's chanting a slogan the strikers used during their demonstrations. *Viva La Causa! Viva La Communidad!* At least he's not resorting to *Viva La Huelga*, as they always did."

"*La Huelga?*"

"The strike. Still, this is not the wisest way to gather our supporters, I'm afraid."

We stand on the outskirts of the growing crowd, and the chanting crescendos as others begin to join in. Silvia, like the men in our group, has gone tense; her fingers bite into my arm. I tighten my hold on her as well—God forbid we get separated. Signs and placards are popping up around the crowd: *QUEREMOS COMIDA,* and beneath that, translated: *WE WANT FOOD.* Other signs make appeals in Spanish and English for due process of law, security, fair wages, education. Despite the press of people, those bearing the signs hold them high.

Luis says something to Silvia, and then, ignoring her frantic protests, he works his way to the front of the crowd to stand by the man with the bullhorn. The man and Luis exchange a few words, and then Luis takes the bullhorn. He says something in Spanish only to be met with a grumble of resistance from the crowd.

"He's asking them to be quiet and calm," Silvia tells me. "He's reminding them that strikes are against the law. He's asking them to put down their signs." Luis continues speaking. "'We are gathered here to work for peace, not for strife,'" Silvia translates. "'A few of us from Kirk Camp have been talking with members of the Farm Security Administration. Some of them understand our concerns. There's talk of improvement—special camps where we will be safe and able to stay in this country, if we are here legally.'" Luis calls for Thomas, beckons to him.

"He is asking Thomas to say more about the Farm Security Administration's promises," Silvia says.

Thomas starts toward Luis. I can't see him now—the people in front of me block my view. I stand on tiptoe, straining to catch a glimpse of him, and as I do, the sound of a gunshot ricochets around the plaza.

Women scream, and men, and children—there must be children in this crowd!—begin to cry. There's a great din of shouting: *"Leva!" "Razzia!" "Raid!" "Roundup!"* I wrap my arms around Silvia. I don't let go of her, though the crowd presses and pushes as people scatter, running in all directions. A stampede—that's what this is. We could be crushed. Silvia and her baby—if she falls down, they could be killed. She cries out as a man shoves us aside, and someone's boot heel comes down hard on my foot. For a moment, that pain surpasses the pain in my head, which has flared again, threatening to obliterate my vision. I look around for help, but Marco and the other men in our group have vanished, lost in the chaos. But then I glimpse the back of Thomas's shirt, his thick brown hair, his skin, so much paler than most. He's forcing his way through the frenzied crowd, trying to get somewhere, trying to get to Luis, who's being throttled by two police officers. "Let him go!" Thomas yells, his voice rising above the din, and then a baton strikes him across the shoulders, and another strikes Luis and they both go down.

The only person I recognize now is Silvia, trembling in my arms.

I hold on to her, and she holds on to me; *juntos, no separados*, we are pushed and pulled by the crowd. Silvia has closed her eyes against her pain and fear; she can't have seen what happened to Thomas and Luis. She doesn't yet know the raw fear opening inside me, the panic of desperation. I need to escape with her. I need to find safety for us. I need to protect the baby.

"Thomas!" I scream. "Luis! Help!"

But then Silvia groans—a low sound, a frightened animal sound—and like that, I understand. Thomas and Luis, Marco and the other men—they're not going to save us. I'm the one who has to get Silvia and the baby she carries to safety. Gunshots sound all around, and my head is about to split open—it hurts so—and there is that meaty sound again and again of fists against flesh and batons thudding, cracking down to the bone. "Get that wetback!" "Catch the roaches!" That's what people—white people—are shouting. Silvia buries her face in my shoulder.

"Come on!" I try to drag her from the fray, only to be swept in another direction. I push my way in front of her. Her arms are around my waist now, and her belly presses into my lower back. I hold tightly to her arms, and we try to move as one creature, intent only on protecting the little life inside her. We stumble and nearly fall. A man lies on the ground before me, his arm twisted at an impossible angle. I try to think what to do—am I able to help him, too?—but the crowd heaves us forward. Using my shoulders, knees, feet, I try to push open a path for us. In this way, we keep going. We stay together.

And somehow, finally, Silvia and I stand at the border of the park. There are palm trees again. We pass through them to the sidewalk. There is our truck, and inside it, our driver—a small, wiry man with salt-and-pepper hair and a hawklike nose. Silvia tries to turn back; she calls for Luis. But I drag her to the truck, fling open the door, wrestle her inside. Then I leap in, close the door, and lock it.

Our driver is bleeding profusely from his forehead. He

can't see for the blood in his eyes. I rip my dress at the hem and bind his wound. Then I turn to Silvia. She is gasping for breath, grasping her belly. Her face contorts with pain. Her mouth moves, shaping words, but she is unable to say them. I don't need to hear them. I know exactly what's she's saying: "Luis? Where is Luis? Where is my husband?"

The truck grumbles to life. The man behind the wheel has turned the key in the ignition. He punches the accelerator, gunning the engine in warning, and then wrenches the steering wheel toward the street. People part before us as we inch our way forward. Others fall down, then scramble up and run away. The truck proceeds slowly, often stopping, lurching as people jump into the bed, escaping the panicked crowd for a moment. I look back to see two children, a boy and a girl, perhaps ten years old, their faces pressed to the back window. "*Ayúdanos,*" the girl cries. I don't know what this means. But Silvia twists around, wincing, and raises her hand, then lowers it, palm down. As one, the boy and the girl disappear from view, hunkering down and out of sight in the back of the truck.

"*Los niños,* Hector. *Bueno?*" Silvia asks.

Our driver nods. Blood is leaking through the rag I wrapped around his head, clotting in his thick gray eyebrows. I tear another strip of fabric from my dress and dab the blood away. Hector maneuvers the truck around a corner and down a narrow side street. It's less crowded ahead, though many people follow in our wake. Hector says something urgently, but his Spanish is beyond my understanding.

Silvia sees my confusion. "*Look* for them, he says!" She

leans toward the window, her gaze raking each shop and alley we pass. "They must be somewhere."

I shift in my seat, searching, searching. People throng around us; some manage to squeeze between the truck and the buildings on either side and run on before us. But there is no sign of Luis or Thomas. No sign of Marco or the other men who came with us today.

Hector has begun singing soft and low, a melancholy folksong I don't recognize. I don't think he's aware he's doing it. He sings as the blood oozes from beneath my clumsy bandages, sings as the blood mats in his eyebrows, sings as it drips into his eyes, sings as he wipes it away.

Todos me dicen el negro, Llorona
Negro pero cariñoso.

It's a long song with many verses, which Hector sings as we turn down one narrow street and then another until Silvia begs him to stop singing and stop driving and stop now, *por favor!*

We are on the outskirts of town, and the crowd has dissipated. Hector parks the truck along the side of the road in the shade of some trees, and—with no threat in sight—the three of us get out. The children are gone; they must have jumped out along the way. Silvia says something in Spanish to Hector: a command, it sounds like. He climbs up in the truck bed and lies down there. With a boost from me, she heaves herself up beside him. Her bag is where she left it, tucked into a corner with her black book. She opens it and takes out a flask, then a needle and thread. As Hector tips the flask to his lips, she looks at me. "Luis said we would be safe." Her voice breaks bitterly. "But when are we ever safe now, really?" She shakes her head, staring down at the wound on Hector's forehead. "Get me something for him to bite down on, Ruth."

I find a stick, take my handkerchief from my pocket, wrap it around the stick. Hector takes it—his expression stoic—and as Silvia strikes a match and holds the needle in the flame, he sets the stick between his teeth. I have to look away then.

"I'm going to find them," I say, turning back toward Puebla. When Silvia doesn't respond, occupied as she is, I set off, running. My head pounds harder with my every footfall. But I run the whole way.

AFTER SOME TIME searching—an hour? at least—I find Thomas and Luis in the plaza, where they returned after combing the streets for us. I tell Luis that Silvia is safe. Repeatedly, I reassure him, until he finally seems to believe me. Only then am I able to ask what happened to them.

With Thomas's help, Luis escaped the police officers. But many weren't so lucky. From what they've heard, the officers, federal marshals, and some of the local farm bosses took away about thirty people. Some are in jail; others are preparing for deportation.

"Two children jumped in the back of Hector's truck. Young children!" I blurt this out. "Do you think—" I draw in a deep breath. "Do you think they found their families?"

Of course Thomas and Luis can't provide me with an answer.

We search for Marco and the other men until dusk, but they are nowhere to be found. So we trudge back to the truck. Hector and Silvia are resting there in the bed. When Silvia opens her eyes to see Luis climbing in beside her, she pushes herself up, sobbing in relief, and throws her arms around his neck. They stay like that for some time, until Thomas persuades them that we must go back to camp. "We've looked everywhere for the others," he says. "Hector needs care, and you do, too, Silvia." Half in Spanish, half in English, she has told us about her concerns for the baby. "We must be very careful now. Or this baby will come too early. *Bebé prematuro.*" Silvia's low voice is hoarse with fear. "*El bebé podría morir.*"

The baby could die.

Luis drives us back to the camp. Silvia sits next to him, her head on his shoulder, and Hector beside her. Exhausted, Thomas lies down in the truck bed. We jounce roughly along for a few minutes, until, rattled, I lie down, too. I pillow my head in my arms, trying to cushion it as I am able. Side by side like this, Thomas and I look up at the black sky. It's cloudless, the stars thick as spilled salt. Even after today, I can't deny that it's beautiful here. Still a Golden Land.

For some it is. But not for others. I can't deny that, either.

I turn to Thomas. "Hector sang a song this afternoon. Over and over he sang it. I wonder if you know what it means."

"Do you remember the words?"

I try to recall the lyrics.

Todos me dicen el negro . . .
. . . pero cariñoso.

"Something like that," I say.

Thomas nods. "It's an old song, very old, and very sad. 'La Llorona.' In English, that means 'The Weeping Woman.' It tells of a woman who drowned her children to be with the man she loved. But he wouldn't have her. She drowned herself then—a suicide—only to learn that she wouldn't be admitted to heaven until she found her children. And so she searches the earth for all eternity, weeping without ceasing. That's the story. I've heard that parents tell it to their sons and daughters to keep them from going out alone at night. You don't want to encounter *La Llorona.*" He is quiet for a moment. Then, his voice harsh, he adds, "Or *El Regreso.*"

"*El Regreso?*"

"The Return—as in repatriation."

The truck turns a sharp corner. My head bumps against the metal bed—I can't help but cry out—and I'm thrown against Thomas. His arms come around me; my head rests against his chest. For a moment we stay like that, breathing in time, even as time seems to have stopped. Then he opens his arms, and I move away. *Separados, no juntos.* Lying beside each other at a safe distance, we silently watch the stars.

IN THE DAYS that follow, Silvia, from her bed, guides me through the pages of her black book, translating the herbs needed to make the special teas and soups that compose her meals now. She translates recipes, too—*pollo caldo,* for example, but the broth of the chicken soup only. Luis and I eat the bits of meat and vegetables she isn't able to consume. I learn to make tortillas: Gently knead and divide flour, lard, and salt, then flatten the balls of dough and cook on their cast-iron pan. I learn to make rice the way Luis likes it, with bits of onion and tomato. Silvia eats plain rice only now. She can also have strawberries and oranges, which I buy from a nearby fruit stand. We often share an orange in the late afternoon, when the cabin is hot and bright and the fruit in my hand resembles a pebbled sun. The torn skin emits a citrusy-sweet mist, and Silvia and I nibble slowly at the segments, savoring the juice and the pulpy white threads that she assures me are good for us both. Almost, at moments like this, I forget that just a short time ago—after Charlie, and then again after expulsion—I thought my life was over. Now I hold happiness again, if only for a moment. I share it with my new friend who relies on my care. I take my duties seriously—more seriously, even, than I did with Charlie in East Texas. My time with Charlie—our brief newlywed season—seems like playing house in comparison to this. My time with Charlie seems like a beautiful dream from which I was abruptly awakened. From it, I learned how swiftly life can be extinguished. Here, there are two lives at stake. So whether we're sharing an orange or I'm busy with simple tasks, I keep watch over Silvia. She must stay quiet, resting until her delivery. She has no choice. The next weeks, if she wants to carry this baby to term, she'll keep to her bed. I'll do whatever it takes to keep her there. And with my days and nights nearly as confined as Silvia's, I must do what I've been avoiding for too long. I must write to Mother and Miss Berger. I must tell them what has happened to me in these last weeks.

I decide Mother will learn that I had a run-in with a teacher—a disagreement. In its wake, the university administration asked me to take a leave of absence. *I'm fine*, I write to Mother. *It's turned into a kind of adventure. I'm gaining real experience. Next year or, more likely, the year after, I'll return to college. Where, I don't know yet, but I'll find the right place, a good place. I still have the money from the insurance company. And where I am now, I don't have to pay rent! They've only asked me to help buy food, which I'm more than glad to do. So, don't worry. I'm really, truly fine! All love to you and Daddy.*

Miss Berger will learn the whole truth. Given that Union University has the Alba Public Library on file as my primary contact, she may have already received notice of my dismissal. If so, I doubt that she's come to any conclusions or made any judgments. She will wait to hear from me. Discreet as she is, she won't have shared the news with Mother. But she will be concerned for me, deeply so, and she has enough to worry about in Alba. I want to ease her concern. Telling her the truth, or at least my side of things, I will try to make things less terrible.

This letter proves the hardest thing I've ever written. The official story, the one Tobias told and the administration believed, yammers on in my head, threatening to drown out my own version. I try and fail, try and fail, and so days pass.

This afternoon while Silvia sleeps, I sit at the table and set my pen to paper, determined. I do not stop writing until it is all laid out before me. The unofficial story—my story. I try not to cast blame in the wrong direction. I try to state the facts and state them simply. The facts, I pray, will speak for themselves. Miss Berger will be the one interpreting them, after all.

The hardest part of my news finally down on the page, I tell Miss Berger where I am now. *I'm living with migrant farmworkers and their families,* I write. I describe Silvia and Luis. I describe the raid in the plaza. *I'm hoping to start teaching a bit in the evenings.* And then I reassure Miss Berger, as I did Mother, that I will return to college one day. I close with a plea: *Take good care and please don't worry. All in all, a fair amount of good has come from the bad.* I include the address of the Puebla post office, used by residents here at Kirk Camp, in case Miss Berger wants to respond.

I set down my pen with a sigh. I feel lighter, the burden of telling—not confessing but telling—lifted. I clasp my necklace—my wedding band and the silver cross—and wait for the black fog. But it doesn't overwhelm me. It, along with the related feelings, belong to the person I was and would have become more fully, I imagine, if I'd stayed in Alba or continued on at Union, under Tobias's sway. Charlie wouldn't have wanted me to be a person who carried such feelings day to day. I don't want to be that person, either, and it appears, suddenly, that I might not be. Despair, guilt, and shame are just one version of the story. I can create another version.

I fold Miss Berger's letter, slip it into an envelope, and set it on the table beside Mother's. Someone in camp will be making a post office run tomorrow. I will send the letters along then.

FOURTEEN

The third week of June, when the last of the cherries are ripe for picking, I finally slip away to a bonfire. Luis is with Silvia. It was Silvia herself who encouraged me—no, *begged* me—to go out for the evening. If it hadn't been a risk to her health and the baby's, I believe Silvia would have shoved me out of the door. I've been hovering over her, she says. Too much energy, now that I seem to have recovered from my concussion, and too little to do but cook, clean, and tend to her needs. Earlier this evening, I asked to braid her hair. That was the last straw. "My hair is fine," she snapped. "Now, *go*. Please!"

I follow the scent of wood smoke through Kirk Camp's narrow dirt roads, which are mostly deserted now. When I reach the edge of camp, I see why: A large number of residents already are gathered around the bonfire. The fire flickers, a bright blaze in the center of the open field before me. People move around it, their bodies dense shadows against all that light. Through the shifting crowd, I see the tall flames shooting toward the night sky, licking and snapping at the air. Given that there's no electrical service in Kirk Camp and the sky is cloudy now, the fire seems all the brighter. There's a large pop, and sparks shower over the crowd, but this only seems to add to the general feeling of festivity. People laugh and talk; children of all ages run and play around the perimeter. All in all, it looks like a great, good time, a kind of reward at the end of the long workday.

I approach the fire, and as I do, I hear Thomas calling for the children. By the time I stand with the others, Thomas and a few other adults have begun the night's lesson. The children are split into three groups, which in essence serve to represent the very young, the older elementary school–aged kids, and a few young people who would attend high school if they were able to do so. The largest group—composed of about twenty of the littlest children—are learning the alphabet in English. The older ones are taking turns reading aloud from battered schoolbooks; there are four groups of about five, each group sharing a book. The oldest of all are learning how to write a formal letter. They stand before two chalkboards mounted on easels, writing down various salutations and opening paragraphs. They appear to be working on requests for job interviews. As I watch, they weigh different versions and make suggestions about which is best.

Each group is monitored by at least two adults—the little kids need four. Depending on the needs and abilities of the child, the adults speak Spanish or English. Thomas moves between the groups, lingering when a question arises, a mistake crops up, or a particular aptitude is revealed. His intensity and focus serve him particularly well in this situation. He seems to see only the child or group of children before him, and I can tell by the way they look at him, lean in to him, listen, and smile that they are at ease with his attention, enjoying themselves.

Only one boy stands away from the others. Short and slight, hunched and restless, he loiters at the edge of things, his hands shoved deep in his pants pockets. His black hair appears to be uncombed; it covers his ears and falls into his eyes. His eyes are further hidden by the spectacles he wears, the wire rims of which glint and gleam in the firelight, as does their glass, which reflects the brightness as a flat sheen. The boy kicks at things—stones, sticks, and dust, and once another child. He does this last on purpose, I'm afraid, for when his victim spins around, he's already darted out of sight. Thomas is aware of all this, I can tell from the looks he casts the boy's way. The boy is aware of Thomas, too. He makes sure that his behavior is benign, if sullen, when Thomas is watching.

Thomas is absorbed in a discussion with the older kids when the boy drifts over to the youngest group. I ready myself to interfere should he attempt to hurt one of the little ones, but the boy seems satisfied with distracting them—whispering, teasing, tugging at clothes and hair. I make my way over to him cautiously in order to take him by surprise. My plan is to distract or engage him. If he simply needs attention, I can provide that.

I'm only a few feet away from the boy when a large, luminous white moth, drawn by the firelight, swoops low over his head. He leaps up and catches it in his hands, then, holding it by its narrow, jointed body, brings it close to the face of the nearest girl. Cringing, the girl leans back, which only causes the boy to draw closer. The moth frantically beats its wings, which must be at least four inches long. The other adult attendants, including Thomas, are unaware of this little drama. The girl's black eyes widen in fear as, slowly, methodically, the boy takes a beating wing and starts to tear it.

Every impulse to be stealthy evaporates in that moment. I am upon the boy, catching him by the arm, wrenching him around to face me. "Don't," I say as the girl gives a cry. The boy stares coldly up at me. The frames of his spectacles are off-kilter; spidery cracks web one of the lenses. I give him a little shake, but his expression remains unreadable. I wonder if he understands English. "Stop that." That's all I can think to say. "*Basta ya.*"

The boy tightens his fist around the moth, snapping its body, crushing its wings. He drops what's left of it on the ground, and when I release him, horrified, he holds up his hand, fingers spread wide. Every line that creases his palm is covered with the white dust that coated the wings. "Stop that," he says, mocking me in perfect English. "*Mujer blanca estupida.*" He spins away from me, then, and runs, disappearing into the shadows that stretch beyond the fire's glow.

The little girl is crying. Other children begin to whimper, too, and parents quickly descend to scoop them up and ferry them away. When something questionable or confusing happens, these people move quickly, I've noticed. They probably learned to do so the hard way. White person, children crying—*vámonos!* Those who linger eye me warily. The children in the other groups have turned restless and distracted, and are watching, too. "I'm sorry," I say, and add for good measure, "*Lo siento*."

Thomas comes to stand beside me. "What happened?"

I try to explain, babbling—at least to my ears—but Thomas nods. "Daniel," he says, confirming something I don't fully understand. He turns to the children and adults who are waiting to see what's next, and announces they'll stop for tonight. They've nearly stayed their typical hour anyway. Nodding guardedly, people begin to leave.

The fire is not the blaze it was when I first arrived. Thomas goes to stir it. "I'm sorry, Ruth. I was hoping your introduction here would be easier."

"I made a mess of things."

He drags over a log on which a few children perched, and drops it in front of me. He sits down, stretches out his legs, adjusts the hem of his trousers so that his prosthesis is all but hidden, then pats the log for me to join him. I stay standing.

"It wasn't your fault," he says.

"Whose was it, then? 'Stupid white woman.' Isn't that what the boy said? He's right. I don't know him, or anyone here, really. Why should he obey me? I interfered where I didn't belong."

"It does take awhile to earn trust in this community, true enough, which is understandable."

I nod foolishly.

"But with Daniel, it's particularly difficult. And even if he trusts you, as he does a few people—not yet me—that doesn't mean he's going to do the right thing. More often than not, he won't. He likes to cause trouble. And he's gotten quite good at putting the blame on someone else. An adult, if possible. An adult who's not of Mexican heritage, even better. It's clear that he's had a decent education in a decent school in the past. From his English, I am sure he went to an Anglo school—maybe in Los Angeles? I don't know. He won't tell me a thing about himself. He'll barely look at me."

"His spectacles are broken."

Thomas laughs dryly. "It's a bigger problem than broken spectacles."

"Who is he?"

"I'm not sure of his last name. I'm not sure of anything about him, really. Someone heard he lives with an aunt and uncle here at the camp. I've yet to meet them. He works in the fields, like so many of the kids. I've seen him out there. Some days he works hard, like a man. Other days he lollygags around. A few times I've caught him sleeping. I'm the overseer; I've got to take him to task then. But if I were him, or any of these kids, for that matter, I'd be sleeping all the time, I bet, and far more inconsistent in my labor. So I ignore his behavior as much as possible. I get the feeling he doesn't have much, and I don't want to jeopardize anything he does have. Kid's got a temper, that's for sure. I've seen him let loose on more than one adult and many children. I've been trying to encourage him to join us at the bonfire and attend the lessons. Mostly, he doesn't. When he does, most of the time something happens like tonight. But I won't ask him to leave, and the other adults certainly won't. Every child, no matter how ornery, is the best hope this community has."

"Which makes my riling him up all the worse." Frustrated, embarrassed, I walk in a small, futile circle.

"I'm glad you came tonight, Ruth. I want your help with all this, if you still feel able to give it. I need all the help I can get."

I look at him. "Teaching, you mean?"

"Teaching, yes."

I shrug. "If they'll let me teach."

"We'll try again tomorrow night. I'll make sure and give you a proper introduction."

Suddenly breathless, I look away from him and into the dying fire.

"It would be good if you could mind a group," he says. "There'd be less running around for me then. As it is now, I just get started on something, and then I have to jump up again."

"I worked with a little girl back in Texas. I believe I'd feel most easy with the younger ones." I keep my gaze on the flames.

"That's fine."

"Good."

We stay very still for a moment, neither of us talking. Then Thomas fills the expanding silence, speaking quickly, fervently. He tells me about the kids, which groups are capable of what as a whole, and which individuals in the groups are capable of more. "It's hard," he says, "the difference in abilities, all because of the education they did or didn't receive. Some of the kids went to schools where Spanish was never spoken in the classroom—it was against the rules. Other kids never went to school at all. The little ones, there's less variety, many of them were too young for school until now. The basics, that's what the little ones need, as you'll see right away, I'm sure. But there may be exceptions among them, too."

"I understand." I say.

He grins, dimples cutting into his weathered face. "I bet you do, college girl." His grin fades. "Listen to me, going on and on. Am I talking awfully loud?"

I can't help but smile. "It's all right."

"You being here could make a real difference, Ruth." Abruptly, Thomas stands. He comes over to me and takes my hand. His hand is smaller than Charlie's, nimbler, but strong, I can tell from his grip. His palm is heavily callused. Sometime tonight, mine has gone clammy; I feel awkward and clumsy and cold.

I find myself shaking Thomas's hand as if we've just struck a business deal. Then I draw away from him, saying that it's time I get back to Silvia. I'll see him tomorrow night. I promise him this.

I head back toward Kirk Camp, moving so quickly that I might as well be trying to catch a bus, or, for that matter, keep up with Thomas, if he were walking by my side, but who, when I cast a look over my shoulder, is where I left him, watching me go. He lifts his hand; for a moment I think he is asking me to wait for him. But then he shoves his hand into his trouser pocket. Confusion further hastens my step, and as I enter Kirk Camp and turn down a dirt road that hides me from him, relief descends. I slow down. Too close, too fast, too much, too strange, too wrong—my hand in his. Slow down.

Thoughtlessly, I enter the shack without knocking to find Silvia and Luis stretched out on their bed, holding each other close. They are dressed, but they appear as flustered as I feel. I apologize immediately and we try to laugh it off. We're unsettled, the three of us, until the curtain falls between us and we take to our respective beds. From the quiet that ensues, I assume they are soon asleep. Only I hold my body rigid so I won't twist and turn fretfully, restless as I am now, and as I am all night.

NEXT EVENING, THOMAS introduces me as Señora Ruth. He mentions that I've been to college. That's his "proper" introduction, and then I am teaching. Of course, I need to prove my worth and win the children's trust. But with some care and concern, patience and perseverance, and a little bit of good humor, I vow I will.

Of course, it takes a few weeks. I stay with Silvia by day and, after Luis returns, do my best to teach the younger children something worthwhile by night. Silvia's due date is still about a month away, but increasingly with each passing day, she experiences stabbing pain that she fears might be contractions. She is often unable to keep her food down, and so she grows weaker. She has gotten to a state where she can barely endure anyone's touch; she says her skin is tender, almost on fire. Luis sleeps on the dirt floor now. Many nights I'm so worried for her—for them both—that I beg to forego the bonfire and stay with them. Now it's Luis who gently pushes me out the door.

I have less trouble keeping my distance with Thomas. I'm polite but aloof; we talk of the children only, and of how our school might improve. I make sure there's always a few feet between us, and that seems to do the trick. We're never in close enough proximity to easily touch. If Thomas notices the change in my demeanor, he doesn't mention it. He, too, is all business.

The boy Daniel is all mischief. He makes unpredictable appearances at the bonfires, and his stays are erratic; like some kind of magician, he appears, disappears, and appears again, never where I expect him. We'll catch sight of him up in a nearby tree, sitting on a branch, listening in. He'll skulk around the outskirts of the older kids, or the younger. Never does he settle down among his peers or sit quietly with the adults. One night he danced around the fire. Another night he threw things at us from the shadows. Thomas and I try to hunt down Daniel's aunt and uncle—though everyone believes he lives with them, no one knows who they are. Try as we might, we can't seem to find them. So we endure his presence if he's not too disruptive. A few hard times, Thomas had to enlist the help of some of the bigger men gathered around the bonfire: They carry Daniel back to camp, kicking and screaming. After one such indecorous departure, ten days pass without any sight of him . . . ten days during which Silvia's pains continue to grow worse. I've made a calendar for her, and every night when I return from the bonfire, I mark off another day, which brings us closer to the time when she will deliver this baby.

By now, I've learned all the children's names, and the names of their families, and some of what they've lived through before coming here. Hard times. *Tiempos difíciles.* It's as I'd expect—little food, unfair pay, relentless, grueling labor for people of all ages, the babies carried on their mothers' backs through harvests, even in the hottest seasons. But hearing it from the children and the parents I am coming to know as individuals—these intimate stories work away at me, change my thoughts and beliefs, until I hardly recognize the woman I once was, who thought deportations were best for everyone involved, and that certain Americans were more "real" than others. I can't sleep at night for the changes inside me, and for Silvia, stirring and moaning in the darkest hours.

I'm tired all the time—more tired than when I was at Union, more tired than I can ever remember being—but I'm not as tired as the people who work in the fields every day, and if they can keep going, I can, too. In fact, those hours when I'm with the children, my weariness evaporates and I'm at my most energetic. They are making progress with the alphabet; some are able to correctly say every letter in the proper order in both Spanish and English, which is more than I can do most days. More slowly, but on the whole steadily, the children are learning to add and subtract as Edna Faye once did. I think of her often; I still pray for her. I long to feel as companionable with these children as I did with her. Maybe someday they will trust me wholeheartedly? Or will I be the one who stops short in the face of our differences, just short of being part of the community? I'm afraid this will be the case if I don't continue to change.

Since I left Union, I've dodged my memories of Tobias— my work with him and my time in his class. These memories make me feel sick inside. But one night when some of the older, more precocious children are giggling and distracted, and some of the younger, less advanced children are struggling to keep up, I force myself to recall at least some of what I learned in Educational Practices. Examples from the textbook and Tobias's lectures descend on me. I hear his voice in my head, see myself hanging on his every word, remember how I ignored the warnings, and feel once again ashamed. But then one idea settles and catches my attention: not a distraction but a possibility. The adults don't have to be the only teachers among us. Let the older children use what they know to help the younger.

I divide my group into five smaller groups of about four children each, then I hand out five of the ten chalkboards that Thomas has managed to purchase in these last months. I set each group different math tasks. I oversee the groups, but with the children helping one another in this way, I'm mostly able to observe. With a few errors, each group manages to move through the addition tables all the way up to five. I gather them together again, we correct what needs correcting, and start in on learning the sixes.

Thomas has been reading *The Story of Doctor Dolittle* to the middle group. The next night, I bring my copy of *The Brothers Grimm* to our meeting. The children practice their sixes together, and as a reward for their good behavior, I ask if they'd like a story. They clamor for one and draw closer around me, settling themselves as comfortably as possible on the ground. I sit down, too. I let the book fall open on my lap The pages flip to "Rapunzel." I stare at the first page and the facing illustration of a girl in the tower. Edna Faye loved this picture best. After one of her visits, Charlie would ask me to tell the story of "Rapunzel"—not the fairy tale but Edna Faye's response to it. "How was our neighbor today?" he'd ask. And I'd describe her gray eyes widening, her hands clasped at her chest, her lingering sweet, sad smile of longing, her questions, her answers to my questions. Charlie loved hearing all this, and I loved telling it to him. He would love that I'm telling the tale again now.

I know it practically by heart. Certainly, I know every detail and twist and turn of Rapunzel's entrapment and escape. But I'm afraid I'll cry if I rely too much on my memory now with Charlie so present to me that I expect any moment he will step into the circle of light cast by the fire. So I ask the children to raise their hands if I say something that's unclear or if they have something to add, and I begin to read the fairy tale word for word from the book.

Soon hands are waving. Sometimes I am able to offer a satisfactory explanation to a question, but other times the children have to help me—those who can translate my English into Spanish or make comparisons to the world they all know. I listen carefully to their discussions, and in this way I learn a little more about each child. Charlie and Edna Faye retreat a bit, and I find myself absorbed with my students instead. They show me yet another side to the fairy tale. While Edna Faye liked the tower best, and I liked the escape, these children are more interested in the woman who's hungry at the beginning. A woman who's hungry, and pregnant, desperate to eat anything—desperate for the plant growing in a nearby garden most of all. The children discuss how it is when people are hungry like that, surrounded by good things to eat that they are not able to have. It is like that all the time in the fields, they say. The woman's condition, coupled with her desire, causes her to beg and plead with her husband to do the wrong thing. When people are desperate, the children agree, they are often driven to do things they otherwise would not do. They might be driven to steal things that don't belong to them, if it meant keeping someone they love alive. And this is how it is for the husband in the story. One night, so great are his wife's cravings, he climbs the wall separating them from the plant she desires—a plant called rapunzel. He picks the plant— "harvests" it, one of the children says, doe-eyed Clara, who spends her days minding her little brother and baby sister. He takes it back to his wife, and the woman devours it. But of course it isn't enough. (It is hardly ever enough, the children agree.) She wants more. So the next night the husband tries the same thing again, only this time he is caught by the woman who owns the garden. She lives in the castle—a very fine house, a *hacienda*, the children agree. The woman is a witch. "*La bruja es mala*," a small boy cries with a shudder. His name is Gabriel. I tell Gabriel—and the other children, who look worried, too—that yes, this witch is bad. "But she's not real," I say. "She's only in this story." The witch catches the man as he scales the garden wall, and she accuses him of theft. She says she will curse him or, better yet, kill him. But the man begs so eloquently for mercy that the witch finally grants it. On one condition. When the man's wife gives birth to their baby, he must deliver the baby to the witch. "Now we get to the best part," I tell the children. "The tower and the escape."

But they don't want the story to continue. They want to stay right there, between house and castle, between good and evil. "It is like Adam and Eve and the serpent," says one of the older girls, Maria. She is all of eight, with two long black braids secured at her temples so that they hang like teardrops against her cheeks. She's made it clear before that she knows her Bible well, and that she's had some previous schooling. In Spanish, she quotes a verse from Genesis 3, then translates it into English: "'And when the woman saw that the tree was good for food . . . she took of the fruit thereof, and did eat, and gave also unto her husband with her; and he did eat.'"

I swallow my surprise and tell Maria she's right. "So interesting. This part of the story is a bit like Genesis," I say.

"Bad things happen to people who do bad things." Maria nods, confirming her assertion, and her teardrop braids bobble.

"That can be true," I say.

"Or when people go where they're not supposed to go." Maria gives her peers a knowing look. "That's why we must never leave camp alone. Bad things happen all the time."

Again Gabriel shudders. "*La bruja es como La Llorona.*"

"I know that song." I sound like a child, piping up eagerly. But the other children keep their sober gazes on Maria and ignore me.

"*Sí,*" she says. For now, she is the authority in the group. She says something in Spanish, then gives me a sober look. "The witch is like La Llorona *and* the officials who want to deport us."

This is not what I intended to happen when I chose to share this tale. I wanted to give the story to the children as a reward and, if possible, teach them a few things, simple things, classic things—about beginning and middle and end, plants and towers and adventurous escapes. I didn't want the children to become frightened, which, from the looks on their faces, many of them are. They're comparing government actions and authorities to evil spells and witches. What will they remember from this storytelling time, and what will they tell their parents? Will they have nightmares tonight because of me?

"But you've done nothing wrong," I say. "As Maria pointed out, the husband in the story got himself into this mess."

The children ignore me, understandably. If I were one of them, I'd ignore me, too.

An older boy named José begins talking about his mother, who is pregnant. Unlike Silvia, she is still working in the fields. Today the two of them were miles away, picking beets. "She is still hungry, though we had some supper tonight. If I had stolen food, maybe she wouldn't be," José boldly says.

"Ruth."

I turn to see Thomas standing some yards away. And then I see my students' parents, waiting and watchful, nearby. Reluctantly, I stand and go to them.

"You all right?" Thomas asks. "The rest of us finished some time ago."

"I'm sorry. I must have lost track of time."

"I can see why." Thomas smiles. "Look at them. They're chattering away. They're interested. Not so shy of you anymore."

"You think so?"

"Look!"

He's right; I can see their enthusiasm. A few children are brave enough to beckon to me; they want me to return so we can resume our discussion. *We. Our.* The children and me. Students and teacher, although I'm the one who is by far learning the most. Smiling, I return to where they sit. Three more children may speak, I say. Then we'll go home to get some rest. We'll resume the fairy tale tomorrow. We'll see it through to its end—the official tale and their unofficial realities, two sides of one coin that add up to a living truth.

FIFTEEN

The next morning, I return to the river to do Silvia and Luis's laundry as well as mine. The older women know me now, as do the little children, and they greet me, smiling and waving me over to stand with them, not at a cautious distance. Their welcome fills me with happiness—unfettered by any other emotion, uncompromised by memory or doubt. With gestures and a few words of English, the women include me in their work. They smile at my clumsy Spanish. The soaking and scrubbing, the drying—they show me how best to do it here. When my basket of laundry is empty, the clothes carefully draped over rocks and steaming in the midday sun, I am nearly as dry as when I arrived. This is thanks to their good direction, and they know it, nodding approvingly. But then the children grab my hands, tug me deeper into the river, and splash me with water. We're playing as before, drenched as before. The women seem bemused by the sight.

When the clothes are dry, I walk with the women and children back to Kirk Camp. It is midafternoon by the time I arrive at Luis and Silvia's. Carrying the full basket in my heavy, sodden clothes has left me tired, and I nearly miss the slip of folded paper tacked on the door. *Ruth* is written on the outside. I open it to see a note from Thomas. *The parents and other adults are asking if we'll work with them, too. If you're able, come an hour earlier tonight, and we'll figure out what we can do.*

Juntos, no separados. In the past, my circle of friends has rarely exceeded two. Charlie and Miss Berger in Alba. Charlie and Edna Faye in East Texas. Helen and, God help me, Tobias at Union University. Now my circle is expanding quickly. Silvia, Luis, Hector, the older women at the river, the younger children there, the children I teach and their parents. And Thomas. I feel wealthy in a way that I never have felt before.

Inside the shack, I put away the clean laundry and make a late lunch of rice and beans for Silvia and me. Well, the beans are for me. She can't stomach beans, nor should she, her book says, for the child to stay healthy in her womb. There's one orange left in the bowl on the table, and I press her to eat it. She starts to peel it, but then she nearly drops it. She looks at me, her large, dark eyes fearful. "I don't know myself," she tells me. Her lack of strength, I think she means. I peel the orange and pass it to her segment by segment. Then I bring her the pan she uses to relieve herself, and when she's finished, I wipe her dry.

"Only a little while now," I remind her.

I stroke her hair, hum songs and nonsense tunes until she sleeps. Then, dropping down on my cot, I fall asleep, too. Luis is home for the evening when I wake. He readily agrees to prepare supper so I am able to leave early for the bonfire, my copy of *Brothers Grimm* tucked under my arm.

While the children watch and play around us, Thomas and I work with the adults who've asked for help improving their English. We sit in two separate circles: I work with the women, Thomas, the men. There are ten adults in each circle. "How are you?" "What is your name?" "Where do you live?" "How may I help you?" We all take turns asking and answering these questions, working on not just the words and their sequence but their pronunciation. Sometimes the questions and answers spark surprising exchanges that end in laughter. In this way, the hour passes. As our time draws to a close, I hear Thomas asking the harder questions, so I feel liberated to ask them, too— the frightening questions, the questions that are frequently an attack, the questions that it is most important to answer correctly. "Are you a United States citizen?" Each woman in my group answers no. "Then where are your papers?" All but two of the women reveal work permits pinned inside the waistbands, pockets, and hems of their skirts. We practice new phrases now: "Here they are." And "Please, look." The two women without legal documents shrink into themselves, their gazes darting around the group, but meeting no one's eyes. *I don't see you, you don't see me.* They seem to be playing this children's game. Only they, like the rest of us, know it is no game. Their fear is palpable.

In this way, the lesson ends. "It is very nice to meet you," we say to one another. And then: "I hope to see you again soon." I extend my hand to each woman, and after some hesitation, each one shakes it. The two women without documents try to slip away, but I catch up and cajole them until, flushed and unsettled, they say farewell to me. I long to tell them not to worry, that all will be well. But I can't think of the words in Spanish, and I'm not sure of how truthful the words would be. I watch the two women hurry back toward camp and whatever awaits them there. I watch until they are lost in the shadows, and then I turn to the children, gathered together and waiting in the bonfire's warm glow.

Thomas is working on a science lesson with the older group; they are dissecting, naming, and drawing the parts of a plant. They're working with flowers—the bright orange and yellow poppies that bloom wild all around us. His other students are divided into groups of two; they are, with varying degrees of attention and success, taking turns reciting important dates in history, related to the United States and Mexico: 1492, 1776, 1865, 1929 for the United States; 1521, 1810, 1848, 1910, 1923 for Mexico. (What these last dates signify, I don't know yet, I realize to my shame.) And then for California, 1850, the year it became one of the states. "The thirty-first." A serious young girl with long black curls falling over her shoulders says this to her partner. "Before that, this land belonged to Mexico."

I do a quick calculation. Only eighty-five years ago, I would have been the immigrant, the alien here, perhaps in need of my own set of legal documents in order to stay.

I sit down with the youngest children, who are, with great care, passing around the book of fairy tales, poring over the illustrations. "*Por favor?*" one boy says, holding the book out to me. "Please," a girl adds for good measure. "What? No math?" I exclaim in mock horror, and to a child, the group exchanges worried glances: That's exactly what they mean. "No math," I agree with a sigh, though of course I want to return to the fairy tale as well. "But tomorrow night," I add for good measure. "*Math.*"

And so we finish the story of Rapunzel, and gradually reach the happily-ever-after end. But the children aren't really interested in that; they seem suspicious of it or disregard it altogether. They want to talk about the beginning again—the hunger and need and what it can drive the most moral of human beings to do. The danger and repercussions of getting caught.

"Should we make up our own fairy tales and illustrate them?" I ask.

Some of the children gasp with delight, others clap or jump up excitedly; a few others are quiet, their expressions doubtful. "*No hay papel, no hay lapices,*" a boy flatly states. Even the giddiest children, and those most proficient in English, don't bother to translate as this irrefutable fact sinks in.

"Don't worry." For once I can say this with utter conviction. Other than for necessities like food, there's never been a better reason to spend my money. "I'll get the paper and the pencils. There will be plenty for everyone."

Tonight, parents seem to whisk their children home more quickly than usual, and I suddenly find myself alone with Thomas. We have avoided this moment until now. But here we are by the lowering fire. His thick hair has grown longer and wilder since my arrival: a lion's mane to match his eyes.

"You can go back." His voice is quiet. "I'll stay with the fire until it goes out."

In spite of myself, my vows and reservations, I go to stand beside him. "I'll stay, too."

We sit together on the ground and talk about the children—the ones who show particular promise and confidence, the ones who show less promise because of a lack of confidence.

"There's a fine line between helping them learn how to survive in the United States and encouraging them to forget Mexico," Thomas says.

It takes me a moment to put into words one of the many things that's been troubling me in the past days. I take a deep breath. "I'm afraid they'll be caught between here and there, unable to call either home. Many of the children are already acting as translators for the parents, you know."

Thomas shrugs. "The children are the best chance the parents have to stay here. They're the reason the parents are here to begin with. And many of them are U.S. citizens after all."

A lock of my hair has slipped from the pins I use to keep it out of my eyes. Thomas reaches out and tucks it behind my ear, then quickly draws his hand away. But still I feel the pressure of his touch where his fingers grazed my ear.

A hard, loud clatter makes us both jump, and then sparks rain down close at hand. Something went in the bonfire, and went in hard. An ember has snagged on Thomas's shirtsleeve; he swiftly brushes it off. The smell of singed cloth—my throat clots with that smell. For a moment I am back in East Texas, and there is a blowout. I jump up and turn toward the fire. A patch of flame has leaped over the stones set in a ring to contain the blaze; the flames lick at the grass, spread. In an instant, those few inches of flame have turned into several feet. Thomas runs to try and stamp it out as a lithe figure darts from the other side of the bonfire—a slip of a boy, trying to run away.

"Stop!" I lunge after the child, seize his arm, drag him back into the light. Daniel, eyes wild behind his broken spectacles, hair wild about his head. He struggles against my grasp, shoves at me, knocks the wind out of me, nearly pushes me down. So I do the same to him, only my weight and force overpower him and we fall on the ground. I leverage myself up and pin down his arms. Behind me, Thomas shouts for help. The flames are leggy, moving ever more speedily through the tall, dry grass and weeds, heading toward the line of trees that borders the field, and toward Kirk Camp. Beyond, all around, stretch farms. What will happen to us if the camp burns down? What will happen to us if the fields catch fire and the crop is ruined? I try not to imagine. I try to keep hold of the boy who is twisting, spitting, and clawing now—a wildcat of a boy. A hot wind gusts, invigorating the flames. From the corner of my eye, I see Thomas rip off his shirt. He uses it to beat down the flames. But it won't take long, it's clear, before the fire will be more than any person, any group of people, can handle.

A man cries out—not Thomas.

I see them then, running toward us from the camp, men, women, and children. They carry blankets, and the slower ones, far behind and emerging from the darkness, lug buckets. The fire is so close to Daniel and me now that Thomas has dropped his shirt; he's pulling me, pulling Daniel, up and away. My exposed skin feels tight and swollen, blistered hot. The thought of Charlie flashes through my mind—what he might have suffered in his last moments— and sets me retching. I stumble over my feet, over Daniel's legs, and wheel away from the fire, sucking in smoky breaths that burn my lungs. *Charlie*—my grip loosens on Daniel, and he wrenches himself away with such force that now he entirely slips my hold. Like a wraith, he is lost in the smoke, lost as Charlie was. But there is Luis. And there is Thomas, the fire dancing too close to his bare chest as he wields a blanket, beating at the flames, trying to snuff them out. And there are two elderly women struggling to carry a bucket of water. I recognize them from the river and try to help.

* * *

IT TAKES NEARLY two hours, but finally, the blaze is out. People exchange words of exhausted relief; those who've suffered injuries return to camp to tend to them. Soon most everyone begins to drift in that direction, and once again, it's Thomas and me, only this time we're standing by the wet, smoking remains of the fire.

"Daniel's gone," I say.

Thomas, still bare-chested, looks up at me. His skin is soot-stained, his eyes bloodshot. A purpling burn slashes the back of his hand. "Did you see where he went?"

I shake my head. I am drenched in sweat, my hair plastered to my forehead and neck. "We could try to find his aunt and uncle again."

"You really think they exist?" Thomas rakes his fingers through his hair, then lets out a sharp yelp and gazes, stunned, at the ugly burn on his hand. It's oozing now.

"Silvia should take a look at that."

"Is she strong enough?"

"She can look. Then she can tell me what to do."

Thomas shakes his head. "But Daniel—he's somewhere, yes? Something's wrong with that boy. I don't want him doing worse harm to himself or anyone else."

"Silvia first. Then Daniel."

"Daniel first. Then Silvia."

Thomas starts walking, and I fall in beside him. I glance down. "You're limping, too. Don't be foolish, Thomas. She needs to tend to your leg as well. Otherwise you won't be looking for anyone or going anywhere at all."

With each step, Thomas's pace increasingly falters. At the edge of camp, he stops walking altogether. He turns to me, his eyes suddenly wide and frantic with pain. "Ruth?" he says, but he's unable to finish the question. He sways, and I manage to catch hold of him, wrapping my arms around his waist. His body is less lean than Charlie's, less lithe and long. His body is denser, more compact, like mine. I am able to support him, bear up under his weight.

Our arms around each other, we move through the camp. The place seems strangely quiet after the chaos. The others must be getting cleaned up, recuperating from the fire inside the privacy of their cabins; tomorrow morning comes earlier than early for them, after all. And so Thomas and I lean in to each other, so close that we move almost as one. But we are not in love. We are not. We are simply trying to keep each other upright and alive. We are simply trying to find the way home.

At last we reach Silvia and Luis's. I can't let go of Thomas to open the door, so I give it a sharp kick. The rope handle jiggles, and there is Luis, peering out at us, his face, like Thomas's—like mine, too, I suppose—blackened with soot. He takes one look at Thomas and opens the door wide. He opens his arms, too. I release Thomas. He falls into Luis's arms. Luis maneuvers him inside and lays him down on the dirt floor. I follow.

"My book—get it," Silvia says from her bed. I go to where she likes the book kept—a high shelf on the wall farthest from the stove, where grease and smoke are least likely to penetrate its pages, and thieves (though I've never heard of thieving at Kirk Camp) are least likely to locate it. I take the book to Silvia. She is sitting up in bed, her hair loose and long, shielding her face as she sets the book on the mattress—her belly is far too big for her to open the book on her lap—and begins to turn the pages.

"Aloe leaves?" I blurt. More than once these last weeks, Silvia has sent me out to her garden to take cuttings from the thriving aloe plant there. The thick, serrated leaves with their small white teeth release a sap that she uses in any number of ways: to soothe Luis's skin at the end of a blistering-hot day, or to heal the calluses that sometimes tear open on his hands. She's applied aloe to my perpetually sunburned face, neck, arms, and legs. But no, not this time. This time Silvia tells me to collect three eggs from the basket by the stove and separate the yolks from the whites. When I've done that, she tells me to take the bowl of egg whites and then, as gently as possible, dip a clean rag into the viscous substance and spread a thick layer of it over Thomas's burned hand. "This will dry," she says, as I carefully follow her instructions. "Then we will peel it away and do it all over again. We will keep doing it until the burn begins to heal. Egg hastens the healing and lessens the chance of scarring. Is he with us?"

I look at Thomas, lying still, eyes closed. But for his breathing, I'd fear he was dead. "He's unconscious, I think. His leg—"

Silvia asks Luis to roll up the leg of Thomas's trousers. She has seen the bloodstains there, blacker than dirt and ash. I have to force myself to look. It's not because I'm afraid to see his injury; it's because I've never see his leg bare. Almost, I feel I'm about to see him naked. I suck in a breath and hold it. Here is his black leather boot, tied on to his metal foot, which is latched at the ankle to his wooden shin. Here is the slight swell of his wooden calf—for some reason, this lifelike attention to detail brings tears to my eyes. I blink them impatiently away to see here, where the tan cloth of his trousers is most stained, the bottom of the thick rubber cup that secures the prosthesis to Thomas's knee.

A smell like iron rises from Thomas's leg, and there the blood is, oozing over the rim of the cup.

Calmly, Silvia asks Luis to remove Thomas's prosthesis. Luis hesitates for only a moment, and then he does so. And there: Thomas's wound. A long splinter of wood juts out of his stump, just above its rounded tip, which is already mottled with scars. I clap my hand over my mouth to muffle my cry.

Silvia turns to me. "Boil water."

I hurry to the stove, where a large covered pot of water always sits. I light the stove. When I turn back, Luis, instructed by Silvia, is beginning to ease the splinter of wood from Thomas's flesh. "Clean rags," Silvia snaps. I get them, turning just as Luis gives a last sharp pull, and the splinter—perhaps five inches long, half an inch wide, and jagged at the edges—dislodges. Thomas moans, his eyelids flutter, but then he slips into unconsciousness again. The piece of wood was originally part of the prosthesis, I realize, seeing it on the floor. This will probably cause Thomas the most pain. The new device, which allowed him such facility of movement, is badly damaged.

By the time water boils on the stove, Silvia, seated in a chair now, watches as Luis does his best to pluck any last bits and slivers of wood from Thomas's skin and the fleshier part of the wound. "There will be infection if we're not careful," Silvia tells me as I lift the steaming pot from the stove.

We soak rags in the boiling water, and when they're cool enough, we use them to clean Thomas's leg. Luis lifts Thomas's thigh so Silvia can swab it, and then she applies salt to the area. She has stirred together the honey and the little bit of sugar on the shelf, and now, much as she did with the whites of the eggs, she slathers on the mixture. Then she swaddles Thomas's knee with the remaining rags, which are clean enough without being boiled, I hope, because Silvia says they must first and foremost be dry.

"That is all we can do for now." Silvia holds out her hands so that Luis can lift her from the chair and help her onto their bed. "We must do it again soon. We will need more honey, sugar, eggs, rags, and water from the pump to boil, and we will need these things quickly."

Without a word, I go to my cot and pull some money—ten dollars—from where I've tucked it, where the cot's heavy tarp meets the wood frame. I press the money into Silvia's hand.

"This is too much, Ruth."

"No, it's not." I look at Luis. "You'll go to the store?"

He nods. "*Mañana.*"

"Nothing is open now," Silvia reminds me. "He will have to borrow the supplies we need."

"Then please, let me pay for everything you have to borrow, then buy anything else we need for Thomas, and food, milk, coffee—*anything* we need." I remember the children, the paper and pencils I promised them, but these things I'll purchase another time.

Luis nods, tucks a blanket over Silvia, who is lying down now. Then, not wasting any time, he heads out the door.

"*Estoy cansada,*" Silvia groggily murmurs as she closes her eyes. Of course she is tired, given what she's just done. Of course she must sleep before she does more.

I turn back to Thomas and catch my breath. He is conscious, watching me from beneath his eyelashes, his mouth taut with pain. I go to him, kneeling so that we can better see each other. Carefully, I smooth his hair from his forehead. "Hello." I try to smile, but then I see the tears standing in his eyes. *Tears.* I've never seen a man cry. Certainly not Daddy. Not even Charlie. I touch Thomas's cheek, and his tears spill onto my fingertips. "Oh, Thomas."

"What kind of man—" His voice breaks with emotion; he can't speak.

I lean closer to him. "Tell me."

"What kind of man am I?" He swallows hard, the muscles in his throat working against the tears. "What kind of man brings such hurt on himself and tries the lives of others?" He slams his hand down on his injured leg. "If *this* hadn't happened, I could have kept working in the field. I could have earned enough money to pay a doctor to care for Grace. I could have *saved* Grace."

I shake my head. "You can't know that. It was an accident. You couldn't help—"

"That's it. I couldn't help. I couldn't help Grace then, and I can't help others now. Not in a way that makes a real difference." He grips my arm, holding on as if for dear life. "Lupe was taken. I couldn't stop that. I couldn't stop Daniel. I couldn't save any of my friends—my family, they feel like—not to mention the people I don't even know who are deported every day. I can't help myself. If I can't help myself, how can I help others?"

"The children you teach. You're helping—"

"For how long? To what end?"

I draw in a breath, and then I say it. "You're helping me."

"Ah." His sigh sounds wretched. His eyes have gone muddy brown, his gaze distant, as if he's looking into the far, far away. He releases my arm and then gently traces the curve of my cheek. "My dear—" He hesitates, and I steel myself for another woman's name.

"My dear Ruth," he says. He shakes his head restlessly and says the word *grace*; whether he's speaking to his sister, or speaking of free and unmerited favor, I don't know.

His head stirs restlessly on the pillow, and I touch his fore-head again. His skin holds the heat of the fire. If he's this feverish, should I wake Silvia? There is her black book on the table. I go to it. My Spanish is stronger now. I turn the pages. I find the word I'm looking for: *la fiebre*. Below that, the neat, antiquated writing says that the body tempera-ture needs to be lowered. Wet towels and ice baths can help.

We don't have ice or a bathtub; nor would I want to move Thomas if we did. The rags are all gone. So I take some of my clothes, run out to the pump, douse them in the cold water, and return to find Thomas, unconscious again. Quickly, I drape the dripping clothes over Thomas's body, leaving dry only the bandages that cover his wounded leg.

Thomas moans, eyes still closed, and his teeth begin to chatter.

"He needs stronger medicine. He must drink it."

I turn to see Silvia awake again, watching from her bed.

"I can make it if you direct me," I say.

Silvia tells me to put another pot of water on to boil, then directs me toward the rows of jars and tin cans that hold dried herbs and berries. Following her guidance, I measure out correct portions, and when the water boils, I brew a foul-smelling pot.

"It will need to cool now," Silvia says. "As soon as it does, he must drink it all."

We sit for some time together, Silvia and I, watching over Thomas. Then Silvia again falls asleep and I watch over them both. Finally, Luis returns. He has managed to borrow a bit of everything that Silvia requested.

Soon we will have to change Thomas's dressings. But with Luis home, I realize I'm desperate for fresh air, just a gulp of it. Maybe a short walk will calm me down. So as he sets the goods out on the table, I whisper that I'll be back soon and slip out the door.

MECHANICALLY, I BEGIN to walk the empty roads. The smell of smoke lingers in the air. Only a few blocks and my feet are dragging. The simple shacks and low buildings show themselves in a new way to me tonight. Each one is as unique as the people who inhabit it. In such extenuating circumstances, people have found ways to build window boxes and grow flowers—many are varieties I've never seen; perhaps they are from the seeds of plants indigenous to Mexico. Here is the Ramos family, their name painted on a piece of carefully carved wood and embellished with the sun, moon, and stars. Here, wind chimes clink musically in the breeze. A lush front garden, a trellis laced with thick vines, a sundial, a white picket fence. And here, a bicycle cobbled together from various sources, a fat tire swing, a hammock made of rope, a car mounted on cinder blocks for repair. Except for the fact that the shacks are assembled from cardboard, rusted tin, freight car scraps, and license plates, this could be a neighborhood anywhere, the evidence of individuals and everyday lives all around.

I stop for a moment at the outskirts of town, near the

same field where the bonfire turned wild. My eyes feel like I've had sandpaper scraped across them. I bury my face in my hands and try to rest.

I hear it then—the sound of a child singing, a voice very like that of the child I heard singing on the Everlys' radio on Christmas morning. The sound seems to be coming from the field. I can't see much through the lingering haze of smoke, but that means that the child, if it is indeed a child, can't see me, either. I start toward the sound. Soon my stinging eyes are streaming. The charred grass upon which I walk has gone blurry. It is hard to be quiet; I stumble over this stone and that scorched piece of wood. The singing stops, and I hear, before I see, someone leap up. Yes, a child, not twenty feet away, standing near the smoking remains of the fire. A boy.

He bolts again—Daniel—sprinting for the line of trees at the far side of the field, which marks the end of Kirk Camp. On the other side is a road, busy by day with all the trucks bearing the camp workers to nearby and far-flung farms. The road is far less busy at night. But if that boy wants to escape for good, it is the place to go. It will be only a matter of time before he hitches a ride, or a farm boss picks him up and sets him to work, or a government official deports him.

I run clumsily after Daniel. Clearly adept at the art of survival, he moves nimbly, swiftly; already he's not much more than a speck of white shirt bobbing in the distance. He vanishes into the trees, but still I keep going, shoes slapping the ground, knees ripping through the tall grass—the fire didn't reach this far—arms churning the air. And now I am among the trees, too, roots tripping me, branches scratching. I glimpse the road, a silver ribbon in the moonlight, slashed now by a harsh yellow glare— headlights!—and then there is the squeal of tires, brakes grinding, a horrible thud, and silence but for an idling engine, a metal door creaking open, and a man shouting in fear and anger.

I burst through the trees. A wide swathe of white light spills over the road, and in the light lies a small round heap that must be Daniel. The man stands over him. He is swearing like I've never heard before. I tear across the gully that banks the road and fall on my knees by Daniel's side.

"He came out of nowhere! *Nowhere!* These migrant kids—they're everywhere! Enough already!"

Daniel is breathing. He stares at me, wide-eyed with terror. I wonder what he can see. His spectacles lie a few feet away, or what's left of them, smashed to smithereens. His arm is twisted beneath his back in a way that is simply wrong.

The man is going on and on, his words hateful. I can't see his eyes for the cap pulled down low over his forehead, but his fists are clenched, and he is spitting another string of profanity.

There's no way I can carry Daniel back to camp. There's no way I'll get him there in time. (In time for what, I don't dwell on.) So I tell the man it's all right. I know it was an accident. Clearly, he didn't aim his truck so he could hit this boy head-on. "I didn't hit him head-on!" the man barks. "I swerved and barely glanced him." I see that the man's truck is indeed stopped at an angle, and I reassure him that, yes, I understand. "You're not in any trouble," I say. "If you'd just drive us back into camp, that's all I ask. Then you can head out from there."

It takes some doing, but in the end, the man agrees. I climb up into the truck bed, and the man lifts Daniel up to me, and I cradle him in my lap like a baby, not a boy, trying to support his twisted arm. We rattle into camp. Daniel won't faint, no matter how much I wish he would. In this way, Thomas had it easier. But maybe the boy will remember how I held him. Maybe he'll remember that someone tried to soothe him, tried to be gentle, and that will help him more in the long run than the sweet relief of unconsciousness. Maybe.

I direct the man to Silvia and Luis's cabin. He helps me get Daniel to the door. And here I am, kicking at the door again, two times in a handful of hours, my arms wrapped around an injured person. And here is Luis opening the door, taking the person from my arms, and Silvia, standing, as she should not. Luis has moved Thomas to my cot; through the crack in the curtains, I glimpse my wet clothes still draped over his body. Head to knees, Daniel is just the length of the table, so Luis lays him down there. I pull up a chair to support his dangling feet.

As I thought, Daniel's arm is broken. While Luis, with Silvia's help, fashions a splint, I stand by the boy's side, smoothing his hair. He looks up at me while Silvia and Luis bind his arm. I remember the song he was singing out there in the field; I wish I knew it and could sing it to him now. Instead, I try to sing a hymn like a lullaby.

There is a balm in Gilead,
To make the wounded whole . . .

In my own plain voice, I sing the hymn once, twice, three times, until Silvia and Luis have finished binding his broken arm. Somehow, Daniel manages to keep still.

Luis holds a cup of tea out to me. I take it. The tea smells nothing like what I steeped for Thomas; it has a thick, sweet, sedative smell. There's a smokiness to it, too—some kind of alcohol, I think. I hold it to Daniel's lips so that he can drink it. When he is finished, his eyelids droop and he whispers hoarse words I can't hear. I bend closer to him. "Tell me again," I say.

He swallows hard and speaks a bit louder. "My mother used to sing that song, the song about Gilead."

I smile at him. "My mother used to me sing it, too." She did, I remember now, along with other hymns, when I was a little child and sick in bed.

I miss Mother suddenly, with a vengeance. But I don't dwell on it. I can't. Daniel's black eyes have fluttered wide open, so wide that a body could fall deep down into them. Daniel's eyes are like Edna Faye's in this way—like Edna Faye, he is a child I will come to love. I know this. He stares at me, riveted on my throat. His lips part; his expression turns to one of longing. He was a troublemaker. I'd nearly forgotten, but now I remember. I fumble with the collar of my dress, concerned for my modesty, though Daniel is, at most, ten years old. He whispers something; again I can't hear him. This time when I don't respond, he repeats himself of his own accord.

"My cross. My father's cross."

My hand flies to the slender chain given to me by Helen, to the little silver cross and my gold wedding band. "You're—"

"Yes."

The boy beneath the bleachers.

"You have my father's cross," he says.

Without another word, I undo the chain from my neck, slip my wedding band from the chain and then into the pocket of my dress. The gold chain, I drape across Daniel's throat so that the cross settles neatly on his chest. He strains to lift his head and see, though the tea is taking further effect, I can tell from his woozy expression. I secure the chain around his neck. It only accentuates his shoulder bones, collarbones, and sternum, which jut out painfully. This boy, like so many, hasn't eaten enough today or for many days. Tomorrow I will feed him something mild but satisfying. Rice. The clear chicken soup Silvia is able to take. I'll feed him something like that, and perhaps he will tell me his story—the one that nobody seems to have heard. For now, he'll sleep, lifted by Luis from the table to the pallet of a single blanket on the dirt floor. He'll sleep with his hand clasped around his father's cross, and I'll lie down beside him, since Thomas is on my cot, and someone needs to be close at hand should Daniel wake. Someone needs to make sure he's as comfortable as he can be, warm and safe and slowly, slowly healing. I'll be that someone—the makeshift family in his life. At least for tonight.

SIXTEEN

Daniel stays on at Luis and Silvia's over the course of the next few days, sleeping, gradually relaxing and warming to us as meals come with regularity and fill his belly. Thomas returns to his cabin the morning after the fire, after Luis promises that he will take the prosthesis to town to be repaired. I visit Thomas every day. We are awkward and shy in each other's company; I never stay long. I simply take him a portion of a meal I've prepared and change his dressing per Silvia's instruction. She has insisted that he take a week to recover; to my surprise, he has agreed. Luis and I cover his duties overseeing the camp; if he's needed to make decisions or give advice, we know where to find him.

Thomas is wary of my returning to the field at night; he's sure the farm owners are aware there was a fire and are watching Kirk Camp now. But I insist. If they're watching, let them see the good going on. There won't be another blaze gone out of control. The children and I have stacked the ring of rocks higher, so that flames can't escape. And while they work with me during our lessons, their parents keep careful watch over our gathering—minding not only the fire but also the surrounding shadows, out of which those who do not wish well could emerge.

In teaching the two older groups, I follow Thomas's suggestions. The younger children, as promised, begin creating their own fairy tales. Though most of them have yet to read any stories besides "Rapunzel," theirs are chock-full of details and motifs reminiscent of Grimm. There are magic beans and plants that grow to great heights and transport characters to otherworldly realms. There are flowers in which whole miniature families live happily, until blight comes or a giant takes a single step and, sometimes intentionally, sometimes not, crushes what has been home. There are runaway children, and stolen children, and royal children who've been told they're the poorest of the poor. And there's the pervasive presence of *La Bruja, La Llorona*—sometimes a witch, sometimes a wicked stepmother, sometimes a wealthy landowner or government official, who hunts children down, separates and divides families, instills fear and causes grief. As the children shape their fairy tales, I transcribe them. And I learn more about their lives, some of which hold events that make the most dramatic and adventurous twists and turns in their fairy tales seem moderate, even mundane, by comparison.

About Daniel's life, I have yet to learn anything, though all of us in our little home—Silvia, Luis, and myself—try to gather information. If Daniel ever chooses to reveal himself, my hunch is that it will be to Luis. Daniel reminds

Luis of his younger brother, and I wouldn't be surprised if Luis reminds Daniel of an older brother, or perhaps his father. Both Daniel and Luis are reserved people, guarded and shy. Luis takes watchful care of the boy, nights when he's home from work—the kind of care he once reserved only for Silvia. Luis is the one who adjusts Daniel's splint while Silvia oversees. Luis is the one who administers the herbs and teas that lessen Daniel's pain and, Silvia promises, will hasten and ensure healing. Luis moves between the two of them, his wife and this child, with a tender attentiveness that, on any given night, deeply moves me. They are creating the rhythms of a family, with their roles and quirks and unspoken understandings. As Daniel, with the resilience of youth, gains more strength and confidence, Silvia grows frailer and quieter. Soon Daniel watches over her as Luis does him. In fact, Daniel displaces me as her caretaker by day. Silvia has a hard time taking food now; she has become a remote, still presence whose focus, it seems, has turned solely interior as she works to bring her baby into this world. The person who best draws her out is Daniel. He's also the person who best encourages her to eat. And if I'm grateful to the boy for this, I know Luis will be indebted to him for life.

By the week's end, most of the young children in my group have nearly finished their fairy tales, all of which have happy endings achieved through a variety of means: gifts and talents bestowed by ancestors, fantastical creatures based on their own legends—forest sprites, mermaids, snakes, and sorcerers who change shape. Sometimes simply cleverness suffices. The children yearn to start their illustrations. So on

Friday afternoon, I hitch a ride into Puebla with Hector and purchase blank notebooks at the five-and-dime—enough for every child in my group, as well as every child, regardless of age, who joins us at that bonfire. I purchase colored pencils and watercolor paints. At the last moment, I remember to add a notebook for Daniel, and then I tuck in a bag of assorted penny candies for him, too. I step outside with about twenty minutes to spare before Hector, who's been asked by the farm owner to pick up some supplies at the feed store, will be ready to go. Bags in hand, I feel the weight of my pocketbook clutched under my arm. It holds the rest of the money I earned as Tobias's assistant. Suddenly, I want to be rid of that money, and as much as I want to be rid of it, I want it put to the best possible use. If there was any danger of Tobias killing my love of teaching, these children have saved it. What better use for the money than to spend it on them?

I turn around and go back into the five-and-dime. I collect more pencils, but I don't stop there. With the clerk's help, I gather reading and arithmetic workbooks, cards with the letters of the alphabet written on them in cursive, so the children can start practicing that. Colored craft paper, scissors, and glue. Boxes of chalk, along with two dozen little chalkboards so the children can save paper. I buy rulers and paste and blunt-nosed scissors. And then I am done. All in all, I have spent more money than I have since I came to California, more money than I have spent in my *life*. Now we just need an actual school.

On the ride back to camp, I ask Hector if he would mind singing a song. *"Cantas una canción? 'La Llorona'?"* Having heard so much about her from the children, I want to hear her song again. Hector shrugs, but willingly complies.

Todos me dicen el negro, Llorona
Negro pero cariñoso.

He sings all the verses and then sadly shakes his head. *"Muy triste."*

He breaks out into a happier tune, a Mexican folk song that's all bouncy rhythm and lilting melody. This song accompanies us all the way back to camp.

It's early evening when Hector drops me off at Luis and Silvia's. I find Daniel sitting outside, his bound arm cradled against his narrow chest, watching Luis chop wood. Luis drops the ax and, eyebrows raised in surprise, helps me unload my many purchases. I feel a flash of guilt—how many people could be fed by the money I spent?—but then Luis says, *"Para la escuela?"* When I assure him that this is indeed for our school, he nods, satisfied, and helps me carry the bags inside. Silvia sleeps through our coming and going; she must be terribly depleted today. I watch her for a moment after Luis goes back out to resume his chore; yes, her chest rises and falls, yes, she is breathing. Then—because my staying here might soon disturb her, and it's a lovely evening, balmy for July in California—I decide to go outside, too. I quietly draw the paper bag of penny candy from where it's tucked among the new notebooks, then ease my way out the door, and sit down beside Daniel. I pass him the bag of candy. His eyes widen. "For me?"

I nod, smiling. "All for you."

He stares into the bag, deliberating for such a long time

that Luis splits five pieces of wood. Finally, Daniel decides on a cherry sour ball. He unwraps it and pops it into his mouth. "Thank you."

"My pleasure. But don't eat too many all at once or you'll feel sick."

Daniel nods. "And thank you for this." He lifts the little silver cross from where it's hanging beneath his shirt, and looks directly at me as he never has, his gaze unabashed and steady. "I thought it was lost forever." He tucks the cross underneath his shirt again.

"You're most welcome."

We watch Luis for a moment, his wiry body moving fluidly and efficiently as he splits the logs, and then Daniel holds out a cherry ball for me.

"Oh, no! It's for you."

"Please. I used to share all the time when there was plenty. Or at least, there was enough."

I take the candy. In this moment, Daniel seems more at ease with himself than I've ever seen him. There is his favorite, Luis, working away, providing as he can, and here Daniel is, holding plenty—something he hasn't had in a long, long while, something unrelated to survival, something for pure pleasure. In this moment, he is what every child wants to be: safe and content.

"There never was an aunt and uncle, you know," Daniel says, his gaze on Luis. "I slept wherever I could. Sometimes a family let me inside. But mostly, I was in the field, or among the trees along the road. A few nights, when there were bad storms, I slept in a privy."

"I'm sorry."

Daniel cracks down on what's left of his sour ball and swallows it. After another long deliberation, he takes out a stick of black licorice and bites off the end. "It's better than living on the streets of Pasadena. That's where I was before I found my way here."

I hold very still, not wanting to startle or disrupt him, only wanting him to keep talking. And he does. He goes on to tell me what happened after our encounter at the football game. He got away from the guard, got home safely, as did his friends. For months, life went on as it always had. But then one day in late January, he skipped school for a lark and roamed the streets with a friend until suppertime. When he went home, everyone was gone. His family had been deported, along with almost everyone else on their street. "There were a few of us kids left together. We managed to get by. Then one day the others got picked up and I was the only one. I'd heard about Kirk Camp. So I found my way here." He doesn't tell me how. He finishes his licorice stick. "It didn't make a real difference, though, being here. I was still alone."

I have to clear my throat before I can speak. "Well, now you're not alone. Not at all."

Luis looks over, wiping the sweat from his brow. Daniel leaps up and goes to him. He takes a lemon drop from the bag and, to Luis's surprise, offers it. They exchange a few words in Spanish that I can't make out. Then Daniel returns to me, shoulders back, head held high. For the first time at Kirk Camp, I have a glimpse of the bold, generous boy who risked so much returning Helen's shoe to me. Like this, I would know him anywhere.

"I'm going to save the rest." He plops down beside me again, rolls the top of the bag closed, then sighs, rests his chin in his good hand, and watches Luis with such naked admiration and loyalty that I have to look away.

"I'm sorry I did all those bad things," he says.

"It's all right." I hesitate, but then I do it. I rest my hand lightly on Daniel's shoulder. "No need to apologize again."

Daniel shifts away from me, ducking my touch. But Luis, he gives me a fleeting smile.

SEVENTEEN

Next day, midafternoon, there's a knock at the door. I open it to find Thomas leaning on his crutches. His left pants leg hangs empty below the knee. He flicks his fingers against that thigh, gives me a tense smile. "Got a favor to ask. My . . . device is supposed to be fixed and ready. Hector said I could borrow his truck to pick it up in Puebla, but I'm wondering if you could drive me? My hand still isn't in good shape, and, well, you know about my leg as much as anyone, I guess. I don't want to make anything worse."

My heart bangs in my chest. He asked *me*. Then again, who else would he ask? Most everyone is at work in the fields.

"Let me think," I say. Daniel can stay with Silvia, and she's sleeping the deep way she does now and again (not often enough), which could go on for hours. "Yes," I say. "As long as we can make it back for the bonfire."

He nods. "If I can, I'd like to be there tonight, too."

"You're able to teach?"

He shrugs. "Least I can do is try."

I let Daniel know what's happening, then we walk to where Hector parked his truck, and Thomas passes me the keys.

As we drive toward Puebla, I glance over at Thomas's burned hand. The surface of the burn is hardening, forming a deep red shield against the tenderness within. But it still looks ugly and painful. He's right. He shouldn't drive. I am just the person available to do so. That's all.

We park in front of the low brick building that Thomas says is the doctor's office. He suggests I look around town while he goes in, but I say I'll just wait in the truck. The cab smells familiar; I've been trying to place it, and now I have. It smells like tobacco and grease—Daddy's smell. Though the odor isn't particularly pleasant, I want to spend some time with it. It brings back good memories of Daddy from when I was a little girl. He used to take me for long drives in the country before times got so hard and we couldn't afford the gas. We both liked to go to abandoned settlements—towns that never made it after the Run. Ghost towns. We'd wander through them, me looking for ghosts, or pretending to. I never told Daddy I was doing this, of course. He's never had patience with such things. He might have gotten angry, prayed me out of my pretending, stopped the drives altogether. I kept quiet. Sometimes I scared myself silly. But with Daddy there, I was never really afraid. Looking back on it, the abandoned ditch-bank camp in San Jose reminds me of those ghost towns. Only the ditch-bank camp was worse, with all those possessions left behind. It was more frightening than any ghost town Daddy ever showed me. The people in those ghost towns took every-thing with them when they left. They were able to do that. And those ghost towns weren't burned to the ground.

I glance across the street, my attention caught by an ap-proaching car. Three cars. Police cars, all. A brand-new Ford pulls up beside them now. The men step out of their cars—the uniformed officers, and the men inside the Ford, who wear plain, professional suits. I recognize the look of these men. These are the kind of men who oversaw the deporta-tions I witnessed.

I want Thomas to see this. I consider going into the doc-tor's office and getting him. But given the necessity and impor-tance to Thomas of whatever's going on in there, I don't want to interrupt his appointment. So I do the watching on my own.

They don't stay long. After five minutes or so, the offi-cials return to their Ford. One ducks inside the car, then im-mediately pops back out; he returns to the police officers, bearing what look to be fliers. He hands the fliers over to the officers, and then they all drive away in various directions.

Thomas emerges from the doctor's soon after their depar-ture. To my surprise, he's wearing his . . . What did he call it? Device. Funny word. Maybe it gets tiring after a while for him to talk about it—though for me, it's gotten easier. Pros-thesis, wooden leg, device—whatever it's called, it's part of life now. I don't think about the fact that he wears one. Un-less, of course, he gets hurt.

Using his crutches, he comes to the truck. "Almost as good as new," he says, rapping his knuckles against his pros-thesis. He cuts me a glance. "Knock on wood."

I roll my eyes. "How's the wound?"

Thomas grins. "That's the best part. The doctor was amazed at how quickly I'm healing—both my leg and my hand. He thought I must have gone to the hospital on the east side of Los Angeles. When I told him about Silvia and her black book, he was flabbergasted. Actually, he seemed a little ticked off. Guess he doesn't like modern medicine being shown up by *la curandera.*"

I smile. "You'll have to tell Silvia."

"Oh, I will. Listen," he says as I turn the key and the truck growls to life. "I've been hankering to get away for a bit, see something different. Have you ever been to the beach?"

I shake my head wordlessly, stung by a memory. Land-locked as we always were, all Charlie and I ever talked about, when we let ourselves dream of college in California, was seeing the beach and the Pacific Ocean.

"All this time here, you haven't gone?"

I manage a shrug. "I've been busy."

"You want to go?"

I nod. "I think so," I qualify, and I can't keep the sadness out of my voice. I wanted to go with Charlie. I planned to go with him. "When?"

"Now," Thomas says.

I gape at him. "But—" I point at his hand, his leg.

He waves my concern away. "I'm better. The doctor said so. Might as well believe it."

"What about the bonfire?"

"I know a shortcut. We'll be back in time. We can't stay long, but we can be there long enough for you to finally see it and me to get some fresh air."

* * *

THE DRIVE TAKES less than an hour. As the time passes, I try to put away my sadness and allow myself to be eager for what's to come. Helen encouraged me to try to do new things in California, but without her influence, I've done only what needs to be done and given little thought to any other adventure. Every livelong day, for better and worse, has been adventure enough. And I've been busy, as I told Thomas. Or—*admit it*—constrained. Ultimately, adventure has always seemed a luxury to me, along with fun. Driving simply for the fun of it, going somewhere I don't need to go, seeing something new—the last time I did something like this was probably with Charlie, exploring our small portion of East Texas, and before that with Daddy, going to the ghost towns—a long time ago. And now I'm the one doing the driving. Years since I've done this as well. I smile at the long lost fun of it—my hands on the wheel, my foot on the gas. I roll down the window, rest my arm on the door, let the hot wind buffet me and tangle my hair. From this distance, at this speed, the world we pass appears to be nothing but a gorgeous garden, Eden before the Fall. Farms, groves, flowers, palm trees, fruit stands bursting like cornucopias with their fare—all this flies by in a bright, ever-changing blur. There's a sedative quality to all this, I have to remind myself. If I'm not careful I might forget that poverty lurks just out of sight.

Thomas points at a sign for Huntington Beach. "Nearly there."

A few more minutes and we're parked in a crowded lot. I am surprised to see that the tall buildings of Los Angeles rise at not so great a distance, and there's an amusement park with a tall roller coaster that undulates against the blue sky. Together, Thomas and I cross the parking lot to the sand.

There, he has to move slower on his crutches, slower than I've ever seen him move, uninjured. The sand makes it tough going for him. He apologizes, but I don't mind going slowly. It gives me time to take things in—the blinding sunlight, the salty air, the people lying on blankets and towels in bathing suits that I'm glad Mother and Daddy don't have to see—the sight alone would age them ten years. We weave through the crowd and around the occasional beach umbrella. The vast ocean winks brilliantly; its waves whisper, *Come here.* Finally, we stand on the wet, packed sand at the edge of the shore.

Without a word, I kick off my shoes and stride into the water, my skirt held above my knees. Warm waves lap around my ankles, now my shins, and now—colder now—at the hem of my lifted skirt. I hoist my skirt up around my thighs and wade still deeper. Bigger waves foam just ahead. The children and adults splashing and playing fall away like sheaves of wheat from my field of vision. In this moment it is the ocean and me, all alone. The salt stings my eyes, but that is not why I'm crying. *Our bed is an island,* Charlie and I used to pretend. When I imagined the ocean with him, I imagined us this way—alone, always alone, castaways together. The two of us as one for eternity. That's what I thought we would be. But now the crowd makes itself known again. Here I am, surrounded by people—an entire community that extends from this beach back to Pueblo and Kirk Camp and beyond. I may feel alone sometimes, but the people in my life, they buoy me up. They anchor me. And if I need them, they'll carry me to shore.

I look back to see Thomas standing at the water's edge, watching me. He smiles and waves. Even at this distance, I can see the dimples creasing his tanned cheeks. Wise man, winsome boy. He seems both. I churn back through the water to him.

"I love it here."

"I thought you would."

Shielding my eyes with my hand, I look out at the ocean. "It reminds me of something. The prairie! That's it! Rolling and endless."

Thomas regards me for a long moment. "You see that, too, then."

"I see it, too."

We make our way slowly along the beach for a bit, then sit on the sand and watch the sun sink toward the horizon. When the ocean swallows it, the beach goes dim and cool. It's quiet now but for the waves' whispering, with all the sunbathers trudging off to the rest of their lives. I could stay here all night. I could sleep with Thomas in the sand or, if a storm comes—which it might, he says, nodding at the clouds rolling in—we could sleep under the shelter of the wood pilings just over there. I say this to Thomas. "Only joking," I say. He smiles, and his smile seems almost sad. "Are you?" Still, very still, I hold myself. Until a breeze stirs, cooling my skin—I'm sunburned again, I realize—and I shiver. Then Thomas puts his arms around me, and I bury my face in his chest. He is warm. He warms my heart. I thank him for this, and though I've done nothing, he thanks me, too.

"You'll catch a chill. Let's go home," he says then.

Home. I smile into the soft cotton of his shirt. Under his shirt, *him.* I smile into him. "Yes. Let's."

I drive us back to camp, and this time he holds my hand. He clasps it so carefully, so tenderly, that it seems he thinks my hand might be hurting, as his is. It takes my breath away for a moment, our hands together like this. But then I'm breathing again, steady and calm. We are safe, together. We won't hurt each other. We know there's too much hurt already all around. I believe this. In silence, we drive the rest of the way to Kirk Camp, hands clasped. I feel the soft throb of his pulse in his wrist. We are alive together, and I thank God. Charlie would understand. I believe this, too. I would wish the same for him, if things had been different, the other way around and me gone. Creature comfort—that's what this is right now with Thomas. And so much, so very much more.

At the camp's entrance, as our headlights cut across the fence, Thomas asks me to hold up for a moment. Then he releases my hand and climbs out of the truck.

I see it, too, the flier nailed to the gate. Thomas returns with it. Together, we read:

Labor Day Holiday This Coming Monday!

The fields will be at rest
As we take the day to honor
Those who have labored.
Picnic and Dance begins at 6:00 sharp, Monday night.
Come one and all.
Food, drink, and music provided.
Work resumes as always
First thing Tuesday.

Beneath this there's a professional portrait of a fine-looking man—the kind of confident man who probably has the wherewithal to become a politician. Thomas tells me this is Mr. Ronald Kirk, the son of Mr. Reginald Kirk, who originally established this farm and recruited laborers from Mexico to work it. "Ronald is a very different man than his father," Thomas says soberly. "Just look at this. Usually, when farm bosses post fliers—about a rare holiday or a health clinic or a camp inspection—they make sure it's also translated into Spanish."

We drive into camp, and as we approach Luis and Silvia's place, we see, down this street and that, police officers nailing the same flier to shop doors, fence posts, and tree trunks. I remember what I saw outside the doctor's office then, and I describe the scene to Thomas—the officers, the men in suits, all of them as white as Thomas or me—and the fliers, now being passed along.

"We have to get to the bonfire," Thomas says abruptly, his voice gone grim. "We have to tell the others."

There is no teaching this night. Instead, children stay close to their parents, and we talk about what the fliers may mean.

THE NEXT DAY, one of the older women in camp stays with Silvia. Thomas, Luis, Daniel, and I walk to the southern border of Kirk Camp, near where I washed clothes with Silvia and the other women, so long ago, it seems now. We're bound for the little church recently established there. It was agreed last night at the bonfire that we needed to meet with people from the other farm camps in this area. The place to most easily convene would be at church. One group is going to the Catholic church in Puebla, where most people attend. We are going to the small Protestant church, held in a cantina, which was a filling station before that, Thomas tells me.

The outside of the cantina is drab and dusty, but inside, it's a burst of color. The walls are painted blue, the tables red, and the chairs green, yellow, purple, and orange. We help a few members of the congregation push the tables to the wall and set the chairs in a circle. By the time the service is due to begin, there are about fifteen men, women, and children sitting in the circle with us. The pastor, whose name is Raphael, leads us in prayer—"*Padre nuestro*," he begins, and then I make out the words *como en el cielo, asi también en la tierra.* The Lord's Prayer. I join in under my breath, quietly matching my pacing to theirs, chiming in on the Spanish words I know. "Amen," we all say. They sing hymns in Spanish, and I listen, trying to translate the words. Then Raphael reads from Matthew 13, the parable of the sower. As much as I'm able, I translate this, too. It helps that I've heard the parable read so many times, I almost know it by heart: . . . *some seeds fell by the wayside, and the fowls came and devoured them up; some fell upon stony places . . . and when the sun was up, they were scorched . . . some fell among thorns . . . but others fell into good ground, and brought forth fruit . . .*

From what I'm able to understand, Raphael suggests in his sermon that although this is usually called the parable of the sower, it might be more appropriately called the parable of the four soils. God the Father, Raphael says, will do His part in our lives no matter what, changing us, sowing hope and opportunities for transformation. But we must prepare the ground of our own lives, our souls. What does it take to do that? We must be caring and, at the same time, fierce. We must scare away the birds—distractions, these may be, that take us away from what's necessary and good. We must cast aside heavy stones, such as grief or despair. We must weed out anger and judgment, and shield ourselves from the scorching sun of doubt that burns faith from our lives. We must suffer ourselves to be broken ground, carefully tilled and tended, knowing that only then can we be fertile and fruitful. "When we are most broken," Raphael concludes, "only then can we grow in God."

These last long months, this last hard season of my life—this is what I've been unable to understand, let alone believe. I understand and believe it now.

We close the service in prayer. Then Raphael nods at Thomas, who stands. In Spanish, he tells the small gathering what I saw in Puebla. He tells them about the *gringos* posting the fliers in Kirk. Members of the congregation murmur; those fliers were posted in other camps, too, though no one saw who put them up.

"I'm afraid we may be encouraged to come together for a celebration," Thomas says in Spanish, "only to suffer a raid and deportation."

La redada. El regreso.

For some moments, no one speaks. There's a clock on the wall; the sound of its ticking fills the room.

Finally, Luis clears his throat. "*Y entonces todo se perdera*," he says, his voice shaking. Thomas nods as I piece together the puzzle of Luis's words: *And then all will be lost*.

There's a long moment of silence before the others start to talk. From what I can gather, most want to leave the area. Today or tomorrow before six o'clock, when the Labor Day festivities are supposed to start, they want to be gone. By the end of the meeting the general consensus seems to be that they will be exactly that—somewhere else entirely, having fled. The gathering disperses quickly then, and our little group heads back to Kirk Camp.

PEOPLE ARE ALREADY packing. For many of them, this is a familiar routine; they work swiftly. Others struggle with decisions. Some of the struggles spill out of homes and into streets in the form of arguments, tears, breathless exchanges, stunned silence. This language I can easily interpret—the language of fear, panic, and conflict. I talk this way to myself as I stuff my belongings into my suitcase, then take many things out again and try to fit the new school supplies inside instead. The quilt takes up so much room, but I can't leave it behind. So when the supplies overflow onto the floor, I grab two orange crates and pack them full, too. Daniel and I help Luis collect their things while Silvia watches numbly from the bed. By nightfall, everything inside the shack that is small enough is stuffed inside something that makes it easier to carry. The rest of the things, the table and chairs, the mattress, cot, and bedding, we'll have to maneuver as best we can. Silvia is dozing again, and Daniel is curled up beside her, so I whisper to Luis that I'm going to find Thomas. "He'll have found someone to give us a ride," I say, desperately hoping that this is the case.

I am halfway to the cabin where Thomas lives when a pickup truck pulls up beside me.

"I bought it just an hour ago," he says as I jump into the cab beside him. "From a man who wanted to purchase bus tickets to Nebraska for his family of five. In places farther from the border the chances of deportation are slimmer, the man heard. It still happens. It's happened as far away as Detroit and New York. But it costs more to transport people those extra miles. So I guess it's not so worth it. Not yet."

We return to Luis and Silvia's, and together we decide to leave at dawn the next morning. We want to get a good night's rest. Thomas, Luis, Daniel, and I decide to stow our goods in the back of the truck now. It is nearly ten o'clock at night when we finish doing so. Our belongings piled on each other rise a few feet above the cab. Luis scrambles up on top, and with Thomas throwing ropes from either side, he helps position them so that when the things are cinched and secured, they are less likely to fall. Whoever isn't driving will ride in the back of the truck with Daniel. That person will be me most of the time, I imagine. Daniel and I will nestle down like Edna Faye and her siblings once did while Silvia stays as comfortable as she can in the cab.

There's not room for every single thing, but Luis and Silvia say that's all right. Like Thomas and me, like the other residents of Kirk Camp, they are hoping that this total evacuation—for this is what it has become—is a false alarm. We're hoping to return soon, when we're sure there will be no trouble and the farm bosses are begging for help in the fields. Who knows? Maybe the hourly wage will go up, so great will be the farmers' needs. "That would be the silver lining," Thomas says. "That would be a miracle," I agree. In my mind's eye, I see snowflakes glittering on blue and red mittens. Charlie's and my mittens, lifted up to the snowy sky on the night Charlie and I fell in love. I don't believe that will be my one and only miracle any more, I realize. This year has held an abundance of miracles. Helen, Daniel, Silvia and Luis, and Thomas—the love I feel for each and every one of them. And my deepening love for Miss Berger, Mother, and Daddy. The black fog lifting, at least for now. God's voice saying, *Go*. Once I start tallying the miracles, they proliferate from one and only to innumerable. And if I allow them—I believe this now—more will come my way.

We've all agreed to travel north for the fall harvest. Luis has heard there are farms up that way that are still interested in hiring Mexican migrant workers. Their labor costs less than that of their white counterparts, after all. And north is farther from the Mexican border. If the evacuation does prove necessary, we're all hoping and praying that north will prove a safer, less volatile place to be.

Thomas has returned to his place and Daniel is already sound asleep on his pallet beside Silvia and Luis when I lie down on my cot for what may be the last time. The curtain is drawn, but I can hear them murmuring in their bed. They haven't said how worried they are about what effect tomorrow's ride on rugged roads will have on their baby, whose birth may be in a matter of days. But I can see it in their faces. I imagine this is what they're discussing now. Silvia gives a little cry of pain, and then I hear her muffled weeping. I saw the back of her skirt tonight, lightly streaked with blood. If Luis could ferry her in an ambulance to the nearest hospital, I imagine he would do so immediately. I know I would. But they've heard the stories, as I have. There's a good chance he wouldn't be allowed through the door. And the trip would put them at risk of permanent separation. So they stay right where they are.

In what seems a matter of minutes, screams awaken me. I leap from the cot and part the curtains. It's Silvia screaming. Though the place is still dark, I can see her at the open door, clinging to Luis, who's being dragged out into the night. The two men who are doing the dragging— two white men in overalls—are cursing at his efforts to resist. Outside, the bright beam of a flashlight wildly ricochets, illuminating a police officer, the gun in his hand, and another man who holds a clipboard, and now Luis's stricken face, as a man pushes Silvia back toward their bed. She stumbles, gasping, and then all in a rush, water spills down her thighs. Her thin nightgown clings to her now, accentuating her legs. She drops down on the mattress and curls into herself, hiding herself from the men who hold Luis, and from the other white men who are waiting outside. Daniel bolts to Silvia's side. He is crying, but he stands between her and the men; he tries to shield her from their stares. Slight and small, he tries to protect her like a man.

But the men are gone now. Luis is gone.

"Go!" Silvia cries.

I run from the cabin to see Thomas trying to push his way through the crowd gathering in the road. There's a cacophonous din of shouting. Two police officers grab hold of Thomas; he struggles, but they're big, burly men, and with his crutches, he's no match for them. Thomas casts a frantic look my way. "Luis!" he shouts. "Help him! Help anyone you can!"

I see Luis then, already a block away, hustled by his captors to a paddy wagon. The two men are unable to shove Luis inside, but when more join them—ultimately, five against one—Luis is unable to fight them off. In the wagon now, he crouches in the huddle of other men from Kirk Camp, men I recognize as the fathers, brothers, uncles, and grandfathers of the children I teach.

Standing beside the wagon, watching as people are rounded up and forced inside, is a white man I recognize. For a moment I can't think where I know him from, but then I remember. It's the man whose photograph was on the flier advertising the Labor Day picnic—the owner of the farm worked by people I now call friends. It's Mr. Ronald Kirk. He wears a pale summer suit, the fabric of which shimmers like changeable water in the swinging, shining beams of the flashlights and kerosene lamps.

Without thinking, I run over to him and grab the lapels of his jacket. "What's going on!" I don't ask this. I shout it: an order to which Mr. Ronald Kirk must respond.

He stares coldly at me. "I believe this would be called a government-sponsored action."

"I call this criminal!" I give him a hard shake, very much as Mother used to discipline me as a child. "Some of these people are U.S. citizens! Others have legal work papers!"

Is it possible that he is sneering? It is.

"And some of them aren't and don't. Still others are known dissenters who've caused a lot of trouble for people like me—their employers, who pay their wages and provide them with homes." He jerks his head toward the inside of the paddy wagon. "Like those men. Give them an inch and they'll take a mile. We don't have another mile to spare. Time they go back to where they belong."

A police officer stands beside me now. His hand comes down hard on my shoulder. "You need help here, Mr. Kirk?"

Again the sneer, the corners of his mouth turning down at the edges as his anger creeps closer to the surface. "What'll it be? Unhand me, young lady? Or would you like help?"

The police officer wrenches me away, then hustles me back to Luis and Silvia's cabin. He shoves me at the open doorway, where Daniel waits, still protecting Silvia. She is sitting on the bed now, and she is shaking. I sit down beside her, wrap my arms tightly around her, draw her close. And then another hand settles on my shoulder, a gentle hand. It's Thomas.

"You okay?" he asks.

"I have nothing to worry about. It's everyone else."

He nods.

Silvia pulls away from me and stands. Blood seeps pinkly into the wet fabric of her nightgown. She takes a jacket, draped over a chair—Luis's worn jacket with its frayed cuffs—and puts it on. She goes to Daniel, takes his hand, and before either Thomas or I can stop them, they run outside.

We go after them, Thomas and I. We beg Silvia to wait.

"They're not taking Luis away without us," she says wildly. "We won't let them."

She and Daniel run to the paddy wagon. Silvia, who leaves a faint trail of blood in her wake, is going with Luis to jail. And Daniel, just a little boy.

"Stop!" I shout.

They don't stop. They are resolute; I can see it in the set of their shoulders. In a moment, they are at the paddy wagon. In the next moment, they have climbed inside. The sweep continues. Other paddy wagons have arrived and two school buses. Our neighbors and friends, the children whose stories I know now, both their real ones and their imagined, and their parents, and the elderly women—all of them are forced to do what they don't want to do, go where they don't want to go. All of them are being taken away.

"We'll follow them," I tell Thomas. "Come on."

EIGHTEEN

We're in the truck, me behind the steering wheel, Thomas beside me. The paddy wagon holding Luis, Silvia, Daniel, and so many others is already gone, but we know where's it heading. So we rattle after it, passing through the camp gates, where Mr. Ronald Kirk still smiles from the Labor Day posters. I turn the truck onto the two-lane road and drive as fast as I'm able.

"Tell me this," I say as we hurtle toward town. "Just this. How long will it keep on happening—the raids and deportations?"

Thomas cuts me a sharp look. "Something will end this hard time. Rain will fall. The dust storms will stop. There will be steady work again. But the conviction that one person deserves something more than another—even when that something is a decent life? Well, that conviction is as old as Cain and Abel, isn't it? I don't think it's ending any time soon."

I press my foot down still harder on the accelerator, and we speed toward Puebla and the pinking horizon.

* * *

WE PARK IN front of the police station and hurry inside. There are people from Kirk Camp being held there along with others who have a history of protests and striking, "trouble-makers," as Mr. Ronald Kirk said. The officer on duty tells us this. He also says Luis, Silvia, and Daniel are not among those being held. When Thomas asks to see the men in the cells, the officer says no. When I ask what will happen to them, the officer says, "Guess." When we ask where Luis, Silvia, and Daniel might be, the officer shrugs. "Try the bus station," he says. I remind him that Silvia is about to give birth, and the officer bristles at my tone. He tells us we better hurry up and leave. Or we'll wind up in a cell with the other troublemakers.

Thomas grabs me by the arm and hustles me from the station. Back in the truck, he points in the direction of the bus depot. I drive there as fast as I can.

The small, grimy place is packed with people from Kirk Camp, all waiting for the buses that will deliver them to Mexico. There are others waiting, too—people I don't recognize.

"They did it," Thomas says, his expression stunned, his voice hollow. "They hit all the surrounding camps. They got everyone they could."

We split up and search the depot. It takes us nearly half an hour to work our separate ways through the crowd. It would take much longer if we allowed ourselves to talk to everyone we know. I gravitate to the mothers of the children I've taught; they tell me, some in Spanish, some in English, some in a melding of the two, that they don't know where they're going or when. They haven't learned a thing other than that they have no choice. They cling to their children; their children cling to them. When the children look at me now, they are silent, guarded. Why trust any white person? They're filled with doubt, as they should be. They've been betrayed.

Thomas talks with the men. In the last years, he's stood beside them during their strikes. He's translated as needed, at times played mediator with the authorities. When we've spoken to everyone who's willing to talk and still learned nothing about Silvia, Luis, and Daniel's whereabouts, we say our goodbyes, and then we leave the station. There's nothing we can do here—not really. Our best hope is to search widely for our friends. Our best hope is to confirm that Silvia is alive, and her baby, and to help them if we can. We make our way to the truck and, driving slowly so we won't miss a thing, we scour the streets of Puebla. It feels futile; they could be behind any door or already gone. But it's all we can think to do. We stop at churches, the doctor's office, every open shop, the Farm Security medical clinic, housed in a tent on the outskirts of town. We ask if anyone has seen a pregnant woman, a man, and a boy. But there's no sign or news of them. When our hunger is too great for us to ignore it, we find an open market and buy a loaf of bread, a few slices of cheese, a jug of milk, and a bag of oranges. Then we pull over to the side of the road in a shady patch and eat our food in silence there.

"We've about run out of places to check," Thomas says as we finish up. "Homes outside of town. They're all that's left."

"We could knock on every door. We could try the next towns over."

"We could." He sounds like he's saying just the opposite. He looks sharply at me then. "The school."

"What?"

"The local public school. It serves the surrounding towns as well as Puebla. It was damaged in the earthquake in 1933. They're rebuilding it, but for now it's a collection of tents and outbuildings. Ezra is there. He's taught there all along, but now he's trying to open up the classrooms to the children of Kirk and the other camps. Or he was. He's a U.S. citizen, and he's a good friend of Luis's. If he got wind of what's happened, he did everything in his power to help. You can be sure of that."

The school is located about half a mile outside town, among the farm fields. The low, humble buildings and tents appear to be empty of people. But there is one car parked near a larger building that once must have been a garage for farm equipment. We stop the truck there. The building's door is closed. Thomas tries the handle; sure enough, it's locked. He knocks; then he knocks again, louder. We wait for a few long minutes. When there's still no sound from within, Thomas yells, "It's Thomas Everly and Ruth Warren. Could we speak with you? We won't take much of your time."

And now we hear footsteps, running fast, running toward us. From the light, quick patter, I'm thinking a child will open the door. And a child does. There is the silver cross, and here is Daniel, in my arms.

DANIEL LEADS THOMAS and me past rows of desks to the back of the building, where Silvia lies on blankets on the floor. She holds a bundle in her arms. Ragged pieces of cotton hide what's inside. Luis kneels beside her. At the sound of us approaching, they look up, their expressions soft and open with wonder. Silvia gently tips the bundle toward us to reveal a pink-faced baby with a thatch of curly black hair, sleeping soundly, thick lashes fanning over smooth cheeks. As she sleeps, her rosebud of a mouth puckers, the sweet sucking motion of a baby trusting she'll be fed.

"A girl," Luis says.

I kneel down beside them. Cupping my hand gently over the baby's warm head, I thank God she's made it this far and pray for her journey to come.

"We named her Milagros," Silvia murmurs. "The name of the grandmother who first wrote the black book—at least, that's what my mama told me." Silvia kisses her daughter's forehead. "And we named her Milagros because she herself is a miracle."

It proves as Thomas thought: Ezra learned of the raid and was waiting with his friend—a white man, a lawyer—as Luis and Silvia climbed out of the paddy wagon. One look at Silvia, and Ezra's friend threatened the police officers present with legal action. "Unless you take her and her husband and son to a safe place for the baby's delivery," the lawyer said. The officers agreed, but only after he'd confiscated all of Silvia, Luis, and Daniel's belongings, as well as their legal documents—even Daniel's citizenship papers are now in official hands. Silvia's contractions were fierce by the time Ezra ushered them into the car waiting outside, and soon after they arrived here, Milagros was born. The ease of Silvia's labor shocked everyone. But Silvia thinks it makes perfect sense. "This baby has wanted out for months. She's longed for this world," Silvia says. "And now here she is, a citizen of this country."

Ezra has joined us by now. I recognize him as one of the men who intended to help Thomas and me remove belongings from the ditchbank camp in San Jose, but who watched it all burn instead. "The authorities will be checking in tomorrow," he says. "With how they've been acting lately, I wouldn't be surprised if they come tonight. You know what could happen then."

Luis shrugs, lifting his empty hands, palms up. *What can we do?*

"We can get you out of here, take you somewhere else," Thomas says firmly. "You might not be deported. Daniel's a citizen, and Milagros, and you have your papers."

Silvia looks at Luis, and he nods in confirmation.

"We've talked about it, Luis, Daniel, and me," she says. "We will go back. No more of this. We're fighting for something we'll never win. Steady work. A future here." She kisses her daughter. "At least we've given her citizenship. So one day she may return. Who knows? *She* may have a future here, if she wants that."

"Maybe we'll be citizens here together, Milagros and me." Daniel kneels down beside Silvia and tentatively touches the baby's tiny hand.

"Wherever you go, may we come visit you someday?" Thomas asks.

"*Juntos?*" Luis knows more English than he lets on.

I turn to Thomas, and he regards me, the question in his eyes. I nod in confirmation. "Together."

"*Claro.*" Luis nods. "*Este es verdad.*" Certainly. This is true—the truth as it should be, I think he means. Thomas and I, together.

But still, I think, this is not the ending anyone wanted. This is not a fairy-tale ending at all.

THOMAS AND I drive back to Puebla, where we buy food for five for a few days, as well as clothes and blankets for Milagros. We spend the night with Silvia, Luis, and the children. *Their* children—not only Milagros but Daniel, too. At least for a while. They'll look for Daniel's people when they get to Mexico, Silvia tells me. They'll do all they can to find his family. And if they don't, Daniel will always have a home with them.

We are sitting side by side on the blankets, she and I, with Milagros sleeping soundly in her arms. Ezra, Luis, Daniel, and Thomas are all outside, finishing the last of the coffee and cleaning up the remains of the supper—canned beans, cucumbers, tomatoes, and bread. For the first time in a long time, Silvia and I are alone, but for Milagros, and for the first time in a longer time still, Silvia seems truly at ease, her expression untroubled, free of fear and pain. Of course, she is exhausted; her head droops forward occasionally as she nods toward sleep. But each time she straightens up with a jerk and blinks the drowsiness from her eyes. When I suggest that she rest, promising that I'll stay by her side and keep watch over the baby, she shakes her head. "Soon," she says. "But not yet. Who knows when we'll see each other again?"

So we sit quietly together, watching Milagros breathe. The rise and fall of her chest, the flicker of her eyes beneath

their closed lids, the slight movement of her fingers or parting of her lips—these things absorb all our attention. In this
way, time seems to both stop and expand, until a question
comes to me, a question I have to ask Silvia before we say
goodbye.

"Why did you take me in when Thomas brought me to
your door that night?" I speak in a whisper; still Silvia inclines her body away from me, protecting the baby's sleep. I
hesitate then, but she nods for me to continue, so I try to
speak more softly still. "Given who I am and who you are,
why didn't you ask any questions?"

It has struck me only lately, considering what we've
faced, considering what she will continue to face—her im-
mediate acceptance of me, along with Luis's. She opened the
door to their home that night, and I followed Thomas inside,
stumbling in weariness, woozy from the blow to my head, all
but lost in the black fog of a sadness that humbles me now,
since I've seen what people like Silvia, Luis, and Daniel endure. How was she able to prepare a place for me—a cot behind curtains—how was she able to share the little food she
had, nurse me back to health, teach me her language, push
me out the door at night so that we could each patch together some semblance of our individual hopes and desires?
If it hadn't been for Silvia, what would I have done? I would
have been without a meaningful occupation, as she and Luis
are now without meaningful occupation. I would have been
without a home, as they are now without a home. I would
have been a stranger in this place, as they are now considered
strangers. I would have been wandering, as they soon will be.
I would have sunk further into bitterness and despair.

Silvia studies her daughter for a moment, as if the answers to my questions might be revealed in her perfect being. Then she looks up at me and smiles, and her smile is sad.

"Two things are both true, Ruth," she says. "We are entirely different. We are not so different. I choose to put my faith in the last."

THE NEXT DAY the police officers come. They want to take Silvia, Luis, and the children back to the station in the squad car, but after much persuasion on Thomas's part, they agree that they can ride with us in the truck. "We'll be on your tail," an officer warns. "So don't even think about trying to lose us." We don't think about it—not when Silvia, Luis, and Daniel have made their mutual decision so clearly known. Thomas, Luis, and Daniel climb into the back of the truck, I drive, and Silvia, holding Milagros, sits beside me. Silvia is still weak, and before I know it, the bouncy ride has made both her and Milagros drowsy. She lies down, the baby tucked safely between her body and the seat back. Soon they are asleep. So it's a quiet trip to Puebla—a quiet trip that goes too fast.

"All the others have already been deported," an officer at the police station tells us as he gives Luis, Silvia, and Daniel their legal documents. "You'll have to depart from Los Angeles, the central train station. There's a train leaving tonight. You need to be on it." When Thomas and I offer to drive them to the station, the officer snorts with laughter. "Not half likely. *We'll* be the ones driving them this time. *You'll* be the ones following."

Thomas and I don't say much as, following the squad car,

we make the trip into the heart of Los Angeles. He looks as I feel: tired and very sad. We arrive at the station only minutes before the train is set to depart. We collect the things we hope are most important to Daniel, Luis, and Silvia—clothes and other possessions, necessary and important. I make sure to collect the suitcase that holds Silvia's black book, though of course the plants and herbs she so carefully tended will now be lost to her forever. Carrying all that we can, we hurry through the waiting area, locate the correct platform, and find our friends there, under the careful watch of two officers. They stand before an open boxcar crowded with people who are making the same journey. *El regreso.*

"A boxcar?" I say, my throat tight.

"Here." Silvia ignores my concern, gently laying Milagros in my arms. "I want you to be the first besides her papa and me to hold her."

The baby gives a mew and looks up at me with wide black eyes. She blinks, studying me. A wise sage, that's how she seems to me. Perhaps she will be a healer, too, like her mother. I bow my head close to hers. "You're a miracle. Never forget that. You can be anything you want."

The conductor blows his whistle, and Luis takes Milagros from my arms. There is an emptiness where her small, warm body was. I turn to Silvia, and we hold each other, and for a moment, at least, that emptiness evaporates.

"*Mi amiga,*" I say.

"My friend," she says.

Thomas helps them lift their suitcases into the boxcar. There's one additional bag that contains food and baby things. But then there is nothing more. Everything else they have to leave behind, strapped to the truck's bed. I hug Luis, and then I wrap my arms around Daniel.

"Thank you," he says, touching his silver cross.

I can't find the words to thank him. I kiss his dark hair instead.

They climb into the crowded boxcar now, this little family, our friends.

For as long as we're able, Thomas and I wait on the platform where we can see them. But soon the train is too crowded to catch even a glimpse of Luis's white shirt, Silvia's yellow dress, Daniel's silver cross, Milagros's curly hair. Still, we wait while the train huffs to life. We wait while it thunders away. We wait, the two of us alone on the platform, while it shrinks to a pinpoint and vanishes altogether. Only then do we leave the station.

In silence, we return to the truck and their things piled high in the bed. All that Thomas owns is tucked away in there somewhere, too—the picture of Lupe and other mementos he has yet to show me—along with what I've held on to from one place to the next and have yet to show him. My wedding dress and veil, the pictures of Charlie and me, the quilt he and I shared, a Bible and a collection of fairy tales, a few clothes, a pocketbook that holds a check, a little money, and a wedding ring, and school supplies that will have no use now if something isn't done. We look at these things, so many of which are not ours. To me, they feel a heavy load to bear.

"What now?" Thomas asks.

I don't know the answer. Unlike our friends, we can go

most any place we want without fear. We are what many call "Americans," at the expense of so many others who are called otherwise. Just look at the world around us, palm trees, and fruit trees, and flowers. A Golden Land, tarnished for me now. Look at it long enough and the black fog will soon cover it all.

Go. Again, the voice, the one I can't ignore. *Go.*

Where? To another college or another job, courtesy of the WPA? To Helen, or Alice and Talmadge, or Mother and Daddy, or Miss Berger? East, or still farther west, so that I may dip my feet once more in the ocean?

Someday, maybe, to all of that. But not now.

Go.

I turn to Thomas. "There are people who try to help, you said."

He cocks his head, confused.

"People who try to return what's been lost or left behind."

"The ones who drive to Mexico, you mean, like Ezra."

I nod. "Like Ezra."

"Yes, there are those who do that. That's what we hoped to do with the cedar chest at the ditchbank camp. But it was too late."

I look at the truck again, the things piled there. "It's not too late now. Not yet."

"Ruth," Thomas says, and then he is quiet. But his eyes are bright with understanding.

I get in the truck and settle myself behind the steering wheel. Thomas climbs in beside me, props his crutches between us.

"It's not going to be easy," he says.

"Far easier for us than for Silvia, Luis, and the children."

"We don't know where we're going."

"We'll go back to the train station, and ask where they were bound." I shrug. "Then we'll get a map—and there will be people to ask."

"We might not find them."

"But we can try. We have that privilege, and with it comes a certain responsibility, don't you think? And if we don't find them, say we don't find them . . . maybe there will be a school that needs supplies."

His eyes brighten with understanding. "You're sure."

I turn the key. The truck rattles to life. "Let's go."

ACKNOWLEDGMENTS

When I started researching *Broken Ground*, I had no idea that I would end up writing about the deportations without due process of untold numbers of people of Mexican heritage, many of them U.S. citizens. In fact, I knew nothing about the involuntary "repatriations" of the 1930s. I started out writing a story about a young woman who, after experiencing devastating loss, makes a journey west to pursue an education. In fact, I wanted to write a novel based on my mother's experience—an experience that has always inspired me, though she never had the chance to speak of it to me herself.

It wasn't too long after I began work on the book that a black-and-white picture popped up on the Web and stopped me short. It showed a crowded train station and cattle cars filled with people. World War II, I thought, the death camps. But then I looked at the caption and read for the first time the word "repatriation," and my understanding of history, as well as my novel, began to change. After some searching, I found other related photographs of displacement and deportation. It took me longer, however, to find credible written sources that confirmed what the pictures showed. There simply hasn't been a whole lot written about this event in U.S. history.

For this reason, I want to begin by thanking Francisco E. Balderrama and Raymond Rodríguez, the authors of *Decade of Betrayal: Mexican Repatriation in the 1930s*, an account that is both substantive and evocative and proved to be my greatest resource of information for *Broken Ground*. Many thanks to the Instituto Cervantes of Chicago as well, particularly Salvador Vergara, who welcomed me into their wonderful library and encouraged me in my research there.

Needless to say, I love libraries, and I think it's about time I expressed my gratitude to the Wheaton Public Library, too—second home of my childhood, go-to workspace of my adulthood. In these last years, I've most often set up shop in the Quiet Reading Room, a room with a view that is not at all my own and all the more precious for that fact. My gratitude also extends to the First Congregational Church of Glen Ellyn, in particular to the Reverend Lillian Daniel, who let me spend time in Sunday school again when nobody else was there. I accomplished a fair amount upstairs in the Temple of Light. And surrounded as I was by the many wooden story figures, the silence there always felt companionable.

I've been privileged to work on two books with Beth Adams. Without Beth these two books would not have come to be. Thank you, dear editor, for being the great guide you are—for listening well, thinking clearly, reading between the lines, and keeping your sense of humor. And to Amanda Demastus, Bruce Gore, Katie Rizzo, and all the terrific folks on the team that is Howard Books: many, many thanks for believing in the manuscript that was and seeing it through to the book it is.

Sandra Bishop, as an agent and advocate, is simply the best. As a friend, she's better yet. Thank you, Sandra, for being courageous and empathetic and wise in the face of every challenge and change.

I am indebted to my friends who are writers, in particular those with whom I meet once a month to hash things out. Beth Franken, Eve Gayley, Sherrie Lowly, and Jack Zimmerman, I'm so glad for you in this season of life.

Joni Klein and Jan DeVries, thank you for Sunday night dinners, ongoing conversations, and a whole lot of music and laughter. Thank you, Cheryl Hollatz-Wisely and Kate Gray, for your deep understanding of what this process takes. Thank you, Cookie Murphey, for opening doors to the past. And thank you, Randi Ravitts Woodworth and Mark Woodworth, for journeying with my family and me down so many roads and over so much broken ground.

And as for my family . . . Magdalena and Teo, thank you for being your beautiful, unique selves. You two are there behind every word of this book. Greg Halvorsen Schreck, thank you for the sacrifices you've made and the support you've given so I could keep on trying, word after word. Thank you beyond words, dearests. I love you.

Finally, to those who live the unofficial stories, and to those who speak what some may prefer suppressed: thank you.